6/16/98

For Ken and Jocelyn

These are my thoughts and
reflections on how the
Silicon Valley phenomena
impacts the life of young
professionals, especially engineers.

I hope you enjoy
reading my story!

Paula Nesreen

High Tech Murder

A SILICON VALLEY MURDER MYSTERY

BY
GISELA NESHEIM

www.startupweb.com

High Tech Murder

Jacket and Cover Design: Muccino Design
Typography and Page Layout: Nicholas J. Vitale
Editing: Beverly McGuire
Photo: Arthur Mintz Photography

Published in association with
Strategic Enterprise Consulting, Saratoga, CA.

98 99 00 01 02 03 04 05   10 9 8 7 6 5 4 3 2 1

ISBN 0-9663167-0-3

Contents

1	The Break-In	1
2	The Body	13
3	In Dar Es Salaam	25
4	The Morning After	41
5	Lunch with Brigitte	53
6	The Latest News	67
7	A Long Peaceful Hike	77
8	News About Jeff	85
9	Company Rumors	101
10	Evil is Lurking	113
11	A Productive Day	127
12	Sudden Bad News	135

13 Dinner with Brigitte   143

14 News from Santa Fe   165

15 On the Way to Alaska   183

16 Thanksgiving 1985   199

17 Leaving Vancouver   221

18 Somewhere in Alaska   239

19 A Weekend in Seattle   255

20 News About Loren Grimm   275

21 A New Beginning   295

Chapter 1

The Break-In

Monday Evening, January 9, 1995

Nothing could match the furor and noise of this storm. Jeff slammed the door of his VW bus, but the usual bang was muffled, almost imperceptible. The storm had taken over. Jeff moved as fast as he could to get out of the pouring rain. There was no need to lock the car; it held nothing of value. Even the old radio had lost its luster. Powerful gusts were often accompanied by an eerie screeching. The wind's sheer force and might created the illusion that the rain was coming down horizontally. Within seconds, Jeff was soaked. He relished the force of the elements surrounding him. That's exactly how he felt inside! In a half-hearted attempt to shield himself, Jeff lifted his parka over his head while tightly clutching his backpack to his chest. One, two, three big steps, and he was out of the rain and under the covered entrance of his condominium building. Vaguely, more due to an automatic reflex than prompted by a conscious act, Jeff tried to shake the rain off his jacket before stepping into shelter.

Mulling over the day's events while driving from work in Mountain View to his home in Menlo Park had intensified Jeff's rage. His mood had been vacillating between wanting to scream out his frustration and fantasizing about punching out Loren Grimm in a great fist fight! Yeah, Jeff would knock him out and get rid of him for good, forever!

"Easy, Jeff, easy! Remember, you can't do anything about it! Calm down, calm down. Wait for the right moment—then move and attack. Be smart!"

Storming up the couple of steps to his first-floor condo, Jeff didn't realize that he was actually talking out loud. As he unlocked the front door and reached for the light switch, Jeff hoped that it would work. The radio had reported electrical power outages due to fallen trees and grounded power lines. The light came on, lifting the darkness of the entry area. Jeff shuddered, thinking what an evening without any electricity would have meant. A wild, jerky movement sent his backpack and jacket flying into the living room. Three quick strides brought him into the kitchen.

"Darn it!" He suddenly realized that he had forgotten to check his mail. Well, he would get it the next time he went out. There were more important things to tackle now.

Intently focused, Jeff surveyed the refrigerator confirming his worst fears—barren shelves. Now what? He visibly cheered up when he found one lonely last bottle of Snapple lemonade hidden in the left corner of the bottom shelf. He opened the bottle quickly while kicking the refrigerator door shut. A large gulp straight from the bottle was followed by a satisfied grunt. That felt good! What next? Jeff hadn't done any grocery shopping for days. He could order a pizza. No, he didn't want to see another human being if he could help it. He opened the cabinet door to the cupboard above the sink. A quick inspection of the shelves yielded a can of pea soup hidden behind the cereal boxes on the right. He seemed to remember seeing some crackers. Maybe he would be lucky again. Sure enough! This was not too bad. He made a mental note to stop at the supermarket tomorrow on the way home. If he had not gotten so caught up in his pet project, he would have done his errands on Sunday. He kept looking through the shelves. Cool! He found a whole box of chocolate chip cookies. Things were looking up.

While the pea soup was warming up in the microwave, Jeff stepped into the living room next to the kitchen and turned on the TV. It was almost 7 p.m. Great—in a couple of minutes he could catch the nightly business report on channel 9. Jeff was an avid investor in the stock market and kept up with the business news, especially everything that related to high technology. However, it was rare for him to be home by 7 p.m. Therefore, he usually had to get his business news from other sources, like listening to the radio while driving and reading the *Mercury News* online.

Big gusts of wind were slamming into the building. Straining his neck, Jeff peeked outside. Wild gushes of water were pouring down from the upper balcony onto his own, forming a growing pool of water. Again and again Mrs. Jacobs from downstairs had pointed out this annoying problem. She could get quite upset about the poor drainage on Jeff's balcony, since the resulting overflow tended to take direct aim at her beloved flower boxes. He was surprised she hadn't stopped by yet to get him to do something. Oak leaves from the big tree at the corner of the condominium complex had probably clogged up the pipe again. For now Jeff would just keep an eye on the problem, since he was in no mood to go out and unclog the drain. After all, maintenance had known about the clogged pipe since November, when he had reported it. Now it was their job to fix it. Hopefully Mrs. Jacobs would leave him alone tonight, but he thought that was unlikely. He had better and more important things to do! He had to figure out what had caused the sudden quick flash on his computer screen. The flash had lasted only a split second, and Jeff had been unable to identify its cause or source.

Jeff's focus was interrupted. Man, that wind was getting violent! The front of his condo was being hit the hardest. The rain was pounding the windows. It sounded like distant drums, which sometimes seemed quite close when sudden gusts whipped around the building. Suddenly Jeff jumped up and ran into his bedroom to check whether he had left a window open, but everything was okay.

On the drive home Jeff had heard the weather reporter on the local radio station talk about more storms sitting out in the Pacific, ready to drench the Bay Area over the next couple of days. Already there were warnings about the likelihood of severe damages due to high winds. The San Francisco airport had closed down for several hours. Without a break between storms, the next concern would be mudslides.

Well, Jeff knew there wouldn't be any in his area. He lived nowhere near the hills, and his community had been around for at least twenty years and had survived plenty of violent storms. Jeff had rented the condo about two years ago. He preferred to stay independent, ready to move anywhere at any time without having to worry about selling a place.

By the end of the business news Jeff had finished his makeshift meal and started to munch away on the cookies. The news had distracted him enough to cool off his rage. He was mulling over some of the stock reports, while staring straight ahead, intensely focused and gazing with a blank stare at something far off in the distance.

Suddenly Jeff came to and realized that the news was over. He turned off the TV. Back to his problem. Gone were the thoughts about stock prices and economic conditions; instead his mind was on only what so far made no sense at all. While Jeff was working on his computer on Sunday afternoon, something had occurred for which he had no satisfactory logical explanation. Since then his mind had replayed the following sequence of events over and over again: The screen had frozen, all processes had stopped, and his computer had flashed a visual snapshot of what he had long most feared—a break-in made visible by the digital life form he had invented!

Surfing the Web one boring Sunday afternoon about eighteen months ago, Jeff had read about the experiences of a Swiss professor at a supercomputer facility in Switzerland. The professor had been experimenting with digital life concepts by simulating biological reproduction on a computer. Leaving the system running over a weekend, he arrived at work the next Monday morning to find his screen covered with moving green-tinged blobs, enlarging very rapidly and quite ominously. The blobs seemed to grow in number and size by consuming each other. At first he was fascinated, but he soon realized that his secured archived hard disk had been breached and was close to being destroyed! Quick action led to the destruction of the unwanted digital being but also destroyed part of the simulation, thus preventing capture of the being for further research and exploration. Similar events had occurred at research laboratories randomly located around the world.

Jeff was fascinated by these developments. Alone over dinner that night he got very excited while trying out some ideas. Why not use such a digital life form to protect systems? Such an artificial intelligence certainly seemed to work well in attacking them! How about creating a life form that could search out, capture, and destroy the programs of invading attackers? That had been the moment of inception for Jeff's ongoing passionate quest!

Jeff had begun private experiments using Tierra as well as Avida software tools. After months of long nights and weekends, he was pleased with his prototypes. He was convinced that using digital life forms could revolutionize system security! He had invented a sensor that could quickly detect any network attacker, not just a digital life form. Jeff's digital security defender would be guarding the system, able to sense any attack and ready to respond *before* a break-in occurred by neutralizing the attack using an adaptable digital life form. Jeff's digital organisms could outthink and outdo the attacker during any attempted break-in!

Jeff's digital defender consisted of a population of self-reproducing strings. The Lan/Wan-complete network security basis was subjected to Poisson-random point mutation detection. His invention could create a large number of living digital police, a population whose sole purpose it would be to detect any kind of attack to the system. Jeff's digital defender would sense and outsmart all attackers by identifying and capturing their pattern of attack. Thus any attacker would be neutralized by the digital security defender, and network administrators would be alerted about any unwanted break-ins by the means of a digital life picture, a digital life snapshot, as Jeff called it.

Yesterday afternoon Jeff had been stunned by what he had seen and wanted to believe that his program had experienced a software glitch. After all, he had never really tested it before. The code that could display attacks in the form of a visual snapshot on the screen was still wobbly. This just had to be a fluke, a software glitch, a false alarm! If it was not a software error, it would mean that somebody had actually broken into Jeff's computer and perused his files, and his digital defender had made the break-in visible by flashing the digital life picture onto his computer screen.

Jeff's mind was racing, and he kept asking himself, Who would break into my computer at home and *why*? What did I really see in that split second on the screen? Am I just getting paranoid, or did it really happen? What if it was a simple case of the CPU freezing and I only imagined seeing a visual? It must have been a fluke, the result of a tired mind that had focused too long and too intensely. It just had to be!

Jeff had gone over his analysis and review again and again. He had spent ten long hours on Sunday trying to find something, anything, that might shed some light on the mystery, yet he didn't know more now than when he had started. The bottom line was that his software was still too wobbly and unsophisticated. Quite possibly his digital security defender had simply acted autonomously and not in response to a break-in. Jeff was angry and frustrated. Well, he'd better get at it again! There had to be a way to trace the source of the break-in—of course, only if there had actually been one! He had thought about it all day long, in spite of a very busy day. There had to be an answer to his dilemma!

During the five to six p.m. product status meeting at Safe Systems, Jeff had gotten into another altercation with Loren. It had taken all the self-control Jeff could muster to stay until the meeting was over. Loren was such an incompetent jerk, as well as a total fake! Yet he could fool most people into believing that he was an expert in all technological subjects. In reality Loren cleverly used those around him by asking questions that gave him access to their ideas and expertise. That was not necessarily bad in and of itself. But then he would turn around and take credit for those ideas!

Jeff could barely contain himself just thinking about Loren. He started pacing back and forth in his living room, totally unaware of what he was doing. He hated wasting energy on useless emotional outbursts. His instincts told him that Loren was up to something. Loren had been feeling him out for a while now. There seemed to be a pattern to his casual remarks like, "So, Jeff, what have you been up to lately? You mentioned digital life the other day, didn't you?" (Jeff was sure he had *not*!) or, "I read something the other day about digital organisms and how they could be used for networking. It was quite fascinating." Jeff rarely minced words, so Loren should have figured out long ago that Jeff had no intention of discussing his personal interests with Loren, or anybody else. Yet, Loren kept coming after him. Why?

Jeff had stopped pacing and had picked up his soup bowl and spoon, heading for the sink. The cereal bowl and mug from breakfast were still there, as well as the dish he had used to warm the soup. He hesitated for a second. Oh, well, he thought, I might as well clean it all up! The kitchen was one area in the house he liked to keep neat and clean. He didn't know why, but he just hated messy kitchens. Done cleaning and while finishing the last cookie, he walked into his computer room.

Jeff had turned one of his two bedrooms into a lab. It looked like a tiny warehouse filled with old and new computer hardware. Cardboard boxes were stacked at random throughout the room. Some boxes were empty, some were filled with reams of computer printouts. One wall was covered with bookshelves filled with manuals, reference books, white papers, and computer magazines. You had to know something about networking to make sense out of the maze of cables crisscrossing, apparently at random, between the three computers, two modems, and printer sitting on a large work table. The telephone looked like it didn't belong, barely recognizable among all those cables. Jeff was rather proud of his setup and had invested a lot of money and time into it.

Back to his investigation! Jeff sat down behind the largest computer, ready to get started, when he suddenly noticed that his message recorder was blinking. He hesitated for a moment, tempted to ignore it, before hitting the playback key.

"Guess who? Yes, it's me. A voice from the past, or should I say an experience from the past? Believe it or not, I am in San Francisco now. Surprise, surprise! How about it? Do you want to get together??? My number is 415-555-3258."

Jeff couldn't believe it. It was Angel! Where did she come from? Hadn't she left him saying it was over, forever, two years ago, in January 1993 to be exact?

Without even thinking Jeff picked up the phone and dialed her number. Darn it, she wasn't home! Where could she possibly be in this storm? The recorder went on, "If you want 415-555-3258, go for it!" Only Angel would leave a message like that.

"Hey, it's Jeff! Is this for real? How long will you be in the Bay Area? Well, I'm home. Where are you?"

Jeff hung up. Hearing Angel's voice again after two long years of missing her had quite an effect on him. Gone was everything that had concerned him so intensely only a moment ago. All he could think of was how great it would have been to be able to talk to her now. He would never get over Angel. Her hold on him was there to stay. Without her presence there was a constant nagging void inside of him, though he had learned to push it back and to deny himself those feelings. How long would she stay around this time before her restlessness would take her away from him—again? Jeff missed her. He would always miss her.

Jeff was leaning back in his chair, eyes closed, daydreaming. A wistful look of longing was on his face. No more anger and rage, only excitement and a renewed, thrilling feeling of just being alive. All of Jeff's senses were centered on Angel, and his thoughts were preoccupied with memories of their past times together. Who cared about break-ins now?

Chapter 2

The Body

Wednesday, October 4, 1995, 9:18 p.m.

Brian sighed with relief as he threw himself into the front seat of his car. His right knee hit the steering wheel. Ouch! That really hurt! It took quite a balancing act, as Brian's mother was fond of saying, to get in and out of the Thing, his treasured and beloved vintage VW. Brian began to curse under his breath, which was rather unusual for him, considering his generally calm and controlled nature. However, in his current highly agitated state, Brian had not been mindful of the car and its inherent limitations.

Now Brian felt wounded in more ways than one. He was still smarting from having spent time at another one of those irritating family get-togethers. Angry and disgusted, he had been berating himself ever since leaving his parents' house thinking, I am an idiot and a sucker. I need to learn to say *no*! Instead, when his sister, Margaret, had called to invite Brian to his father's birthday party, he had said yes. It would have been so easy to excuse himself, explaining how busy he was at work. It wasn't even a white lie; it was the honest truth. "Idiot!" he scolded himself again, this time out loud.

Since Brian had started the car his mood had begun to improve. It felt good to put physical distance between himself and his parents' house. He knew just what to do when he felt this way. He would go to work! He needed to immerse himself in an activity that would require all his focus and concentration. Work could do that. Work would definitely relieve these horrible feelings. It had always worked. He avoided thinking about why it worked. That it was rather late in the day to go back to work might seem strange to most working people who were enjoying a relaxing evening at home, but it was nothing out of the ordinary for Brian and his fellow engineers. He was pretty sure that he would have company.

Brian checked his watch to determine how much time he had wasted at the birthday party. He was eager to get something done, to make up for the wasted time. He should get to work by 9:45 p.m. Good. Traffic was light this time of day. Brian's days usually started around eleven a.m. or noon and most of the time he worked till midnight or even later. Most engineers in his building kept similar hours. For reasons none of them would be able to address even if they tried, they liked to work this way. It was a way to keep alive fond college memories and created the illusion that nothing had changed since then. The engineers felt as if they were still free, not bound to any organization's rules or structure. Brian and his fellow engineers were trapped in a time warp of their own choosing, living in a self-created world, isolated and protected from all intruders and outsiders.

To hear the engineers tell the story, it was more along the line of why they didn't understand why others couldn't see and appreciate the obvious advantages! To work late into the night meant no phones, no interruptions, no meetings as well as fewer people around and therefore an increased likelihood of total focus in and absorption by one's work. "And besides," Brian figured, "engineers just like being different!"

The muffled, mesmerizing sound of the VW engine in the Thing silenced all outside noises and lulled Brian into a state of no worry, no concern—just peaceful satisfaction. To say he was proud of his bright yellow Thing was a definite understatement! He had bought the car four years ago. Today the Thing was almost twenty-one years old, a true treasure! The car's engine had been rebuilt just before he had purchased it and he had, with great care and love, given it a loud canary yellow paint job.

Brian was now leaving the southern part of the Bay Area and approaching the freeway that would take him north to Sunnyvale, where he worked. He had started at Atlas five years ago, right after graduating from the University of California at Berkeley with a master's degree in computer science. Back then the company had about 160 employees and had been in existence for only eighteen months. When Brian joined Atlas, the company was still privately held by the founders and venture capitalists, making it a true high-technology software startup.

Many engineers desire to be part of the early stages of a Silicon Valley high tech startup. Others might point out that many startups fail and do not survive, frequently falling into complete obscurity, never to be heard of again. Venture capitalists even have a name for it, "crib death syndrome." But beyond that the fate of failed startups is shrouded in obscurity. Nobody is interested in writing stories about failed dreams, because, after all, who would want to read them?

Even if Brian had known about these failed ventures, he still would have maintained that joining Atlas was not risky. When he had made his decision, he could see only the possibilities for and potential of Atlas products and nothing else. Maybe deep down Brian had been vaguely aware that the future of the company was uncertain and unknown. But those kinds of thoughts led to nothing good and made Brian feel stressed and overwhelmed. Therefore he focused on the personal satisfaction he felt over being able to show what he could do.

Though money is important to engineers like Brian, simply because a certain salary range is the easiest way to measure one's perceived contribution to the goals of the company, the real issue always boils down to "How much am I worth to them in the form of stock options?" A hot startup always has an edge, even when competing with much better salaries offered by more established companies. A benefit package at a startup can include stock options in the price range of $1 to $5, especially for someone who joins the startup during its very early stages. The lower the price of the options, the better for their holder. The inherent lure is that the startup may become a publicly traded company some time in the near future. The day its stock is offered to the public through an initial public offering, the price of $1 to $5 can rise to anywhere from $10 to $20. Who wouldn't enjoy these kinds of lofty returns? Yet Brian had never openly considered whether it was important for him to make a lot of money, because he simply didn't feel comfortable about money in general. He just wanted to see the startup and, more importantly, its products succeed. Therefore, he didn't perceive any risk whatsoever when joining Atlas.

Brian had been lucky, and his decision to join Atlas had paid off. Today Atlas had 1,800 employees, was quite profitable and successful in its field, and had made a name for itself by keeping up with each major technological breakthrough by launching complementary software tools for various market segments. Since 1992 Atlas had been a publicly traded company, and Brian was actually pretty well off, at least on paper, since he preferred just holding all his stock options and saving them for the future. It was just another way of avoiding thinking about subjects that made him feel uncomfortable.

As Brian drove down the highway, he began to reflect on the earlier events of the day. He had left work at 6 p.m. to attend his father's birthday party. Though he realized it was a childish excuse, he nonetheless blamed his sister Margaret for the bad evening. She always succeeded in making him feel guilty about not wanting to attend family functions.

Family and family relations were subjects Brian didn't like to talk or think about. Why did parents always have to try and change their children's lifestyle and habits? If he ever had kids, he definitely would allow them to be more individualistic! Then again, it was difficult to predict what he would do in the future. The more he struggled with his family, the more he questioned whether he ever wanted the responsibility of having children.

Any casual observer would have been only too aware of how much Brian resented spending time with his family. He looked rigid and stiff around them. He resisted being drawn out of his protective shell to engage in what he called "meaningless chatter." At times he looked like a volcano ready to go off without warning. While at the birthday party, in order to put a distance between himself and his family, Brian had started to think about rerunning certain code at work. He felt so close to a solution, yet major parts of the code kept crashing, and so far nobody on his team had been able to come up with a solid fix. But instead of creating a longed-for diversion, thoughts about work had actually increased the irritation he felt over wasting time with his family. Oh, how he wished he had never come!

Three months ago the pressure at work had become extremely intense. One of the top engineering teams was designing a new security tool. The product was scheduled to be released within the next two months. Once a new product reached the final stages of the design, Brian's test diagnostics group got involved. This group was headed by Bob Laidlaw and tested all new software tools to make sure they worked with Atlas's latest system software. What Brian liked about his job were getting to know a lot of different software tools and becoming an expert for each successive version of Atlas's system software.

To put in at least sixty to eighty hours each week was just part of the job. It was a given, though not an always openly acknowledged fact of an engineer's job description. The engineers were used to it. Nobody seemed to question it. At peak production cycles some actually worked three days a week nonstop without going home, right through the night. It was not unusual to find a couple of engineers still at work at 3 or 4 a.m. The ones keeping these insane hours were young, single, or had been married only a few years. Their marriage partners were still hoping for a miracle that would never come: the day an engineer agrees with his wife that in order to have a healthy and sustainable relationship, they also need to spend more time together! The ones who had children usually had learned to modify their lifestyles at least a little, but only after getting pressure from their wives, who frequently had to remind them to stick to earlier promises to make time for the family. Yet nobody really wanted to talk about these pressures openly. They were in this together, and, more importantly, they were changing the world!

By now Brian had left the freeway and had entered the small access road leading to Atlas. His building was at the end of the road. Brian circled the building to get to the back parking lot. A creature of habit, he parked his car in its usual spot, on the western side of the building. While getting out of the car and locking it, he looked around to see who else might still be in the building tonight. Since it was crunch time, he expected to see a number of cars, yet he identified only six familiar cars. Maybe this was one of the nights most had chosen to go home a little earlier. Among the six cars in the parking lot Brian recognized Jeff's old VW bus. A smile appeared on his face. Maybe he could have a little chat with Jeff. He liked Jeff. He felt comfortable around him, though he couldn't express why.

A long time ago Brian had started memorizing license plates. He didn't try to. It just happened. All numbers somehow seemed to take on a life of their own. Upon sight they were stored in his mind, just like that! Brian checked his watch. It was 10:06 p.m. He approached the backside entrance. Just around the corner, barely visible, partially hidden by the trash containers, he noticed a seventh car, a black Camaro equipped with fancy gold trim. It looked like one of the latest models. Gee whiz! he thought to himself. Somebody must really like flashy features! He had never seen anything like it. Who would drive something like that? Brian was sure that this car had never been in the parking lot before. He couldn't picture any of the guys he knew driving it. Strange. But he could be wrong. Sometimes people were quite unpredictable about what they liked. The license read 4PRIS 1830. Maybe somebody was picking up a friend.

As Brian reached the back door of the building, he fished in the back pocket of his jeans for his ID card to unlock the electronic security door. His building housed roughly 100

employees and had three labs, one downstairs and two upstairs. The vice president of research & development,
Loren Grimm, and his two directors of engineering, Bob
Laidlaw and Scott Jones, were located upstairs, together
with their support people. Most engineers worked downstairs.

After opening the door, Brian slipped his badge back
into his pocket. As he entered he heard a faint sound like
somebody running off in the opposite direction. The sound
seemed to be coming from an adjacent corridor.

Why would somebody be in such an apparent hurry?
Brian stopped for a moment and listened. No more sound.
It was quite quiet now. Maybe he had been mistaken.

Brian decided to stop at the little break room for an
espresso. A good strong cup would get him going. There
he met Loren Grimm. Brian thought to himself, "Oh, no!"
Where had Loren come from, and what was he doing in
the downstairs break room at this hour of the day? Brian
hadn't heard any additional sounds, just the noise of somebody running down the hallway, away from the break
room. He hadn't heard Loren. Loren must have soft shoes.
Brian looked at Loren's shoes. Well, it was hard to tell.
Loren briefly greeted Brian as he checked his pockets for
change, and after retrieving some coins, he deposited them
in a soda machine. Brian tried to avoid Loren whenever
possible. He simply didn't like him. Though Loren Grimm
was in charge of the new security tool product, Brian's own
involvement with him was limited, since Brian belonged to
Bob Laidlaw's group.

Brian had mumbled a short greeting and tried to avoid Loren by busying himself with his espresso. At the same time he wondered why Loren was getting his soda downstairs, when his office was upstairs and a little kitchenette was right next to his office. Also, Loren usually left by the front door. Brian tensed up. Loren had this air about him. He came across as either patronizing, stuck up, arrogant, a know-it-all, or a combination of all of these annoying traits. "What a night," Brian thought to himself. "I got away from my family and now Loren!" But Loren seemed preoccupied, and after a couple of general exchanges he said good night and headed for the same door through which Brian had just entered. Brian started to relax. That hadn't been too bad after all!

The milk was steamed. The espresso was just running through. Brian was all set now, eager and ready to tackle his code. The building was really quiet, the way Brian liked it. Suddenly there was the faint sound made by the closing of the front door. Who was leaving or coming in through the front door? Brian knew every sound the building, the people, or the machines could make. What he had heard was the closing sound of the door facing the east side of the building. He had heard no sounds while talking to Loren. If others were still working tonight, they had to be in one of the labs.

Brian's cube was the one just before the end of the row, on the left, in the corner, with a window view. Right across from him was Jeff's cube. Jeff was a contractor who had been assisting Scott Jones's team for the last three months.

Scott was the head of the design team working on the new security tool that Brian's group was now testing. Jeff liked to keep to himself and didn't socialize much, but he and Brian would chat every now and again when they needed a break. Brian liked talking to Jeff, so he decided to look for him. He had to be around, since his car was parked outside. Sometimes Jeff stayed late, though not as frequently as Brian. With espresso in hand, Brian walked into Jeff's cube and froze. His entire body went numb, and his right hand released the cup spilling its content of freshly brewed espresso and hot, steamed milk onto the floor. Brian didn't even realize that he had dropped the cup, and that, fortunately, the hot brew had missed his body. All he saw was Jeff lying on the floor, face down and bleeding from a wound in the back of his head.

"Jeff, Jeff, are you okay?" Hardly knowing what he was doing, Brian leaned over Jeff's body, hoping he could hear him breathe. He felt sick to his stomach. Without realizing it he said out loud, "Jeff is dead. Jeff is dead. I know it. I feel it." Hearing his own voice scared Brian even more. It sounded hollow and was filled with terror. In an attempt to control the intense panic and naked fear he felt, Brian reminded himself, "Don't touch anything, don't touch anything. The police wouldn't like that!" Incapable of making himself check Jeff's pulse and overcome by a great need to escape, Brian fled to his own cube. Still feeling cold and numb but with a heart pulsating out of control, Brian picked up the phone and called the onsite security people. Let them call the police.

Chapter 3

In Dar Es Salaam

Thursday, October 5, 1995, 1:22 p.m. Local Time

"Come on, come on! Answer the phone, Jeff!! *Now!*" The recorder clicked on. "Hi, this is Jeff."

Totally disgusted, Angel slammed down the receiver. No use leaving a message. She was going to be en route most of the day. She wanted to scream, swear, throw a fit—but she was at an airport, not really the place to make a spectacle of yourself. Besides, what difference would it make? Jeff certainly wouldn't hear her! Her heart was pounding like a hollow, rhythmic echo, seemingly urging her on. To what? She checked her watch. Local time was eleven hours ahead of Pacific time. Jeff should be in bed sleeping. It was 2:22 a.m. on Thursday in California. Where was he? Where could he possibly be? What was going on?

Why did Angel suddenly remember the scary dream that had awakened her around 6:45 this morning? A wave of powerful emotions rushed through her body, causing her to feel cut off from the world around. An unknown force was holding her and pulling her away from what was real, pushing her into a dark and scary bottomless pit. It was so frightening and felt so intense. Calling on all the energy and willpower at her disposal, she tried to stop getting sucked up by this powerful dark force. "I have to fight! I have to fight!! Or I will lose myself!" She thought she had yelled out loud, but no sounds were coming from her lips. There was a deathlike silence all around her. The only sound Angel could hear was the relentless beating of her heart. Oh, to be able to just crawl into a hole and cry and let go. But there was no hole, no refuge. This was an *airport*!

Where was Jeff? Why didn't he answer his phone? Assuming he was still at work, she hadn't called Jeff's home phone till 8 p.m. Pacific time, 7 a.m. local time today. At first she had called from the hotel where her travel group had been staying. They had left the hotel around 10 a.m. for a flight to the Kilimanjaro International Airport. Shortly after arriving at the airport in Dar Es Salaam, they learned that their flight was delayed. Sitting around the airport— waiting—only heaven knew for what—had only increased Angel's tension and fearful apprehension. She felt on edge and didn't know why. Over the course of the last hour she had dialed Jeff's number again and again *every* five to ten minutes. Never mind that it was night in California! Now she felt drained and overcome by cold, naked fear.

Why didn't Jeff answer the phone??

Angel's colleague Lise had been waiting for Angel not too far from the phone booth.

"Any luck?" Lise inquired. Lise's face looked open, vulnerable, soft, inviting and mostly comforting. But Angel hardly noticed her or much of anything else. Everything seemed blurred and distant. Angel just shook her head in response to Lise's question. Lise came over and put her arms around Angel. For a moment it seemed as if they were the only living beings in this busy, bustling airport. It was just the two of them—and Angel's fear.

Lise knew how upset, frustrated, and scared Angel was by now. In a moment of weakness and despair Angel suddenly buried her face in the refuge of Lise's warm and comforting arms, fighting back her tears. However, Angel didn't give in for very long. She hated being perceived as weak and wimpy; yet around Lise she didn't mind quite as much letting her guard down, even though it was for just a short moment.

Angel liked Lise, and the two of them had become quite close on this trip, which had started back in San Francisco on July 15. The tour was scheduled to return on October 15. It was one of those fancy packages that supposedly offered the most spectacular and unusual sights and locations while also promising the most incredible adventures. The package included a two-week cruise as well as a safari. By now Angel couldn't even remember the name of most of the places they had visited, and she hated all hotels, even the luxurious ones she usually enjoyed so much. To make matters worse, she had been terribly seasick during the cruise in Asia. What a life! What a mess! Why did she ever go on this stupid trip? Jeff had been right. She should have stayed in San Francisco.

Lise and Angel were group travel companions working for the same agency. Lise held a senior position and, as Angel had learned on this trip, was quite a seasoned traveler. Lise had joined the agency almost eight years ago. Unlike Angel, who could get irritated by frequent changes in schedule and the peculiarities and fastidiousness of these well-to-do leisure travelers, Lise seemed able to just go with the flow. No matter how fussy and demanding the group was, she still had kind words for them and seemed to truly enjoy them, warts and all. Angel found this absolutely amazing. Her patience with the travelers had worn out after three weeks, and the remaining trip had become more unbearable with each passing day. She must have been nuts when she signed up for this three-month tour to Asia, India, and Africa. She had wanted a wonderful adventure, and what did she end up with? Only misery. Nothing had worked out the way she had wanted it to! Since September she had been counting the days till their return to the States. Just ten more days, and they would finally be back—to what? What was waiting for her?

Angel was obsessed with nagging thoughts and questions. Why did it seem that days dragged on more when you allowed yourself to be openly impatient? Each day spelled unbearable dread and boredom. How could she possibly survive a one-week safari in the Serengeti plain? She wasn't interested in seeing any wild animals and was clueless as to whether she had ever wanted to see any in the first place! What was the big deal about going on a safari? Didn't people have anything better to do with their lives than seeing the world? Well, she certainly didn't.

Jeff had been right. The whole tour guide idea had turned out to be as disastrous as he had predicted. Why did it always take an experience, and mostly a horrible one, for her to learn what she could or could not tolerate? Nothing could hold her attention and interest for very long. Why? What had she hoped to get out of this trip? She had no idea. However, she was only too aware of how irritated and frustrated she was by now!

While resting in Lise's arms, Angel marveled at how calm and centered Lise appeared to be all the time. She was thirty-eight years old, about ten years older than Angel. In her twenties Lise had been married briefly. It hadn't worked out. Angel was amazed at how well Lise had recovered from that experience. The only other divorce Angel knew intimately was that of her parents, and it had been a real war, with acts of revenge and retribution on both sides. Lise in contrast showed no signs of bitterness. When Angel had asked her about her experience, Lise had said, "We were both very young and had no idea what we were getting into. We needed to grow up and solidify who we really wanted to be."

Angel had no idea what Lise meant by that. But Angel loved Lise's warm, comforting, and all-understanding attitude. Lise was the first close woman friend she had ever had aside from her childhood friend Maggie. Angel had learned through painful experiences that women resented her because they felt intimidated by her intellect, energy, and intensity. She figured it was mostly the intensity that scared them away. She wondered why Lise wasn't scared off or intimidated.

By now Angel had regained some of her composure. She had pulled herself away from the warm refuge of Lise's arms, afraid to give in to feelings she could not control. Looking self-conscious and feeling rather exposed, she wiped away some stubborn tears that simply wouldn't stop flowing. "Oh, so what, it's just Lise. It's okay," she thought. But it was not okay, and she knew it. She couldn't stand feeling this vulnerable.

Lise sensed how uncomfortable Angel felt and tried to offer suggestions that might have a calming effect on her.

"Maybe Jeff left town for a couple of days."

Angel's voice sounded a little better and less shaky when she responded, "No, that couldn't be it. I talked to him last Sunday. Let's see, that was on October 1, and we arranged that I would call him again on Wednesday or Thursday. I've usually called him around 9 p.m. his time, if it worked out with the time zones we were in. We've pretty much stuck to the routine of calling twice a week since the beginning of the trip."

"You really love him, don't you?"

Angel just nodded, and again tears welled up in her eyes. She quickly rubbed them away. When the flow would not stop, she covered her face with her hands. Oh, this was so hard to deal with!. She could have never admitted her real feelings for Jeff to anybody else but Lise.

After leaving the phone booth, they had walked to the end of the departure lounge and had sat down where there were fewer people. Angel had found a tissue in her purse and kept dabbing her eyes.

"You know, Lise, the worst part is that I had this recurring dream the last couple of nights. That's why I'm so emotional. I don't understand what the dream is trying to say, and that's why I'm so scared. Did you ever see the old movie "The Song of Bernadette?"

Lise nodded, waiting for Angel to tell her about the movie's personal significance.

"I always cry when I see that movie. Isn't it horrible that nobody believed Bernadette, and the whole village thought she was making it all up? The church people were the worst! Anyway, what I'm trying to say is, I always relate to Bernadette's feelings of not being understood and nobody believing her vision. I guess that's what you would have to call it. And that's how I feel when I have foreboding dreams. I don't want to talk about them, because I figure everybody would think that I'm just crazy anyway. And you know, some of my dreams have actually come true! That's when I *really* feel like Bernadette! Do *you* believe in dreams?"

"Actually, I do. I think dreams are a way for us to learn more about ourselves. But go on."

Angel was looking out of the big window of the airport, but she didn't really see the scenery or anything else around her. She seemed to be far away. Her voice was halting at first. Slowly, sentence by sentence, she managed to get more focused.

"Well, like I already said, I don't seem to be able to make any sense out of the dream. But I've had the same dream several times, and it seems to get more intense and detailed as it repeats itself."

I'm back at Smith College. Everything seems familiar and yet strange at the same time. I feel separated, eerie, and isolated. I find myself getting increasingly anxious, but I don't understand why. I seem to be lost. I don't like what I'm feeling and am looking around for a way out. I start running. I'm running through one of the dining halls at Smith College.

Then the scenery changes abruptly, and I'm no longer at Smith. Instead I'm in an elevator. The elevator reminds me of the elevators in my father's office building in downtown Manhattan.

I don't know why, but for some reason it is imperative for me to get to the fourth floor. What is even stranger is that I seem to be very high up, which means that I need to go down to reach the fourth floor. I press the elevator button for the fourth floor. Then I become aware that the elevator keeps moving down, passing the fourth floor. Suddenly the elevator stops. I look at the sign above the door to figure out what floor it is. I read 209B. The doors stay shut. The elevator is just sitting there, motionless. I start to wonder where floor 209B is. I didn't even know that this floor existed! I panic. I am very distraught and feel out of control, but I can't figure out why. The panic intensifies when I become aware that I am not alone. Somebody else is with me in the elevator and has been there all along. I wonder why I didn't see this person before. It's a male figure. I am unable to identify what the male looks like. His face is blank.

I sense danger! And instantaneously I become aware that the male figure wants to hold me captive in the elevator and doesn't want me to exit. I feel enclosed and trapped and try to move away. But he comes after me, grabs me and his arms hold me in a tight grip. I struggle to get away from this figure. In the midst of my struggle, quite miraculously the elevator door opens to floor 209B. The opening of the door seems to have distracted my captor, and I manage to get free and make a run for it. Then I remember that this is the wrong floor. I was supposed to go to the fourth floor. But now it is too late, and this is the only way out, the only way to escape from the male in the elevator. But what about getting to the fourth floor? What if I don't find my way back? Floor 209B seems to be below the fourth floor, but I'm not sure. I wonder what kind of floor would be called 209B. I feel terribly confused and frightened.

Hoping to regain my bearings, I look around. What happened? I am no longer in a building. Rather I am in a wide open countryside. The scenery has a ghostlike quality; everything looks pale and hollow. It frightens me, though I don't know why. The sun is just about to set. Pretty soon it will be dark. My anxiety increases. I feel so lost. My fear and panic increase with each passing moment. It makes me want to run. I am running and running as fast as I possibly can . . .

Another shift of scenery. Suddenly I am in a small town. Then I remember that I have to get to the fourth floor. It was terribly important; how could I have forgotten? I keep looking around, hoping to find a way back to the fourth floor—my real destination. I pass through several streets, but they do not lead to where I want to go. Full of anxiety, I find myself running rather aimlessly up and down the streets. Suddenly the lights in all the houses go out. My panic intensifies! I feel like I will be lost forever and will never make it back to where I came from and where I really live and where I belong. Getting to the fourth floor is vitally important, a necessity! That's where I am from, and that's where I belong, and I want to be there so much! It hurts so terribly not to be there!

Now everything about me is colored in a gray dusk. All that's left of the sun is a tiny glimmer on the horizon. The houses around me look like the houses in Kitzbuehel, Austria. Terrible dread overtakes me. Then I suddenly feel like an unknown force is chasing me and is about to overtake me in order to extinguish and annihilate me forever.

"I am so frightened that I wake up." Angel took a deep breath. She felt exhausted and drained. While telling the dream, she had experienced and relived its every moment and emotion.

Lise looked concerned. "I'm glad I didn't have that dream. It sounds terribly scary. How are you doing now? Are you getting better? Does it make more sense to you now that you've talked about it?"

Angel still seemed far away as she tried to relate how she felt about the dream.

"Nothing about the dream makes sense, and that's what scares me the most, probably, at least that's what I am thinking right now. The dream uses Smith College as a reference point. But I am not sure why, nor do I have any clue as to what it means. Remember I told you I finally had enough of the conventional college ways and quit in the middle of my junior year? I went home for the Christmas break and did not return to classes at the end of January 1988. Instead I took off to Europe and ended up in Kitzbuehel, Austria, for a couple of years. I was running away from all sorts of things. It seems I'm still running. At least according to the dream . . ."

A dark shadow fell over Angel's face. Her voice had become almost inaudible. Again she started to cry. The tears just came. She couldn't stop them.

Lise nodded and waited for Angel to calm down. Angel had told her about the years she had spent in Kitzbuehel and the subsequent disappointment over a broken relationship.

After regaining some composure, Angel continued.

"Every time I think about the dream I think about how I am running and running and how scared and lost I feel. The scariest moment is at the end of the dream, when I have the sensation that something is about to take me over, and this something, which is totally undefined, will actually swallow me up, and then I simply won't exist anymore. It's just nuts, but the dream always makes me think of Jeff, and I don't know why. There's no good reason for it. Also, I can't figure out at all what those numbers mean. Why does the dream seem to imply that I am trying to get back to the fourth floor because that's where I really belong?"

"Well, do you feel lost and lonely when Jeff is not with you? You've certainly missed him a lot on this trip, right? That might explain why the dream reminds you of Jeff. As to the numbers and the floors, maybe you are just longing to be yourself, though the dream also seems to say that you are struggling to figure out who to be. You are running and looking for something that seems to be about you."

"Yeah, that's true. But there has to be some deeper meaning to the dream. You see, Jeff has never even been to many of the places that appear in my dreams, like my time in Kitzbuehel."

"Can you identify any feelings inside of you that might express that you are longing to be set free, to be more real?"

"Doesn't everybody feel that way? Of course I do!" Angel's voice rose and became almost defensive.

Lise quietly said, "No, not all people feel so strongly about wanting to be more real and authentic. They neither search for more authenticity nor bother thinking about who they are. They just accept themselves and their circumstances. They are unconcerned about what drives and motivates them. They just are."

"Well, that sounds horrible, at least to me! There has to be more to life than the obvious. There has to be a reason why I'm here in the first place. After all, without a purpose, life would be meaningless. I would just be a chance of something, something that I had no control over. No, no, I wouldn't be able to handle that. There has to be more to life than that. And I have been trying to figure that out ever since I was little girl."

Angel suddenly looked like a lost little girl.

Lise was quiet for a moment. She didn't want to upset Angel. Finally she said, "I, too, want my life to have meaning. It's just that each of us has a very personal way of defining what is meaningful. In any case, as to your dream, you are probably not going to find a perfect explanation, but you could try to think about what it is that you always want to run away from. You see, what I am trying to say is, it might help if you were willing to face what is chasing you. And I don't mean that literally. It would just be an attitude. You could try to be *open* to face *whatever* you are afraid of and tend to run away *from*. Does that make sense? Do you understand what I am trying to say?"

"Yes, I think I do. I'm not sure though, but what you say does seem to make sense. Then again, to be honest, I'm mostly quite disturbed that Jeff is in none of the scenes in that dream. Where is he? Is he the male figure in the elevator? I don't think so. And who is the male figure?"

Lise thought for a moment and then replied, "I think in life we have to work through our struggles individually. Others, no matter how much they love us, can't really help us. As to the male figure, I do believe that each human being, whether male or female, also has the opposite characteristics. In this case, you, being female, would also have a male side. Since knowing you I have observed that you use your mind and logic to control your unwanted feelings, especially when you get scared."

"Meaning what exactly? What are you trying to say? I think I lost you now," Angel said.

Lise hesitated again. You didn't have to be with Angel for very long to realize that she had rather strong opinions, which she defended vehemently at all times. Right now

Angel just didn't seem to be very open to a new way of looking at life. Therefore, Lise said, "I can certainly understand why you are worried about not reaching Jeff. You are wondering whether this is a bad omen for the future, right? You are wondering what role Jeff will play in your life? Is that it?"

Angel just nodded. Again she was fighting back her tears before being able to respond.

"You see, I've had other dreams, equally scary. And somehow they always seem to highlight me alone, scared, running, or something not working out. In one dream, while I was on that trip with Jeff last summer, he was part of the dream. We were about to embark on a train, but he insisted on running back to another train to get something. I woke up before knowing whether he got back in time or missed our train!"

Recalling more dreams and feelings turned out to be too much for Angel, and she finally let go and broke into loud sobs. Lise moved closer and hugged her tightly. After waiting a couple of moments and after letting go of Angel, Lise said, "I would be pretty concerned myself. Have you tried calling somebody in the States who could possibly call Jeff?"

Angel found another tissue and wiped away the latest onslaught of tears.

"I've thought about that. I could call my good old friend Maggie. I have the number where she works. But I don't really want to get anybody else involved. I feel kind of stupid. It's just that I can't shake off the dream . . ."

"How about calling the company where Jeff was working and getting information that way?"

"Well, I've thought about that, too. But again, I would feel like an idiot. What would I say?"

Nobody who had known Angel would have recognized her now. Her usually sparkling eyes were dull, and the flaming red color of her tee-shirt intensified the pallor of her face. Angel closed her eyes and slumped into her seat, settling into a helpless fetal position. Lise waited, her face expressing support, comfort, and encouragement.

After a little while Angel opened her eyes again. "You're probably right, Lise. There is nothing wrong with calling Jeff's company. And if I look like an idiot, that's okay, too!"

Angel checked her watch. Their flight was supposed to take off soon.

"Let's first get to the Kilimanjaro International Airport, and once we're settled at the hotel, I can try calling Jeff again. The weekend is coming up. We won't leave on the safari till Monday. So, if I can't reach Jeff over the weekend, I'll call Atlas, the company he works for, on Monday."

Lise nodded. At that very moment their flight was announced over the speaker. They stood up, picked up their bag and headed toward their gate.

Chapter 4

The Morning After

Thursday, October 5, 1995, 10:00 a.m.

Brian's grip was uneasy. Looking down at his right hand, he noticed that he was visibly trembling. Taking both hands, he was finally able to push his security badge against the electronic sensor to gain access to the building.

Ever since last night Brian had felt trapped in an emotional time warp. He kept seeing the same picture, over and over again—Jeff motionless on the floor in his cube. The way Brian experienced this emotional memory was that he actually felt imprisoned in Jeff's cube, forced to see the same scene again and again. Each flashback sent a wave of shock and horror through Brian's entire being.

Last night had been the most horrible night of his life. First the police had kept him at work until almost midnight. The whole experience of dealing with them was just a blur now. He remembered nothing. There had been no letup or relief, not even after leaving work. With his mind spinning and his emotions out of control he had become a total wreck. And the intensity would not let up. It must have been close to 5 a.m. before utter exhaustion finally gave way to a numbing sleep.

The police had ordered Brian to be available for additional questioning today. He dreaded having to talk to the police. It was crazy, but the only feeling he could identify was that somehow, and he had no idea why, he felt like he had done something wrong. Why would he feel that way? After all, he only found the body . . .

Entering the building in a stupor, Brian didn't see Michelle until she had called out for him several times.

"Brian, Brian, wait, wait for me! I want to talk to you!"

Michelle was running toward him from the other end of the hallway. The sound of her footsteps reminded him of the noise he had heard last night. It felt eerie and scary! Brian assumed that Michelle had been on the lookout for him. She seemed to be on constant alert, always wanting to know everything that was happening in and around the building. Her desk was upstairs, right next to a window that overlooked the back parking lot, where Brian always parked. She must have started running downstairs right after spotting his car, which everybody knew because it was such a rare and unusual vintage. Some not-so-friendly co-workers who considered Brian standoffish and arrogant loved to use the car as an excuse for spiteful and often cruel personal attacks. But Brian had learned long ago that it was best to just ignore such remarks and to appear unconcerned, making him appear even more standoffish.

Today Brian actually welcomed Michelle's sudden interruption. Still numb and full of a sense of dread, he was glad to see her cheery face and to become enveloped in her positive attitude—truly a welcome interruption from his gloomy thoughts.

Brian kind of liked Michelle. Not so long ago he had even had a crush on her, though he would have strongly denied it. She was about five-feet-five, probably twenty-five years old. She had long, straight blond hair, and dark brown eyes. Right now Michelle's eyes were glistening like deep charcoal, reflecting feelings of high intensity and making Brian, who already struggled keeping his own feelings at bay, notice her even more. Her clothes, her movements, everything about her accentuated her vitality. She seemed to have no constraints and was a force with which to reckon.

Michelle had decided long ago that she wasn't going to worry about what others thought of her strong, energetic personality and her choice of clothes. Wearing the latest fashion trends was Michelle's forte and delight, and she loved it. She knew that even extreme styles that might have overkill on somebody else looked just right on her. Michelle was sure of herself and her choices, because she knew by instinct what colors and styles suited her best and didn't mind looks and stares. Actually, she seemed to be inviting them and enjoyed the pursuant interplay. Since most of the one-hundred-plus people in Michelle's building were male engineers, she had plenty of opportunity to show off her flair and have some fun. This was her stage where she could perform and show off! However, away from her stage her flamboyant style invited frequent biting criticism and gossip by female coworkers. But Michelle believed that they were just jealous, and that settled it for her!

Today Michelle wore a very short, red, long-sleeved trapeze dress with a twenty-inch rim of ruffles made of the same material as the dress. The short dress exposed well-shaped legs clad in tight black leggings accentuated by black platform pumps sporting big silver buckles. The dress's neckline was low cut, but not tastelessly so, and around her neck Michelle wore a little white scarf with big black polka dots, the kind of scarf Andre Agassi sometimes wore around his head. The pattern of the scarf was perfectly matched by big white ear clips with tiny black polka dots. To top it all off, Michelle wore a black leather vest. Any observer would have had to say she was prepared to defend her turf. Sheer energy in motion! To share in it was the desire of many!

Before Michelle's promotion to the position of executive secretary to vice president of research & development, Loren Grimm, she had worked for Brian's boss, Bob Laidlaw. During those days Brian used to drop by her desk at least once a day. But Loren made Brian feel uncomfortable and uneasy, so he had stayed away more and more. He wondered if Michelle had noticed. Well, not unless she cared about him. With hushed voices and pompous self-righteous attitudes, her critics delighted in insinuating that Michelle and Loren were more than boss and secretary, but Brian refused to believe this. He was certain that Michelle didn't like Loren. Besides, he couldn't stand all that gossip.

Gasping for air after her run down the hallway, Michelle now stopped right in front of Brian and exclaimed, "Brian, you must be so upset! I've been thinking about you ever since I heard about the murder and how you found the body. What a horrible thing to have to go through! You must feel awful!"

Somehow Michelle always put Brian's emotions into words. It was like magic, and frequently he was quite taken back and didn't appreciate this characteristic of hers. But today her words had a soothing effect. He felt comforted and understood and said, "Yes, it was awful."

Brian had been meaning to say more but sensed that he was about to be overcome by strong emotions. Suddenly he realized not only that last night's experience had been quite overwhelming, but also that he now seemed to be in the center of a lot of unwanted attention. This kind of exposure caused him a great degree of personal discomfort and intensified the sense of dread and uneasiness he had first experienced last night. As if she had been reading his mind, Michelle said, "Brian, everybody has been asking for you and wants to talk to you."

Brian panicked. This was not good. No, not good at all. Finally he managed to say, "I'm not sure what there is to tell. Probably a couple of the other guys who were here last night would know more than I do. I only found the body."

The last sentence was barely audible, but Michelle didn't seem to notice. She was too caught up in the excitement of the events. Brian, in contrast found it painful to relate to Jeff as a body. It was so final, so over, so . . .

It was just horrible. All night long he had been wondering—who would want to kill Jeff and why. Had Jeff been aware of somebody approaching him from behind? Did he know the person? Did he die right away? The police had done a preliminary search last night, but aside from questioning Brian and the other four engineers who were still in the lab, nothing had really been discussed or explained. The police team had been very tightlipped, and Brian and the other four engineers had been told to be available for more questioning today. After an ambulance took Jeff's body away, all that remained were a chalk outline on the carpet and a yellow demarcation strip in front of Jeff's old cube. After Brian and the other engineers had left last night, the police had blocked off the building. Sometime late last night or early this morning they must have re-opened the building to allow people access to their workplaces.

It wasn't so much the circumstances surrounding Jeff's death that preoccupied Brian, but rather one single thought: Why had Jeff been killed? Without understanding why, there was no closure for Brian; and without closure his general feeling of malaise was getting worse by the second. He could not rest. His mind kept searching for a satisfactory resolve. There had to be an answer. It was a *must*! To believe otherwise was unacceptable to Brian and out of the question.

Michelle had tagged along to Brian's cubicle. Suddenly she froze in mid stride, staring at the yellow demarcation strip still blocking the entrance to Jeff's cube.

"Doesn't it just give you the creeps thinking about what happened here?"

Brian wouldn't look up and didn't answer. Instead he had quickly sought refuge in the familiar surroundings of his workplace. There was no way he was going to look.

"Brian, it must have been horrible for you when you found Jeff last night. And then, to top it all off, you were more or less all alone in the building, late at night, and it was dark outside. Ugh . . ."

Brian was frantically thinking of something to say that would stop Michelle from evoking the disturbing, unforgettable, and nightmarish picture of last night, which was now permanently stored in his brain. Fortunately Michelle never stayed too long on any subject, and so she soon turned around, entered Brian's cube, and sat down on the extra chair. Loren probably wasn't around, and even if he was, it didn't seem to matter much to her. She never seemed to experience any time pressures at all. How enviable!

Brian settled into his chair at the computer and listened to Michelle detail what had transpired so far this morning. It wasn't as tough as he had feared. Actually he was glad for a short reprieve from all the obsessive thoughts that had been running through his mind without aim and purpose. Now he could just look at her and listen.

Evidently Loren was not even in the office yet, and Michelle didn't know why, but she did know that the police had contacted him, and so maybe Loren had met with them already, possibly at the police station. Word had spread like wildfire all throughout the company. Somebody, Michelle assumed one of the engineers who had still been here last night, had sent an e-mail to the company's internal newsgroup. Since 50 to 60% of the employees read the general newsgroup, probably just about everybody had read about last night's tragedy by now or would certainly read about it some time during the day. All who had read the first e-mail had probably forwarded it to somebody else, like a chain letter. Brian figured that many had also forwarded the message to friends and contacts outside of the company. By now the news had probably spread throughout Silicon Valley and possibly beyond. Though Brian never read any newspapers, he assumed that the morning papers had carried the story as well.

Brian grew restless while listening to Michelle chatting away. Ten minutes was about his limit. Michelle seemed to sense this. She suddenly got up and told him she had to take care of a couple of things but would keep in touch.

"Let me know if you find out anything else, promise?" Without waiting for an answer, she jumped out of the chair. Turning at full speed, the ruffles of her dress lifted just a smidgen, and off she was!

Two seconds later her head popped back into Brian's cube one more time. "By the way, Mike, Steve, and Allen asked about you several times this morning before you got in. I promised them I would ask you to stop by to see them when you arrive. Okay? Look for them in the lab. You will, won't you?"

"Oh, oh, yeah, I guess so . . ." Brian's mind was racing. He would have to ignore that request for now. He could not deal with them and/or possible questions about last night. At least Michelle had left. He was alone with his thoughts. Good.

Brian decided to focus on his e-mail first. Just as he had figured—lots of them. He was sure most of them were about the murder. There it was—for the first time he had called it a murder. It felt ominous, and he couldn't get rid of the sensation that a black cloud was settling over the day, and especially over him personally.

For the next hour Brian read most of the fifty-five e-mail messages in his mailbox and replied when necessary. Two-thirds of the messages were about the murder. He scanned only a few of those and ignored the rest. But a couple of the others required his immediate attention since they related to his current project. He also had to check his voicemail box. He generally hated having to deal with voicemail messages and figured they, too, were mainly about Jeff's death. But he would have to listen to them since he was expecting to hear from the police about possible further questioning.

"Brian, Brian!"

He turned and was surprised to see Michelle back again so soon. Now what did she want?

"I got a call from Lieutenant Woodraw, who wants to talk to you. And guess what, it's a woman, and she is the chief investigating officer for this case. She wants to see you at 11:30 a.m., here. Can you make it? I'll confirm it back for you, okay?"

Brian had frozen inside. He felt like running away and hiding. Slowly he said, "I guess I have to. Yes, please confirm it for me, and thanks, Michelle!"

Brian checked his watch. That left him only about twenty-five minutes. Darn it, this was not going to be a good day! But now he had a good excuse for not stopping by the lab to see the engineers who had been in the building last night and who had been asking for him.

The phone rang, and without knowing what he was doing Brian picked it up.

"It's Michelle! It's all confirmed for 11:30 a.m. I put you into the conference room usually reserved for Loren. The lieutenant will be seeing others there as well."

"Okay, Michelle, thanks."

Brian spent the next fifteen minutes going over all the specifics of last night one more time. Maybe he had missed something. Maybe he didn't remember a specific that could turn out to be vitally important. He wished he knew what Loren had been doing here last night. Loren seldom stayed past 8:00 or 8:30 at night. What had he been up to? Usually Loren liked to chat, but not last night. He had been pretty short when they had met in the break room.

And why had Loren exited through the back door? His car was always parked in front or to the side of the building. Brian was certain about his observations. Loren owned a black BMW convertible, and Brian hadn't seen Loren's car in the back parking lot. This was puzzling. Maybe Loren had bought a new car. Could the flashy Camaro belong to

Loren? Michelle would have told him if Loren bought a new car. He should check with her.

What about the noise he had heard, followed by the sound of footsteps running away from the break room? If Loren didn't own that Camaro, who did? Somebody from Atlas, a visitor, or possibly a friend picking up a friend? However, there had been only five people in the building, including Brian. The Camaro was no longer parked in the back when Brian had left last night. The police and security people had come in through the front door of the building. They might have never seen the Camaro. If somebody had indeed been running in the opposite direction when Brian had entered the building last night, then it was possible that this person could have walked around the building to the Camaro parked in the back. Loren might have seen somebody . . .

Brian interrupted his thoughts and checked his watch again. He had to get to the conference room fast to meet with the police investigator. What was her name again? Oh, no, he had actually forgotten her name . . . He should have written it down when Michelle told him. Brian felt distraught, like a failure. Well, he would have to manage!

Chapter 5

Lunch with Brigitte

Thursday, October 5, 199, 12:12 p.m.

Brian checked his watch and panicked. Oh no, it was past noon already! Now, to top it all off, he would be late for his lunch date with Brigitte. Irritation combined with a vague feeling of guilt surged inside of Brian, immediately followed by intense rage. Since Brian didn't want to give in to the rage, he tried to bottle up what he felt, and this in turn made him feel trapped. Nothing was working anymore. In a desperate attempt to gain control, Brian admonished himself sternly, "Stop everything! Focus and act!"

This sounded fairly easy, yet thoughts about Lieutenant Woodraw and his meeting with her not so long ago kept interfering. Brian had hated the meeting and wished he could forget about it. To him the lieutenant appeared controlling and antagonistic. He had disliked her upon sight and blamed her for causing him to feel like he had done something wrong. Why would he feel so guilty? He certainly hadn't committed any murder! Well, anyway, for now he was definitely going to forget about her. First things first, his lunch date with Brigitte—for which he was late.

Brian's mind was racing again. What if he rushed? Could he still get to the restaurant by 12:30 p.m. after all? Nope, not much of a chance for that. Suddenly the explosive rage inside of Brian took over, and, just like that, he knew that his life was out of control—all because of this murder! In hindsight it would have been advisable to call Brigitte this morning to ask her to please wait for a call from him to confirm lunch. However, she might have started asking questions, and Brian wanted to avoid getting into a prolonged discussion over the phone. Now here he was, racing out the back door of his building and taking off as fast as his car allowed. Brian felt tempted to speed overtly but opted for staying within the speed limits. He held to the belief that if a majority of people on the road break traffic laws, there will be only chaos. And he hated chaos!

The inner turmoil continued. Should he tell Brigitte about the murder, or should he wait for, well, what really? A better moment that would probably never come? Brian wished that somehow the murder would vanish into thin air, never to come back to haunt him. Should he talk to her about the events, or shouldn't he?

But why would he *not* want to talk to Brigitte about last night? Why all this hesitation? Brian finally concluded that he preferred dealing with his problems on his own. Until Jeff's death he had never even considered turning to others to talk about how he felt or why. Furthermore, he felt lost. He had no idea what kind of relationship he had with Brigitte. Would he feel comfortable talking to her or not?

Yet thinking about Brigitte had provided a needed reprieve from fretting over Lieutenant Woodraw. The title "lieutenant" certainly described her well. She had made Brian feel like a small child. He didn't know why. It bothered him, though.

Back to Brigitte. Should he or shouldn't he talk to her about the murder? Brian tossed this around for a couple more minutes and concluded that he might as well tell her. He sensed that he needed somebody to just talk to. However, this meant that he had to be willing to be open to her endless questions. Sure, most of the time he liked it when she engaged herself in his world by asking lots of questions. He was aware that he liked responding by providing answers, but only if it touched on areas involving his expertise. And he was no expert on murder and feelings of gloom and doom. Definitely not!

So that was decided. He would tell her! But what exactly would he tell her???

By now Brian was approaching downtown Mountain View, and he was thankful that his mind was momentarily distracted by heavy traffic. Brigitte had found this brand new Thai restaurant. Whether it was the latest story, a news item, a technology, or, like in this case, a new restaurant—Brigitte was au courant. He loved that about her. Brigitte worked as a marketing associate for a small marketing consulting company called Creative Strategies. She had joined them four years ago, right after graduating with a major in psychology and marketing from UCLA. She loved what she was doing. The office consisted of Alan, his partner, Steve, Brigitee, and one administrator.

Brian could hardly believe that he had been seeing Brigitte for almost seven months now. Strangely enough, it appeared to be both longer and shorter, depending on how he looked at it. When he considered the length of time they had known each other, he immediately became concerned that she would read too much into the relationship, a term that made him nervous. Friendship sounded much better, safer. Yes, they were friends . . .

Brian checked his watch again: 12:30 p.m. It would probably take about ten more minutes to get to the restaurant.

There, it had happened again! Suddenly Brian saw a clear image of Jeff, lying on the floor, motionless, and so foreboding. Something inside seemed to take over and bang, there it was. Though it never lasted long, it scared Brian. He had no control over its sudden appearances. This strange phenomenon had started the night before after he got home. It was powerful enough to override all facets of Brian's life. Desperately trying to wipe out the image, he focused even more intently on his driving.

By now Brian was approaching the vicinity of the restaurant and headed for a nearby garage. Within a couple of minutes he parked and rushed down the stairs from the third floor toward the restaurant across the street. Out of habit he had quickly looked around the garage but had not seen Brigitte's light blue Golf.

As Brian had expected, Brigitte had decided to be seated and was waiting for him at a table for two.

Oh, wow, she looked really great! Her smile was bright and cheerful; her hazel brown eyes expressed warmth and comfort and seemed to be inviting him in. Her dark blond hair was short with pageboy fringes. Well-outlined lips underscored her symmetrical face features. Brian really liked that blouse she was wearing! A pattern of circles about one inch in diameter was just a shade darker than the silvery bluish color of the blouse itself. The pattern and color combination gave a subtle yet elegant impression. The pants matched the blouse but had no pattern. As always, Brigitte wore quite unusual silver jewelry, a choker with matching earrings. He couldn't remember ever having seen her wearing gold or costume jewelry. Some day he would get up the nerve to ask her why she always wore silver jewelry. Brigitte had style and class. The smooth lines and designs of the clothes she liked to wear always conveyed an understated elegance. Yes, indeed, Brian concluded with a sigh of relief, having lunch with Brigitte should be very enjoyable.

Brigitte studied Brian's body language as he approached her and sat down with a heavy sigh. Something was really bugging him. He probably didn't even know that one of his shoelaces was untied. Brigitte had never seen him like this before. He seemed out of control and fragmented. His eyes looked absentminded and were clouded over by glasses speckled with dust. He also needed a haircut. But this was not the time or the place to bring up dirty eyeglasses and haircuts. Brian was not in good shape, she could tell!

Believing that some things in life have to be confronted head on, Brigitte immediately asked, "Brian, what's up? It's not at all like you to be late! What happened?"

Brian didn't realize that his face and body language had given him away and had made him an open book. Adjusting himself to being with Brigitte, he responded, "Give me a couple of minutes. I need to clear my mind. Let me pick something really fast, and then I can talk to you."

It took about thirty minutes for Brian to tell Brigitte about Jeff's murder and all it entailed. Right after he got into his story, Brigitte realized that she should just listen. She felt all of his anxiety and concern. Her face softened and expressed soothing empathy. Asking questions would not work. Brian needed to talk, and talk he did. There had been some awkward moments, but all in all he had managed to tell her as much as he could handle right now. After he finished, he realized that it felt as if a huge load had been lifted off his chest, a load that till then had just about immobilized him. His emotions seemed to have settled down, at least a little bit. He felt less overwhelmed and less out of control.

They had enjoyed their food and were now finishing their iced tea. Delicious!

Brigitte knew it was okay to respond now. Brian had settled down. She was fascinated by the story he had told and wanted to get involved and learn more about what might have been going on in Jeff's life.

"Brian, don't you think we should figure out what Jeff had been working on lately? I just can't imagine that his murder wasn't also somehow linked to his work. How long had he been at Atlas?"

Brian didn't mind addressing facts he knew well. "Roughly three months."

"That's all? It might be important to find out where he worked before, and on what. What do you think? Did he know many people at Atlas? Didn't you once tell me that he was kind of a loner?"

"Yes, Jeff was definitely a loner. As I said earlier, he was writing code that would enhance the security features of one of Atlas's new products. He was quite an expert on system administration and also specialized in security software. Jeff and I never discussed the details of his work. He belonged to a different engineering group, the one headed by Scott Jones. Bob Laidlaw leads my group, and we're testing the operating system software. However, we also get to know each new software tool to a certain degree since we have to make sure it runs on the system software. Security features are especially important for the growing Internet market. Like other software and hardware companies, Atlas wants to launch products for this new marketplace. The general public is still apprehensive about how safe the Net really is for certain transactions."

Brigitte nodded knowingly.

Brian continued, "The team was really lucky to get Jeff. He had been quite sought after because of some work he did about a year ago. Jeff had received job offers from several companies, but he chose to work as an independent contractor for Atlas. He told me once that being autonomous was more important to him than getting the kind of benefits a permanent job might offer.

"Before joining Atlas at the beginning of July, Jeff had spent several weeks traveling through the Alaskan countryside. I think he liked fishing and the out-of-doors. He had talked a little about the trip right after he started.

"Jeff believed that you could learn a lot more and enhance your knowledge in your specific field by moving around from company to company. But Silicon Valley was his base, and he wouldn't have taken a job anywhere else. His grasp and understanding of what everybody in the related industry was doing were tremendous. As far as he was concerned, you limited yourself if you stayed with one company for an extended period of time. He also believed that success can breed complacency, which in turn can kill any desire to explore new and untried ideas. Jeff definitely wanted to be challenged at all times."

Brigitte's mind started drifting off. Jeff sounded like quite a guy. Was it too much to hope that some day Brian, too, would be willing to define himself and his goals more clearly? What would it take for Brian to come out of his protective shell and boldly state what he believed in and why? What was it that made Brian so cautious and tentative, especially about his personal life? Over the last couple of months she had tried to draw him out again and again on this very subject. However, it had been to no avail. Suddenly she became aware of Brian's voice again. She hoped that she hadn't missed too much of the conversation!

"On the side, not as part of his work for Atlas, Jeff seems to have been working on a digital life system security tool. He talked about this only once, and just in general terms. Evidently his old roommate from MIT is now at the University of Santa Fe and is also doing experiments using digital life concepts. Jeff seems to have had quite a bit of contact with his old friend."

Brigitte thought for a moment and then said, "Jeff seems to have been really interested in inventing something totally new. Wow, that's fascinating! It makes you wonder why he came to Atlas, doesn't it?"

"Well, I couldn't say. I don't even know for sure who hired Jeff. I think it was Loren Grimm, the vice president in charge of the new security software tool. He's the project leader. As I already mentioned, Jeff was an expert for system security software in general, and Loren needed him. As far as I know the Atlas product had nothing to do with Jeff's own digital life invention. Furthermore, Jeff told me shortly after he came to Atlas that he and Loren had previously worked together at another company, so they must have known each other. I think that's why Loren hired him."

"I seem to have read something somewhere about digital life software. Digital organisms are really a form of digital intelligence, right?"

Brian nodded.

Brigitte was getting excited. She loved to learn about new technological concepts. "Wow, that sounds like a big deal, don't you think? Could it be possible that Jeff had invented something that a lot of companies might be quite interested in? What if Jeff's invention is connected to his murder?"

Brian didn't like it when Brigitte jumped to conclusions that could not be supported. He hated sheer speculation about any subject.

"I think that's quite a leap of thought. How could you back this up? As far as I'm concerned we know almost nothing, at least no facts. It's just speculation." Brian actually looked a little annoyed.

Brigitte, however, never gave up easily and enjoyed entertaining almost any idea or thought. Besides, this was not speculation; this was following her intuition. Experience had taught her that it was useless to waste time discussing the differences with Brian. Undaunted by his take on it, Brigitte remained firm in her belief that ideas didn't have to be supported or proven; they had to be explored without mental constraints. You never knew where an idea could lead you. The process was very exciting!

"I know, I know. But believe me, facts aren't the only thing that makes the world go round! I've been quite successful in life by being open to, well, whatever, and I believe in exploring ideas that can't be supported initially but might make sense in the long run. Really, what is there to lose? Don't look at me that way! I know, I'm probably confusing you. Whether based on sheer speculation or not, I still think that we should figure out what was really going on in Jeff's life and with his work. It might just pay off. Who knows?"

Brian sighed. He felt crushed and confused. He could understand why Brigitte wanted to find out what had been going on. But what about him? Did he really want to find out why somebody had such a strong motive to kill Jeff?

"Brian, do you think you could get access to Jeff's system at work?" Brigitte was relentlessly focusing on how she could learn more about the murder and Jeff.

"Why, what are you thinking of now?" Brian had become as stubborn as a mule, determined *not* to get involved.

"Well, you have to start somewhere, and his system is as good a place as any."

"To do what? What do you mean? I don't think I get your point." Now Brian tried to avoid the issue by acting confused, but it was just an unconscious reaction on his part.

"Oh, sorry, I guess I was jumping ahead again. I assumed you would be interested in finding out why Jeff was killed. I thought that's why you told me this whole story or . . . ?" Brigitte was attempting to get Brian involved by challenging him and was quite aware of what she was doing.

Now Brian was indeed confused. That's not why he had talked to Brigitte! What had led her to that assumption? He had never really thought about getting involved. That was none of his business. What was she talking about?

Without waiting for a reply, Brigitte continued.

"Well, I for one am quite curious by now and intend to learn more. I'll talk to my manager, Alan, tomorrow. He knows a lot of people in the Valley. Networking is his thing, I mean 'people networking.' I'm sure he could get some information on Loren Grimm's background, and maybe he can find out where and when Loren and Jeff worked together."

Brian was still stubbornly refusing to go along with Brigitte's idea. "Do you really think we should get involved? What if the police find out? I'm sure they don't want us poking around."

"But Brian, I'm only suggesting that we look for possible clues in Jeff's files. That's all! It's really no big deal, is it? You do want to know why Jeff got killed, don't you?"

Brian didn't answer. He was thinking. He felt boxed in. What was he supposed to do? He finally said, "I guess I could look through Jeff's files." This was just a halfhearted attempt to please Brigitte and not at all a decision with which he felt comfortable.

"Look, Brian, it's just an idea. It doesn't mean that you'll really find anything. So will you check out Jeff's system?" Brigitte knew how reluctant Brian was, but she was determined not to give up. Sometimes one just had to push Brian a little for his own good!

Brian nodded, but he still didn't feel comfortable.

Brigitte knew that it would take Brian a while to recover and mull things over in his mind before he felt comfortable with her idea. Since she had to get back to work, she said, "Well, we'd better get going now. I have a busy afternoon ahead. Let me pay today. It's your turn the next time."

Still feeling dazed about what he might have signed up for, Brian didn't even protest and just said, "Okay."

On the way out they agreed that they would be back in touch over the next couple of days, or sooner, depending on what each of them would find out by doing their research.

"Brian, you look all worried again!"

Brian was stunned. How did she always know how he was feeling??? It was true that ever since they had left the restaurant the old feelings of dread had come back to haunt him—again. She hadn't really helped matters. He wished she hadn't started talking about getting involved.

"I just feel so bad about everything." Brian's body language and voice clearly expressed his despair and hopelessness.

"But why should you feel bad, and about what?" Brigitte tried to calm him down and reassure him.

"I keep thinking, what if I had gotten back sooner, or what if I had never gone to my father's birthday party in the first place? Maybe Jeff would still be alive now . . ."

"Brian, stop talking that way. You're always way too hard on yourself! You can't control life. Life just kind of happens. We have to make the best of it. That's all we can do. I know this is hard for you, and believe me, I'm quite sad about Jeff's murder. But we can't do anything except try to find out who killed Jeff and why—and that's what we *will* do!"

Brigitte knew there were no words that would make Brian feel better. So she simply gave him a quick hug and left, heading for the fourth floor, where she had parked.

Brian walked toward his car on the third floor, again left to himself and his thoughts. Not so long ago being alone with his thoughts was something he had relished. Now he hated it and found it quite unbearable.

Chapter 6

The Latest News

Thursday, October 5, 1995, 1:55 p.m.

Upon returning from lunch Brian found the following note stuck to his computer screen:

Brian,

I need to talk to you ASAP!

It's about your interview with the police.

Call me right away!!!

　　Michelle :-)

Why couldn't people just leave him alone? Brian was visibly upset; his body looked rigid and tense. Not even the "smiley" on the note could wipe away the huge frown on his face.

On the drive back from lunch, Brian had been looking forward to the protective solitude of his cube and to long, quiet hours immersed in his work. Since his lunch with Brigitte he had become irritated. He couldn't shake off feeling let down and disappointed. Talking to Brigitte about the murder had not made him feel better, as he had hoped it would. Nothing took away the hold the murder seemed to have on his life. Absolutely nothing! Brigitte's passion to play detective and to get him involved was quite upsetting as well. He was angry and somehow blamed Brigitte. He didn't feel like snooping around in Jeff's files! That was police work. He wished he had had the guts to just say no. Why couldn't she understand that he was under a lot of pressure at work? Brian's irritation increased. Now random thoughts were racing through his mind. He had no control over them, and as a result he felt more and more drained and devoid of energy.

Michelle's note had triggered another wave of anger and frustration. But he liked her! Why did he get mad at her? Brian felt confused. What should he do now? Where should he start? He felt so lost . . .

If only Brian could turn back the clock to just a week ago, when life had been comfortable and, yes, kind of normal. He might even say life had been enjoyable back then. His work had been the center of his life and had made him feel safe and even had provided him with a sense of identity. Oh, how he longed for that old routine of work, work, work.

Brian sighed deeply as he took the note off the screen and moved it to the outer frame of his monitor, where it became part of a collection of many other notes upon which he had yet to act. Becoming aware of the collage of notes in front of him, he had to work hard to disengage himself before feelings of guilt took over and made him feel like a failure. How much unfinished business did all these notes really represent? He shuddered inside and pushed the thought away.

As far as Michelle's note was concerned, Brian knew that he was just postponing the inevitable. Michelle would show up, just like she always did. But he could have never thrown her note away. No, that would have been wrong. Brian knew what might help—he had to get back to work—now! It was imperative! Slowly the anonymity of his cubicle and the familiar surroundings created a safety buffer between Brian and the world around him. He started to relax just a little.

First Brian needed to log on to his system and check his calendar to find out when and where today's new product meeting was scheduled to be held. Okay, that wasn't till 4 p.m., and the conference room was just down the hallway. It was 2:12 p.m. now. Brian became annoyed again. Though he had enjoyed his time with Brigitte, he now wished he had worked instead.

Furthermore, why hadn't he told Brigitte that he thought it was stupid to play detective? It was none of their business. He was such a sucker! He always seemed to fall prey to Brigitte's powers of persuasion. She should know that he wasn't the type who liked to get involved. What was wrong with that? Who said he had to get involved? Why couldn't some people just be different? How foolish would he look if he backed out now? Would it impact his relationship with Brigitte? Probably.

Brian pondered this for a while and concluded that he already was involved, whether he liked it or not. Brigitte was probably right. He just needed some time to think it through. However, this was work, and that's what he had to do—now! After all, that's what Atlas paid him for. But how could he work if he was unable to focus because he didn't know how to deal with the murder?

The temptation to just ignore the murder and his promises to Brigitte was great. But what about personal integrity? Brian had considered Jeff a friend, one to whom he had hoped to get closer. Brian believed in loyalty. How involved would he have to get for loyalty's sake? He wondered how one measures loyalty. If Jeff had been in Brian's shoes, Jeff would have wanted to solve the puzzle of the murder and expose those who were responsible for it. That's what Jeff would have done, so, that's what Brian should do. He started to feel better. He had resolved one of his dilemmas.

It was time to check his e-mail again. Ugh—another thirty-six messages! He checked for familiar addresses to see if any were from his team members. Yes, but only twelve messages were related to his project and required immediate attention. All others could be ignored for now.

One by one Brian went through the twelve messages and responded when necessary. Nothing was really crying out for attention in reference to his project, so on the spur of the moment and without giving it much thought at all, he decided to go home after the new product meeting. Yes, that's what he would do! He needed to put some physical distance between himself and the horror of last night. He was sure he would feel better after that. The new product meeting was at 4 p.m. Having made a decision about what to do next he figured he might as well experiment and log on to Jeff's computer. Brigitte wanted him to look for anything that might look like a possible important clue.

The police had blocked off Jeff's cube, so Brian could not work on Jeff's computer, not that he really wanted to. It would give him the creeps. He decided to log on from his own computer. Within minutes Brian had become totally focused and concentrated on his task. The password was not too much of a problem. Everybody more or less knew how to circumvent those. What next? He had to decide where to look first and for what. But how would he know what to look for? It also occurred to Brian that he should check if anybody else had logged on recently. This might be indicative of something, a possible first lead.

"Hey, Brian!! So you *are* back from lunch!"

Totally startled, Brian turned around and saw Michelle.

"Oh, hi, Michelle!"

"Why didn't you come and see me? Didn't you get my note? I stuck it on your screen!" She moved very close and looked around.

Brian felt miserable and wished he could hide. Michelle seemed cross with him and was probably disappointed in him. Hoping to prevent a conflict, he quickly pointed to the note stuck on the edge of the monitor. He noticed with relief that her face became friendly again.

"Sorry, Michelle. I simply got caught up with some e-mail and work . . ."

Still sulking a little, she said, "But I have something really important to tell you!"

More guilt! Brian had let her down! He felt compelled to show her he cared. Still reeling inside from the sudden shift in focus, he nevertheless tried hard to please Michelle by listening to her story.

For the next twenty minutes Michelle explained in detail what Lieutenant Woodraw had been up to today. Michelle found it important to point out that her boss, Loren Grimm, still hadn't shown up and Lieutenant Woodraw seemed annoyed by it. But Loren had made an appointment with the lieutenant for the next day. Michelle couldn't figure out why Loren was being so difficult and seemingly unwilling to meet the police. Also, Michelle had no idea where Loren was today. She had called him at home but had not reached him. There had been a number of appointments on his calendar, and he had sent her a voicemail asking her to cancel them all. What did that mean? Where could he be?

Brian started to wonder why Michelle told him all of this. What did this have to do with him?

Michelle believed that Loren had been in the office early in the morning, even before she had come in. She usually showed up between 8:30 and 8:45 a.m. Her clue was that Loren's appointment book was missing. Michelle was certain the book had been on his desk the day before when she had left around 6 p.m. For as long as she had worked for him, about nine months now, Loren had never taken his appointment book with him. If he had to see somebody after work or for a breakfast on the way in, she would give him a printed note as a reminder.

Brian had trouble following Michelle's story which appeared incoherent. There was no apparent logic. Even concentrating harder didn't help. Increasing pressure and frustration started building up inside of Brian. The part about the appointment book was interesting, though. Brian made a mental note of it.

Michelle's personal involvement with the police had been more limited. They had asked her a couple of general questions. The lieutenant had mostly been interested in Loren and his whereabouts and how long Michelle had worked for him.

"Brian, now tell me what you and the lieutenant talked about!"

Oh, great, there it was. He had definitely tried to avoid getting into that subject. This time Brian actually considered coming up with an excuse regardless of the consequences. He tried to gauge Michelle's general disposition. Would it work if he pretended to be busy? No, not based on past experiences. Michelle could be relentless in pursuit of a story, or rumor, or whatever struck her fancy.

To share that he hadn't particularly enjoyed the lieutenant and had found her annoying and irritating would make Brian feel very exposed. So what should he say?

"Well, you see, first of all the lieutenant wanted to get all the facts regarding who had been here at work last night and at what time. So I explained when I arrived here last night, where I'd been and when and from where I entered the building."

Brian didn't mention to Michelle that he had run into Loren in the break room, nor did he tell her about the sound he had heard of somebody possibly running away from where Brian had entered. He had told the lieutenant about these two observations, though she had seemed oblivious as to their possible implication. In any case, it was safe to say that she had not shown much interest, nor had she asked any follow-up questions.

Brian certainly didn't want to tell Michelle that he had felt quite uncomfortable during his meeting with lieutenant Woodraw. He couldn't read the lieutenant and didn't understand her line of questioning. Whenever this happened, he would either drop the discussion or try to identify another person's thought pattern. After all, if you didn't know where somebody else was going with their logic or intent, how could you prevent uncomfortable surprises? How could you feel safe and secure?

"The lieutenant had wanted to know which team had people working late last night. She seemed to be looking for a possible link. We spent most of the time talking about what Jeff had been working on as well as things like how well I know—excuse me—how well I knew Jeff. And stuff like how long Jeff had been here at Atlas, where he had worked before, and who he had been close to."

Brian hoped that Michelle would be satisfied. Not yet.

"Well, that explains why she asked me for the name of Jeff's contracting company or temp agency. I told her that Jeff worked as an independent contractor. Atlas actually listed him in the category of consultant. The lieutenant probably wanted the names of Jeff's previous employers. Did you know that Loren and Jeff knew each other from before? Loren mentioned this a couple of weeks ago. Personally, I don't think Jeff liked Loren. They didn't seem to get along. I remember asking Loren when the subject of Jeff came up back then whether they had worked together before. I was surprised when Loren kind of brushed it aside and just said that Jeff was a strange character and that nobody really knew him well."

Finally Michelle seemed to be satisfied. She had gotten Brian's input, and more importantly, she had been able to tell her own story. As usual, and without much ado, she suddenly got up and, after a cheerful "see you later," was gone. Most likely she hardly remembered that she had actually sulked not so long ago and had been quite upset with Brian.

Brian sighed heavily, but this time it was a big sigh of relief. Back to work—actually, back to Jeff's computer files.

Chapter 7

A Long Peaceful Hike

Sunday, October 8, 1995, 12:50 p.m.

Tranquillity and serenity filled the air, stimulating Brian's senses. From a source deep inside himself he responded by yielding to its allure. The experience was intense yet non-threatening. What caused this strange phenomenon? Was it the sun's rays, giving life and energy by taking away the darkness and fear? Or was it the gentle breeze, which moved, stirred, and caressed all of creation? Full of joy and without restraint, nature and all living creatures joined in playful interaction with the sun, air, and breeze.

Brian had become a part of this magical orchestration. He, too, had given himself over to the beckoning of a powerful and all-imposing force. He felt fearless. While the magic lasted, there was no distinction between reality and illusion. All boundaries were extinct. Brian had become one with everything around him. He felt safe, protected, and whole. He existed. There was meaning and purpose.

Brian wished he could prolong these glorious moments. He had never considered identifying what exactly touched him so deeply. At times he felt a deep sadness upon returning to the fragmented reality of his life. Why wasn't it possible to save and store what he felt so intensely, to dispel the gloom and darkness that were sure to follow?

It was Sunday. Three days had passed since Brian had found Jeff's dead body. He was certain that the events of that night would change his life and perception of life forever.

A strong urge to get away had prompted Brian to rise early today, and by 9:15 a.m. he had been on freeway 101 heading south to Coe State Park. On this October morning, after some particularly hot Indian summer days, thick, heavy fog had brought about needed relief from oppressive heat. Shrouded by the darkness of the night, and becoming visible only during the first light of day, a cold, wet blanket of fog had slowly crept in from the Pacific Ocean, enveloping the entire Bay Area. The drive through the gray mist had contributed to Brian's sense of alienation and intensified his desire and need for escape. The veil of fog had not lifted till Brian had hiked for about ten minutes. Then, quite suddenly and triumphantly, the sun burst forth, basking the whole world around Brian in beautiful, warm, invigorating sunshine. How powerful and glorious!

All day yesterday Brian had considered inviting Brigitte to join him on this outing. In the end he concluded that he desperately needed time alone—solitude. He understood that sometimes he had to create a physical distance between himself and the daily grind of unrelenting demands at work. He also needed to remove himself every so often from the pressure he felt from too much contact with people—even Brigitte.

Brian had hiked for almost an hour before his fear, tension, and stress slowly faded into the background. Then, like the fog, these nasty companions suddenly disappeared all together. But Brian knew this miracle wouldn't last. Those bad feelings were always lurking somewhere, demanding and forcing their way back onto center stage of Brian's life. Was there no permanent cure or remedy against these attackers?

Since Wednesday night, the night of Jeff's murder, Brian's stress had never left him and was far greater than any he had ever experienced before. Not one hour had gone by since that fateful moment when he didn't wonder whether life was ever going to be the same again. Some inner voice seemed to be raising all sorts of questions Brian could not answer. What was going on? Why was he questioning the purpose of his work? What had brought this about? He tried to clear his mind and pretended to leave these unwelcome, gloomy thoughts in the dark oak grove through which he had just passed. With renewed vigor, he picked up his pace as he entered a flat, open meadow. He started to feel better again.

During his college years Brian discovered that in order to maintain some degree of sanity in his life, he needed a regular quiet time all by himself, if possible experienced in the wide open spaces of nature. It was then that nature became his own private sanctuary.

On Saturday Brian and his team had labored fourteen hours nonstop to catch up on their project. Why did it always seem like they were falling behind, unable to meet set goals and deadlines? He had been at work from 11 a.m. till 1 a.m. To maintain focus had been painstakingly difficult for Brian and had depleted all his energy. As a result, simple errors ate up additional time and energy. A seething rage accompanied each slip of concentration. To make matters worse, the team had run into a couple of major product design snags. Though able to identify their cause, a quick resolve or workaround had not yet been found. The next couple of days were critical. Any delay could spell disaster and meant missing the targeted product completion date.

Brian wondered if the police had investigated Jeff's files. If they had considered that Jeff's death might be linked to his work, then Brian certainly was not aware of it. He had called Lieutenant Woodraw on Friday when he realized that he had forgotten to tell her about the Camaro he had seen on the night of the murder. She had mentioned that she had finished her interviews with Mike Fitzgerald, Dona Gee, Steve Butcher, and Allen Parker, the other four engineers who had been in the building on the night of the murder. None of them had mentioned the Camaro. However, this was not surprising, since they had been in the lab and the car was gone by the time the police had arrived.

Though hesitant at first, Brian had nevertheless talked to Mike, Dona, Steve, and Allen about the role Jeff had played on their team. Dona had been the most helpful. She appeared quite emotional about the murder.

It wasn't till later on Saturday afternoon that Brian had a chance to talk to Dona alone when she was in the lab all by herself. Knowing how shy and reserved she was, he had hoped to get her feedback while nobody else was around. He had often wondered whether her shyness was due to her background (she had come from Hong Kong to study at Berkeley and then decided to work in the States) or because she was the only female engineer on her team. He had asked her whether she would be willing to assist him in investigating any possible link between Jeff's work and his murder. At first Dona had been hesitant and quite fearful. Brian almost gave up. He never tried for very long to per-suade anybody. It seemed purposeless. He wasn't sure why Dona had come around, but in the end she did agree to research some of Jeff's latest work, probably because she had really cared about Jeff as a person. Brian had also sensed that, like himself, she wanted to understand why Jeff had been murdered.

The murder had upset and frightened Dona. The police had talked to her only about her whereabouts that night. There had been no specific questions about Jeff's work other than determining that she and Jeff had worked on the same team for the last three months.

On Saturday afternoon Brian and Dona had quietly left the lab and gone to Brian's computer. Dona had agreed to join Brian for a quick global review of Jeff's files, hoping they might find some clues. Anything was better than noth-ing! Before Michelle had interrupted Brian's first attempt to peruse Jeff's files on Thursday afternoon, he had figured out Jeff's password and had quickly glanced through the e-mail log. After that interruption Brian had been too upset and irritated to pick up where he had left off. However, his earlier hunch was confirmed Jeff had indeed had intense contact with the University of Santa Fe, and Dona was sure that it had to do with Jeff's personal digital life experiment. After a couple of minutes of research, Dona tensed up and wanted to leave. She seemed nervous and rushed. Maybe, like Brian, it frightened her to be across from where Jeff had been killed.

"Brian, I have to leave now. I'll come in on Sunday. I'll look through Jeff's files and all his e-mail, and, if possible, I'll identify all contacts Jeff had over the last three months.

"I especially want to look for Jeff's last summary of his work assignments. Jeff updated this document each time we met for our weekly product meeting on Thursday morning. I'm sure he finished it on Wednesday. I want to find it. It could be important. I'll contact you on Monday morning."

That had been the extent of their exchange on Saturday. What if Dona really discovered something important? Was that too much to hope for?

On Friday night Brigitte had called, and they had brainstormed any possible motives for the murder. Brian had not been in a good mood then. He could feel that Brigitte was still pressuring him. She had convinced Brian to ask Michelle a couple of more questions relating to the characteristics of Jeff's relationship with Loren Grimm. In the meantime Brigitte's manager, Alan, would make a couple of phone calls to learn more about Safe Systems. As of Friday Alan could confirm only that Loren Grimm and Jeff had worked together at a company called Safe Systems. By calling a couple of other people Alan hoped to get more details. Brigitte felt it was especially important to ascertain when exactly both Loren and Jeff had worked at Safe Systems and what their relationship had been like. Brian didn't know Safe Systems at all. According to Brigitte it was still a small and privately held company.

Then the strangest thing happened. On Saturday afternoon, while working in the lab, Brian overheard the tail end of a conversation Mike and Peter were having about Loren. Evidently Loren had been one of the founders of Safe Systems, and according to Mike, Loren and the other two founders had parted on less than friendly terms. Mike hinted that Loren's departure had been sudden and had led to many speculations.

Brian suspected that Brigitte's real intent for calling on Friday night had been to make sure that he hadn't chickened out and was still committed to investigating Jeff's files for possible clues. He definitely did want to pull out. It really wasn't any of his or anybody else's business. It was police business, and to get involved could only lead to trouble. But he had promised Brigitte, and now he felt trapped. During the phone call on Friday night they had also made dinner and movie plans for Sunday night. Brigitte would pick the movie. Brigitte invariably picked independent and foreign films. Most of the time Brian was quite happy with her choices. However, without her, he would have never gone to see any of them. This was a new and unexplored world for Brian, and he didn't always deal well with the emotions triggered by some of these movies. The plan for Sunday was to eat at one of the Vietnamese restaurants in downtown San Jose and then catch a movie. Afterward they would probably stop for an espresso.

Thinking about his plans for Sunday night had made Brian aware of the passing of time. He checked his watch. It was almost 2 p.m. Brian figured he would need another thirty minutes to get to the parking lot. The path he had chosen was quite time consuming. He had stopped only once, for lunch, unable to resist lying under an old oak tree, daydreaming. He had rested for about twenty minutes, while eating his lunch and staring into space, feeling care-free, detached, and somehow suspended. Now Brian had to make up for lost time! He had arrived at the park about 11 a.m. That meant he had been walking for almost three hours so far. Though he felt physically tired, especially in light of the few hours of sleep he had had, some of the peace and wholeness he had felt was still with him.

Chapter 8

News About Jeff

Monday October 9, 1995, at the Kibo Hotel Near the Kilimanjaro, 7:53 p.m. Local Time, 8:53 a.m. Pacific Time

Angel made no attempt to conceal her rage and frustration. With a voice dripping with sarcasm, she chose words that were meant to strike like bullets.

"I don't seem to understand. What do you mean when you say that you can't connect me with Jeff Williams?"

"I am sorry, but I am just not able to."

"And why is that? Can you at least tell me why?"

"Miss, I am really trying, but I am just the operator here. As I told you already, I don't have a listing for Jeff Williams."

"And I told you that this is impossible, and I even gave you the extension for Jeff Williams. Do you want me to repeat it?"

"No. I wrote it down. You said it was 1632, and I have rung that number several times, and it seems to be disconnected."

"Disconnected? That's a bunch of baloney! Get me somebody else! Anybody who knows more than you do! I told you already, I'm calling from Africa, and this is *extremely* important! Why can't you get it?"

"I'll try human resources one more time. Maybe somebody has come in by now. Really, Miss, I'm trying my best!"

Angel was fuming. Unable to stop the onslaught, she had been buried by a huge tidal wave of emotions. First she had felt a cold steel trap, gripping, then snapping tight shut around her heart. Intense rage and fear were followed by a pervasive feeling of darkness and emptiness. Life as she had known it seemed to be extinct. In its place there was only a cold and barren void. Angel felt ravaged, exposed, and helpless.

And now a stupid operator had put her on hold. Angel waited four endless minutes and almost hung up before a distant, female voice broke the deadly silence.

"Hi, I'm Helen Archer in human resources. I understand you're Angel Blank, and you're trying to get in touch with somebody at Atlas. How can I help you?"

Again Angel did not hide her sarcasm and rage.

"I'm calling from Africa, and this is extremely important. I need to talk to Jeff Williams—*now!*"

Suddenly the line went all quiet, and for a moment Angel thought she had been disconnected.

"Are you a relative of Jeff's or close to his family?"

"What has that got to do with anything? No, I'm not! But if you must know, I'm a very close personal friend."

"You might want to get in touch with his family. Do you know his family?"

"Don't give me this garbage! What are you talking about? Tell me what's going on! I'm Jeff's closest and most intimate friend. There, does that count for anything at all?"

Another pause.

"Who are you, anyway, thinking you can tell me what to do? I have a simple question. Just answer it: How can I get in touch with Jeff Williams? Is that so difficult?"

The voice came back, and this time it was soft and calm and spoke very slowly. "I know this must be a terrible shock for you, but I have some very bad news. Jeff is dead, he . . ."

"*What*? What are you saying? What do you mean? No, no, there must be a mistake! You can't mean this! You don't know what you're saying!"

In an instant Angel's heart broke apart. One piece died, leaving the remaining part helplessly struggling to function on its own.

"Miss Blank, please, try to stay calm. I am so very sorry to have to tell you this. But Jeff was found dead, apparently murdered, last Wednesday night, here in his office. The police are still investigating the case. His parents were notified last Thursday. You might want to contact them. The funeral will . . ."

Angel hung up. She didn't want to hear more. Besides, she would *never* attend Jeff's funeral. Funerals were for the dead, not the living. She wanted Jeff *alive, now!*

Wednesday, October 11, 1995, 11:23 p.m. in a Hotel Room in Amsterdam

Where had Angel been since Monday night? What had her life been like? She had no idea.

Now it was Wednesday night. Angel was lying on a bed in a hotel room at the airport Hilton in Amsterdam staring at the ceiling, eyes red and swollen, convinced that she had ceased to exist. It didn't just *feel* like life was over. It *was* over, *period, end of message*!

It wasn't that Angel had never experienced painful and trying times before. This was different. This time despair had taken over every facet of her being. Angel's mind was spinning out of control as she tried to think. How could she get out from under this load of unbearable, painful and, suffocating emotions? There was no answer, no way out . . . There was only a lifeless void.

One thing was certain: Without Lise's assistance, Angel would have *never* gotten out of that godforsaken place—Tanzania. It certainly wasn't the country's fault! No use blaming the country. But what about her? What about her feelings? What was happening to her—*now*? Why did she seem disconnected from herself? Why couldn't she think? Why didn't she feel anything at all, even though the rage had subsided to bearable levels? Now she was just numb. No feelings, no nothing. No life.

And how come Angel had ended up stuck in Africa anyway, where you couldn't even get a flight out when you wanted to? She had missed the Monday night flight on

KLM from the Kilimanjaro International Airport with an eighteen hour stopover in Amsterdam. By the time she got the news about Jeff it was too late to get to the airport for a 9:10 p.m. departure. She was forced to wait till Tuesday night. A long day filled with waiting and waiting and waiting, for what? She felt like the sand in one of those hourglasses; each time the sand ran out, the glass turned itself over miraculously and the whole process started all over again. The sand kept falling at the same steady pace, and nothing could stop it. It was a horrible feeling! She felt caught and trapped. There was no escape and no hope of ending this ongoing agony!

Lise had organized Angel's departure while Angel had sat around, staring into space. Her look was empty, blank, and dead. Now and again her eyes spilled a flood of tears. Angel remembered somebody telling her a long time ago that tears could soothe your soul and could make you feel better, but it was a lie. It wasn't so. She didn't feel better, and her soul was dark, black, and void—without hope.

Lise assured Angel that nobody at the agency would object to her leaving the tour early. Who cared? Angel sure didn't! What did it matter? They had been scheduled to return on October 15 anyway. Time, dates—it all did not matter anymore and maybe never would again! Only one thing mattered right now—she had to get back to San Francisco and find out what had happened! That's what was keeping her going, well barely, anyway . . . The whole tour thing was like a blimp that came and went. She had no idea why she had ever wanted to take that horrible job in the first place.

Why did Angel even bother thinking about any of this now? Why ever think again? Why live?

Angel had felt this way before, in Kitzbuehel in the fall of 1992. Then, too, her world had come to a crashing halt. Damn life! Damn whoever was in charge of this pitiful existence! And damn all those idiots who pretended life was all thrills and fun! Damn everything and anybody! Damn God, too! Angel realized that this was tough to do, since she didn't even believe a God existed. Well, darn it, anyway! Damn whoever was responsible for this messed up rotten world! There—*now* she felt a little better, just a tiny bit at least . . .

Then the sobs started again. Angel's whole body was hurting by now, not just her eyes. Lise had offered some pills that might calm her down, but Angel refused to take them. Never! She *wanted* to suffer, she *wanted* the pain! At least it was real! Without the pain Angel felt as if she were locked into a vacuum, feeling neither dead nor alive. The pain proved that she was still alive. Anything was better than nothing.

Angel deserved this. It was all her fault! Over the years, ten years to be exact, there had been many opportunities for her to commit to a serious relationship with Jeff. But no, she had to wait till it was too late. They should have taken the plunge and gotten married back in 1993. Yes, and then *none* of this would have happened. Couldn't have! Jeff would have never gotten killed if she had been around. Oh, she was such a fool! What was she thinking?

Nobody knew the future. Why was she kidding herself? How childish to believe that different choices might have prevented Jeff's murder. It still could have happened! She had to snap out of this. That was *all* there was to it! But how?

The sobbing got worse . . .

Exhausted from all the crying and thinking, Angel drifted off into a numbing sleep . . .

Thursday, October 12, 1995, Somewhere in First Class en Route from Amsterdam to San Francisco

"Miss, would you like a pillow?"

Angel shook her head. Couldn't those idiotic flight attendants see that she wanted to be left alone? What else was she supposed to do to signal her desires? She was hiding under a black cap pulled way over her face and was wearing dark sunglasses to cover her red and swollen eyes. She was extremely relieved that nobody was sitting next to her. If anybody had taken the seat next to her and had started talking to her, she probably would have screamed and yelled and gone berserk.

Angel wanted to be alone. That's *all* she wanted right now.

Since leaving Africa Angel had been thinking about wasted opportunities. She was convinced that her life would be very different now if she had taken advantage of earlier opportunities, but she hadn't! If she hadn't wasted what life had offered her, Jeff would still be alive now, and they would be happy together, she was sure! But how does one make opportunities count instead of wasting them? How does one know beforehand what works best? Angel's mind was spinning . . .

Angel started to think about the past. Crushed and broken by another disappointing relationship, in this case with Greg, a guy she had dated for two years in Kitzbuehel, Angel had come home for Thanksgiving in November 1992. She had no idea how long she would stay. She told her mother that she had come to celebrate her grandfather's eightieth birthday party on December 16, but she could tell that her mother hadn't really believed her. Then the bomb had hit. Her mother had told Angel that she had filed for a divorce. Her father had moved to Manhattan. To come back to all this bad news after her own misery made her want to run away again, and this time she had really wanted to stay. Now what? That's when she had started to think about Jeff and the past and how different he was from everybody else she had known since dropping out of college.

What do they say again, distance makes the heart grow fonder, or did it? Oh, Angel didn't really believe in such silly things, but what if it was true? At least she could try and find out.

So Angel had called Jeff's parents in Hartford and found out that Jeff was coming home for the holidays on December 23. She surprised him and simply showed up unannounced on December 26, 1992, declaring herself to be his surprise Christmas gift. It had been wonderful to see that special look on his face! That's when Angel knew that he still loved her. But Jeff had also been quite taken aback, and she didn't blame him. Their contact had been minimal since she had dropped out of college in January 1988. Just like that—she simply quit. Wouldn't even tell him why. Didn't want to. Hadn't really known herself, nor did she want to. How do you explain that you are just following some force that seems to be driving you on and on toward something? She just knew she had to quit. They had been dating for two years, and then she had simply taken off. Though Jeff kept pressing Angel for good, logical explanations, all she could say was that she just had to, that she needed to find herself.

So, after being gone for almost five years, Angel knew that she had to be careful or Jeff would feel overwhelmed. Also, she understood that he had been very hurt when she left. Jeff needed some time to adjust to the new situation. So she explained that after traveling around Europe for almost two years she had landed in Kitzbuehel, where she had stayed since 1990. She had become a ski instructor and had taken some art classes at the university in Innsbruck. The art classes had become boring after a while. Then she found this old artisan who was well known for his woodcarving skills. They had hit it off really well, and he had taught her all about woodcarving. She had spent lots of time at his workshop. It had been a refuge for her soul. She didn't know how much this experience had meant to her until after she had left. Even right now, on the plane from Amsterdam to San Francisco, she missed Alois and everything he represented.

Angel's most valued treasure, created during her time with Alois, was a small horse whose outlines were carved into an eight-by-nine-inch block of wood, left unaltered in its rough natural shape. By giving Jeff this gift on December 26, 1992, Angel gave him part of herself. The horse symbolized who Angel had become while gone. Angel believed the horse could bridge the gap of time and the alienation that had set in and make up for the separation of five long years. As usual, Angel expected Jeff to understand this special, deeper, symbolic meaning. But he didn't. She had been very disappointed.

Yet Jeff was drawn to the horse and kept stroking it, feeling its outlines and curves and the texture of the wood, asking how long it had taken her to carve it, what kind of wood it was. The gift gave each of them time to readjust, to get over the initial awkward moments of seeing each other again.

This first surprise meeting was followed by several trips into Manhattan. Each time they had stayed overnight at Angel's grandfather's apartment on Park Avenue. Her grandfather had welcomed them with open arms. Jeff liked Angel's grandfather very much. However, pretty soon Jeff started fussing, as Angel called it. He had never felt comfortable in Angel's world. So much money, so much glamour, so much of everything he wasn't used to! Yet it had been an exciting time, and Angel kept entertaining him, and he got caught up in her energy and lust for life. They had fallen in love all over again. Their most special moments together had been on New Year's Eve! They were in love, more than ever before, it was as simple as that! That night Angel surprised Jeff and told him she was planning to visit friends in California, and how would he feel if she stopped by and visited him as well? She had made up the visiting friend part, but he didn't have to know that—at least not yet!

So together they had flown to San Francisco on January 3, 1993. Angel had stayed for two weeks. And it had been a disaster! Neither of them quite understood what had gone wrong, but it seemed like absolutely nothing had worked out. She had griped about Jeff having to work "all the time," as she had called it. He had accused her of "being a rich spoiled brat who had no appreciation for people who had to earn a living the hard way and who was only satisfied if she was the center of all the attention!" And on and on it went.

Since Angel's disappointing visit in California their communication had been limited to a couple of letters and cards now and again. Heartbroken and feeling like a total failure, Angel was convinced that no male would ever understand and accept her. So she ran away gain, back to Kitzbuehel, the only place that seemed to welcome and accept her the way she really was and where she had made a kind of life for herself. Greg had left anyway, so why not go back? He wouldn't be around. But there was Alois and there was woodcarving.

The next time Angel set foot back onto American soil was in December 1994. Again she used her grandfather's birthday as an excuse. The real motive for leaving Kitzbuehel was the death of her beloved Alois in September of that year. There was nothing left for her in Kitzbuehel. To now find out that her grandfather was *also* not feeling well was even more distressing. At least her parents' divorce was settled. This was the first time that her mother told her that she had actually filed for a divorce back in 1991 but hadn't wanted to tell anybody until it looked like a financial settlement was imminent. Her brother Michael hadn't been home much either during those years. Since he was four years younger than Angel, they had never really been that close once Angel had left for college. Now her mother explained that there were trust funds for her and her brother that needed to be settled legally. Angel hated all this talk about money. That's all her family seemed to care about! However, she quickly realized that the money would allow her to do whatever she wanted. She had already made one decision—she would stay in the States now and make a go at it. This running away didn't do her any good. Besides, it seemed so childish now. Also, Europe had lost its appeal.

A friend of a friend had told Angel about a particular tour agency in San Francisco targeting the well-to-do who were forever looking for ways to entertain themselves and were interested in seeing everything. As usual she acted before thinking and got the job due to her connections without even having to interview. Oh, well, it was just a glorified tour guide job, anyway. To be honest, she only took the job to be closer to where Jeff was. Why was he the one who always was on her mind when she tried to figure out what to do with her life? When would she finally accept that they couldn't get along for any length of time? They were from two different worlds. They had tried before. It never worked!

Angel figured that by now Jeff was used to her sudden appearances and disappearances. So on January 9, 1995, she had left him a voicemail announcing she was in San Francisco now. That was the beginning of the end. Not just the end of Jeff and Angel, but the end of life itself . . . At least, that's what Angel believed while en route back to San Francisco on October 12, 1995. It was over. They could never start over again. The end. No more life for Angel.

In hindsight Angel believed that there had been many foreboding signs foretelling today's misery. Her grandfather had fallen ill with pneumonia in February of this year. She had postponed starting her job and had flown back east for three weeks. Her beloved grandfather had not recovered and had died during her visit. Angel had gotten severely depressed and didn't even listen when she was told that she had inherited a lot of money. First Alois, now her grandfather. Her first impulse was to bury the pain and to get busy. She had convinced her travel company to let her come along on the company's next tour, though she had not been scheduled for it. She had spent six weeks traveling through South America. That's when she had become close friends with Lise Shepard. Lise was the first close woman friend

Angel had ever had. She hadn't let on to Jeff how depressed she had really been. She didn't want him to feel sorry for her and to engage in acts of chivalry or something even more horrible by becoming her so-called savior. Jeff could get that way, and she hated it. That wasn't the love she wanted. No, she wanted to be loved for *who* she was and *how* she was. They had to be equals, very different equals, for sure, yet equals still! Each would allow the other to be a strong individual. Support would be expressed by just *being there* with the other, kind of like "coming alongside" and not leaving, no matter what! So she had told Jeff that Lise had been quite instrumental in helping her deal with her mourning. Then she had fallen back into her "running away mode" and had taken off on a two-month trip to India and China. Fortunately, Lise had been along on each trip.

Today, on the plane, Angel saw a distinct pattern in her life. Certain choices she had made in the past now looked like crossroads, meaning she could have taken an altogether different road and not just the one she had been aware of at the time. How could this be?

Running back to Kitzbuehel in 1993 had been such a crossroads experience. After all, Angel did not have to run. Right now something inside of her seemed to be nudging her, conveying a strong need to examine her current choices more carefully and to become more aware of another crossroads symbol. What was in front of her? How many roads were there? How would she choose this time? Would she run away again?

Angel decided she actually hated all those crossroads experiences. Just thinking about their implications made her feel uneasy and scared. Really, how was she supposed to have known which road in life was the best one to take? Now it made sense, but not earlier on. Yet if she looked at her relationship with Jeff, she certainly could have tried to work on whatever it was that seemed to kill their so-called love so quickly! Instead she had run away. One could say that life had actually presented her with another choice in June of this year. Another crossroads experience? It hurt a lot to admit it, but it was true Angel could have stayed with Jeff, like he had asked her to, and she could have quit her silly job. That's what she should have done! Why hadn't she? Angel hated herself by now.

Finally utter exhaustion took its toll and provided Angel with some reprieve. Lulled by the droning sound of the airplane engines, she fell into a dead sleep.

Chapter 9

Company Rumors

Monday October 9, 1995, 10:53 a.m.

A split second after Brian had entered the building on Monday morning he heard a voice call out his name from somewhere in the building, not too far away—"Brian, Brian, wait a minute! I need to talk to you!"

He turned around and saw Michelle running toward him. Just like last Thursday, she seemed to know exactly when he would show up! How did she spot him the minute he entered the building? Michelle's ability to always know what was going on and where everybody was never ceased to intrigue and puzzle Brian.

He wished he could have made it to his cube without being noticed. Michelle probably had more news, most likely bad news . . . Solitude, away from the outside world, in the safety of his cubicle, at least for a couple of hours—that's all Brian wanted and needed right now. A refuge, oh, how he longed for it! Brian actually felt something close to outright resentment over this unexpected interruption. For a split second he considered telling Michelle how he really felt. No—impossible, he couldn't. "So then suffer," Brian told himself. "That's the price you have to pay for not speaking up!"

With a voice resonating with a certain amount of hidden exasperation Brian said, "Hi, Michelle. How are you doing?" What a stupid thing to say! He was such an idiot sometimes. He hated himself at moments like this. Anybody looking at Michelle right now pretty much knew. She was excited, intense! The intensity was all around her like a cloud of pungent perfume. Her face and gestures said it all.

Even Michelle's long, blond hair communicated action and vitality while bouncing back and forth, mirroring her every move. She was sheer energy in motion. And it was all coming his way, and Brian couldn't stop it. Oh, well, deep down he still liked her. What he didn't like when talking to her was the way her emotions seemed to overwhelm him. He couldn't describe it any better than that. All he knew for sure was that it always took him a while to recover from the impact she seemed to have on him. Brian hadn't always felt this way around her. Either he or she had changed. Ever since she had begun working for Loren she appeared more forceful. Was it because she saw herself as having more power in her new role as executive secretary? Brian wasn't sure. She certainly had more access to the internal workings of top management and relished being "in the know."

Michelle gave Brian some time to recover after she pounced on him so suddenly. Without being aware of it, she was able to read another's feelings by picking up minute changes in body language, and she adapted herself instantly to fit the need of the situation. Therefore, she waited patiently as Brian went through his morning routine.

First, Brian went to his cube to get his favorite mug. Then he returned to the break room and actually took time out to clean the espresso machine before brewing his espresso and steaming the milk for a perfect cafe latte. Michelle had tagged along and hadn't left his side, all the while making some small talk about this and that. However, she saved the important news for later, when Brian would be done with his morning fix. Michelle had long given up wondering why engineers chose to be so particular about, among other things, something as boring as making a cup of coffee. What could possibly be so important about a perfect cup of espresso? But that's how these engineers were, and she was not interested in changing them. Live and let live—that was her motto in life.

As Michelle accompanied Brian during his morning routine, she remembered the fuss and mini revolt created by jealous employees in non-engineering buildings a couple of months ago. They felt that *not* having an espresso setup meant that they were inferior and less important in the eyes of the company. People could be so silly! Michelle hated such pettiness! Of course, in the end Atlas had relented, and by now every company building had the same expensive Italian espresso equipment that previously had only been installed in the engineering buildings. What would people want next? Would they ever be satisfied?

After Brian had finished his morning ritual and they had arrived back at his cube, Michelle knew it was okay to start talking.

"You just won't believe what I heard the other day! A bunch of creeps over in building 5 have been complaining loudly about the food served at the beer busts on Friday afternoons. Can you believe it? After all, it's free. They get to spend time goofing off rather than working. What else do they want?"

Watching Brian get his cafe latte had probably triggered the food story, but with Michelle one never knew for sure. The stories just seemed to come out of nowhere.

"And that's not all! At the last admin meeting I attended—you know, we get together once a month—I heard something even more amazing. By the way, you won't believe the stuff you hear at those meetings."

Brian had no idea what might be discussed at those meetings, even though Michelle kept him abreast most of the time.

"Anyway, the latest problem they are trying to fix, so to speak, is the infighting between individual groups who sponsor breakfast treats, mostly on Friday mornings—like the bagels and fruit and coffee cake I always get for all of you here in the building. Well, in this building we don't have a problem. We all get our treats on Friday. But in some other buildings different functional groups sit next to each other, like for instance in building 3, accounting sits right next to order administration. So, let's say accounting get their treats on Monday morning and order administration get theirs on Friday morning. As a result there are treats on two different days. Would you believe that this causes infighting? Accounting complain that order administration are eating their treats on Monday morning and want to put a stop to it! Their reason? Our department is charged with the expense, and this gives us exclusive rights to the treats. I ask you, what's the big deal? Atlas pays for treats for accounting *and* for order administration! Yes, it's true, the expense does get charged to each department's budget. But it's all paid for by Atlas money. However, they don't see it that way! I'm telling you, things are getting worse around here all the time. Everybody is so fussy and so spoiled and, like little kids in a sandbox, they're throwing sand at each other!"

Brian had followed this story only vaguely, and it had left him confused, wondering what the real point might be. But he chose not to say anything. Fortunately, though, the story had given Brian time to sort through a number of issues in his mind and to recover from the shock of having to deal with Michelle first thing Monday morning.

On the drive to work Brian had concluded that the Sunday hike had indeed done him a lot of good. He felt less fragmented, and after an initial shock he had even been more open and willing to deal with the unexpected presence of a rather intense Michelle full of wild stories about "freebies!" Brian was faintly aware that the hike wasn't the only reason for his improved mood. He knew only too well that Brigitte and the time they had spent together last night had a lot to do with how he felt right now. Maybe Brigitte was even the main or only reason for this cozy feeling inside. However, to explore such a possibility was way too scary and had overtones and implications best left alone. Instead Brian had told himself several times since Sunday night that he certainly had enjoyed being with Brigitte and had forced himself to leave it at that.

Seeing Michelle evoked more daydreaming about Brigitte. He recalled those special moments that had made him feel so connected to her. There was a certain similarity between Michelle and Brigitte. Both of them had a lot of energy and drive. To Brian, Michelle's energy seemed out of control and always coming right at him. It was different with Brigitte. Her energy was contained inside of her rather than directed toward Brian. However, once she had decided on a certain goal, she was relentless in its pursuit. Brian figured that in spite of such apparent luster even Brigitte felt insecure at times. He had wondered if she ever really needed support and comfort. Last night had been one of those rare moments when he had seen a side of Brigitte he had not seen before. For the first time ever he had been able to discern that she, too, longed for somebody who could understand her dreams and her hopes. This had meant a lot to Brian.

The movie they had seen had triggered identical reactions in Brian and Brigitte. For Brian it had taken a lot of explaining by Brigitte to understand her interpretation of the film's meaning and to recognize that he actually agreed. She had patiently tried to describe to him what in the movie had spoken to her and why. He, too, had felt emotions during the movie, but couldn't really explain them in words. The movie "A Month by the Lake" depicted the struggle of people having to come to grips with longings and hopes that Brian never would have admitted having. Brigitte had expressed her own position by asking herself out loud in her discussion with Brian what human beings can and cannot do to support longings in a friend and/or partner. She maintained that there is a part inside all of us that struggles to be authentic and longs to find fulfillment and completeness. Per Brigitte, it is possible to share this struggle, but the responsibility for this quest belongs to each of us individually. We will always be alone and separate in our individual walk—at least according to Brigitte. But we can share these experiences with each other.

Brian had felt too apprehensive to ask questions, and so he had not understood everything Brigitte had said. Part of the discussion had left a fuzzy picture in this mind. He had been unable to follow her entire train of thought. Brian was not used to talking about subjects like identity, authenticity of being, fulfillment, and raison d'etre, as the French called it—at least according to Brigitte. Brian didn't like it when Brigitte used terminology he couldn't grasp. Yet, there were those rare moments, like last night, when some of the things she had talked about suddenly made a lot of sense. He had enjoyed that feeling.

During the earlier part of the movie, as personal conflicts arose between the movie characters, Brian had found himself getting ready for a big disappointment and was quite relieved when instead there was a so-called happy ending. It had been a struggle for the characters, but they had made it! Brigitte, in her usual forthright manner, had of course immediately tackled the question the movie had raised to her—how unacknowledged longings and fear of exposure could kill a relationship. Intense fear could lead somebody into denying all emotions that could not be controlled. After initial apprehension, Brian had found himself caught up in Brigitte's discourse. Though he couldn't really explain why, he felt closer to her after the discussion than ever before. Now he hoped that this feeling would never end. He began to wonder if he was just a dreamer.

Michelle interrupted Brian's daydreaming.

"Brian, I had wanted to stop by on Friday, but there was no time. The day was wild because Loren had been out all day Thursday. I still don't really believe what he told me. He claims that he got called to a sudden meeting with this outfit down in LA. Rumor has it that Atlas is considering some kind of joint venture with them. I don't think Loren is really all that involved in it, though I believe he wants to be. If my sources on executive row are correct, and I believe they are, it would mean that we'll actually merge with this company. Wouldn't that be something?"

"Which company are you talking about? I don't think I ever heard about this. What are you saying?"

"Well, that's just the weird part about this whole thing. Nobody seems to know who they are and what they do. The rumor didn't mention any specifics. But then rumors never really do."

"Then how can you be sure about anything you heard?"

"Oh, trust me, I can be sure! You see, first I hear tidbits here, then some more from somebody else. And then suddenly it all begins to make sense to me. It's like I suddenly see the whole picture, you know what I mean? And then, just like that—I just know! Anyway, that's how it works for me. I know you engineers never believe in anything like that, but trust me, I've been right so many times, and that's why I believe in my gut instincts."

Ever since Brian had met Michelle, he had gradually come to accept that if anyone had a sixth sense, it must be her. How else could she always be on top of any and all news happening around the company? Brian had to admit Michelle had been right before about some of her crazy suggestions and ideas. However, her tendency to talk about her ideas and gut feelings in extremes, using heavy-handed generalizations, made it tough for Brian not to be skeptical. It wasn't really that she generalized. Rather she seemed to leave out a lot that Brian considered important and necessary. Instead she lumped everything together into some kind of whole and always appeared to be jumping to conclusions. Furthermore, she perceived the world around her from a feeling and, therefore, subjective viewpoint only. Take for instance the rumors about the merger. Without hesitation or concern she presented her conclusions as facts, even though these conclusions were based on gut feelings only. She had no need for a rational framework. She actually believed her perceptions were rational, even though they seemed irrational to Brian. He also knew from experience that it wouldn't bother her at all to find out that she had been wrong! Sometimes he envied her. Basically Michelle's ideas were as freewheeling as she herself appeared to be. For her to have ideas and opinions required no premeditation or forethought. And if her ideas didn't come to fruition, it would be no big deal either. She would simply try something else.

"Anyway, I can tell something's up. I just know it! Loren's been in a terrible mood since all of this started last Wednesday. He also got called to see the president, who is apparently ticked, at least according to his admin, Barbara. Barbara and I get along well, so I hear a lot.

"But this is different. This has to do with the case. Evidently John, Barb's boss, is very angry that we're written up all over the papers because of the murder. To get more of a story, journalists started calling the president's office. All of the executive secretaries have been put on alert and are fielding the calls and passing them on to public relations. Boy, do they have their hands full right now! Did you see the paper on Friday and the article today?"

"No, I don't get a paper."

"Well, you should. Anyway, you won't believe what the reporters came up with and what they said about us, I mean Atlas. Apparently there is this talk that the team Jeff was on has some breakthrough technology, and this outfit Loren supposedly visited on Thursday is developing a product that would complement the tool Jeff's team has developed. So now the papers are trying to figure out what it all means. Barbara says that John is furious, absolutely livid! Of course she won't tell me exactly one way or the other what is really true and what isn't. But John certainly hated what the press reported."

Michelle had come to the end of her story and looked quite satisfied. Brian knew that she never lingered once her story was told. This made it easier for him to just go along for the ride. She also didn't expect him to offer any opinions or conclusions. She just wanted to tell her story. As soon as Michelle had left, Brian decided to start his day by checking his e-mail, since he was waiting for a message from Dona.

Brian logged on and shuddered. Seventy-two messages—how was he ever going to get anywhere? Once he had started going through the messages one by one, his usual focus and concentration returned. Gone was the annoyance he had felt over the barrage of information that had run interference in his life.

What Brian was most interested in and what needed to be taken care of right away was everything related to his project. What he hoped to find was a message from Dona. Yes, there it was.

Date: Sun, Oct 8, 1995 2:36 PM PDT
To: brian@cicero.atlas.com
From: donag@tree.atlas.com
Subject: About our talk on Saturday

Brian,
These are my findings:
1) Jeff's contacts over the last three months:
    I found nothing. It appears somebody deleted all of
Jeff's e-mail as well as his e-mail address. I know for a fact

that he kept a personal file of important messages in his mailbox. At other times he would file the messages catego- rized by subject.

On Monday I will contact our system administrator, saying I am looking for important product information in old e-mail messages. As you know, a server backs up all e-mail correspondence overnight.

2) Jeff's last documented product status report.

I had more luck with this. Apparently Jeff sent out a hard copy report by interoffice mail on Wednesday, the day he died. The report wasn't delivered till Friday. Interoffice mail can be slow. Jeff usually sent out his reports by e-mail. To send his last report by interoffice mail was an unusual occurrence.

I also noticed that this report was quite different from the one Jeff had brought to the new product meeting about two weeks ago. Obviously he had gotten farther along in his work, but something seemed to be missing that had been included in the earlier report. I spent most of the remainder of my time yesterday trying to ascertain whether what was missing had been replaced by new, updated information. Partially this was correct. I then determined that some of the missing data was quite important and as a result the document was no longer as useful and as pertinent as the earlier version had been.

I will be in around 10 a.m. on Monday.
Dona

Michelle seemed to have been right again with one of those crazy hunches of hers. Something strange was going on. Something very strange . . . Now it was 10:50 a.m. Though he felt pressured by his workload, Brian decided to look for Dona. Her findings intrigued him.

Chapter 10

Evil is Lurking

Monday Night, October 9, 1995, 8:44 p.m.

If it hadn't been for the faint ray of light emanating from the dim hallway fixture, the apartment would have been pitch dark. Yet the light was not strong enough to dispel the hovering shadows in Brian's living room. Brian was lying on the sofa, listless and motionless, totally unaware of his surroundings. His body was barely recognizable in the dark shadow cast by the back of the sofa. Brian was scared, very scared. He could not recall ever having felt this scared before, except maybe in a nightmare. He also felt numb all over.

Last Thursday, the day after the murder, he had experienced similar sensations. But this was worse. It had all started the day after the murder, when fear and anger had risen from the depth of his unconscious and had taken over his life. Since then he had felt out of control. This begged the question whether he had ever been control in the first place. What had happened? Why was he feeling so terribly gloomy, empty, and hopeless? He had never had any feelings like this before, or at least he had never been aware of them.

In a sudden flash of insight Brian concluded that what he felt could be compared to a computer experiencing a system crash and shutdown. There were ways to deal with system crashes, but Brian had no clue what to do about an emotional crash. How did one restart one's internal system? Worse yet, how could one possibly make sense out of this deluge of unknown and disturbing emotions? Brian wished he could isolate some of those feelings, line them up and reflect upon each one separately and sequentially. That would allow him to determine a workable solution. A strong sense of urgency demanded that he act, do something, anything, so that he could regain control! This vague unknown felt so threatening. It left him with the notion that he no longer really existed.

Driving home from work this Monday evening Brian had felt chased by an unknown force of evil, out to do him harm! He also felt trapped. There seemed to be no escape, no place to run to and hide. Hide from what—and why? Where was the answer to this unknown? Whoever or whatever was chasing him was about to annihilate him. Brian was sure of it! But how did he know? And why did it matter?

Brian felt it, that's how he knew. What was wrong with him? How could he be sure about what he felt? For that matter, how could anybody ever really determine reality on the basis of their emotions? Brian had never really bought into the concept that when you feel something, this also means it is real and exists. It didn't make sense to him. He needed some logical explanations. He wanted to be sure. After all, how could one *know* for sure what one felt? Is that what was going on inside of him right now? Was he trying to ascertain his own reality, while having this internal dialogue? It was all so confusing and overwhelming. He no longer knew what was real and what wasn't.

Suddenly, at work, Brian had experienced an unquenchable desire to flee. But work was where he felt good and safe. Why would he want to run away from it now? It wasn't stress he had felt. Brian knew all about stress. No, this was quite different. It definitely was fear, unadulterated, cold, naked fear. Convinced that everything in life could be mastered by careful and intense introspection, Brian had tried and tried to make sense out of what he felt, yet he had failed. All these unknown feelings had escalated, leaving him in total despair!

This process had started after Brian had met with Dona. He had gone over to her cubicle just before lunch today. Based on Dona's e-mail there was reason to believe that her findings could shed light onto the murder mystery. At first Brian had felt upbeat and hopeful. He agreed with Dona that it was important to note that Jeff had sent his last product status report by interoffice mail. Nobody in the group, and this included Jeff, had ever used interoffice mail as a substitute for e-mail. Yet, one could argue, that might just have been a coincidence. But neither Dona nor Brian could explain why Jeff had altered his report. It wasn't just that a specific page was missing. No, it was a paragraph here, a sentence there. Dona had carefully examined the two reports. Highlighted sections in the two-week-old report identified what was missing in the last report, the one Jeff had sent by interoffice mail on the day of his murder. Dona had explained that what Jeff had left out was extremely important and critical. Without this information the product would be flawed. She doubted that this had just been an oversight on Jeff's part. This begged the question, what had motivated Jeff to change his report?

Dona had become increasingly emotional and agitated while explaining her findings. Brian had never seen her that way before. Her already rapid speech had increased, and her Chinese accent had intensified, making it harder for Brian to follow her discourse.

Dona was convinced that by omitting critical information, Jeff had wanted to communicate that something was not the way it was supposed to be. She also believed that her research on Jeff's computer on Saturday had exposed her and might have drawn the attention of the killer. Once the killer learned about her involvement, she would become the next target. She acted as if she expected somebody to show up right then and there, and as far as she was concerned, she would definitely be the next victim!

During their meeting Dona had looked around again and again, spoken in hushed tones, and rushed to get the meeting over with. Though lacking any kind of tangible proof, Dona was nonetheless certain that the person who had deleted Jeff's files, mailbox, and e-mail address also had to either be the killer, or be working with the killer, or on the killer's orders. It took somebody with system administration skills and access to internal passwords to delete a mailbox. Such changes usually took weeks, yet Jeff's mailbox had been deleted within a couple of days. Dona believed that only the killer would have something to gain from wiping out all of Jeff's files. What if the killer had stolen Jeff's files by copying them over to his or her system before deleting them? What if several individuals were involved, possibly some from inside the company and some from outside, and what if they were all working together? Dona wanted nothing else to do with Jeff's murder. She was done!

Brian wondered whether a changed report and missing files could really cause somebody to get this scared. Dona didn't seem to be the kind of person who panicked easily. She was quiet, reflective, and careful. What had happened?

Lying on his sofa in the darkness, Brian sensed danger all around him. This was no game. This was murder and a killer was out there somewhere . . . Dona must have sensed the same!

Brian had arrived home about an hour ago. He had been lying on the sofa ever since. He hadn't even thought about eating. He had no appetite. Suddenly the phone rang. Brian considered not answering, but thought or hoped that it might be Brigitte. He sat up and reached for the phone on the little table next to him.

"Hello."

"Brian, where have you been?" It was his mother. Oh, darn it, this was absolutely the worst time to have to deal with *her*!

"Oh, hi! How are you, Mom?"

"I'm fine. I've been calling you for days! Couldn't you get yourself an answering machine? Everybody seems to have them these days. Why do you always have to be so different?"

She paused for a moment as if waiting for a reply. But Brian knew that if he didn't answer she would just go on. And she did.

"Why didn't you call me and tell me about the murder? To think you had just come from our birthday party and then you discovered a murder! And I had to find out about it from the newspapers! And you know I don't really trust them. Did you read about it in the paper? Oh, never mind, I forgot you don't get a paper. I just don't understand you sometimes!"

Brian thought to himself, "Actually, you never understand me. And I don't understand you!" But he said nothing.

His mother went on and on. One rhetorical question was followed by another. Brian had learned long ago that he didn't have to answer all these questions. Instead he simply shut off and was hardly aware of what she was saying. He had been through the same scenario so many times that he knew just when to make an agreeing sound or express concern, or whatever it was his mother wanted to get validated.

Brian promised to call his mother if he found out anything that the newspapers wouldn't or couldn't know. After all, he was kind of an insider, right? He did not mention that he was trying to find out who killed Jeff. Besides, deep down his mother knew that Brian wouldn't call her. Brian expected her to call him again, hoping to find out more. He hoped he wouldn't be around when she did. At least she never called him at work. She knew he rarely answered his phone, and leaving a voicemail was useless. She had tried that. He simply never called back. Once he had explained that he was too busy at work to deal with personal phone calls. His mother seemed to have accepted that.

A long time ago, Brian couldn't quite remember when, he had given up trying to explain himself to his family. Most likely it had happened gradually. They were just too different. Sometimes he felt a real agony inside when he remembered the isolation and abandonment of his years at home. There had been no support, no validation, at least not the kind he had needed and longed for. Brian didn't like remembering. It was too painful.

Brigitte had tried several times to draw him out and to talk to him about his family and the past. However, she soon realized that in response he would shut down and withdraw. She had learned not to pry too much anymore. As far as Brian was concerned the past didn't really have anything to do with who you were now. So far in his life, this belief had stood the test of time.

Tonight wasn't the first time Brian wished he had taken a job in a totally different part of the country to be farther away from his family. Unfortunately, though, the best opportunities for somebody with his skills were still here in Silicon Valley. Also, it probably wouldn't help. His mother would still call him.

After what seemed like an eternity but in reality had taken only five minutes, his mother hung up the phone. Almost without thinking Brian lay down on the sofa again, still unaware of the darkness around him. It was as if there had been no phone call. His mind started working again. How much did he really want to find out why Jeff had been killed? Was the danger he sensed for real?

The meeting with Dona had been quite unsettling. How much had it impacted him? Could it have just been nerves that made Brian believe somebody had followed him home from work this evening? He didn't want to think about it. He was probably imagining things. This only happened in movies or on TV, right? Yet he couldn't shake the feeling off. He really believed he had been followed home.

Was the car Brian had noticed while driving home really the same car he had noticed on the night of the murder? He had always prided himself in his ability to recognize patterns. He possessed an uncanny ability to immediately become aware of shifts and deviations in any typical pattern of everyday life, in this case the flow of traffic. However, he had never before been forced to test these skills during such unsettling and nerve-racking circumstances. The car in the parking lot had been a black Camaro with fancy gold trim and many extra features. It had a distinctly flashy look. Brian still remembered the license plate, and he had also written it down and had checked it when he got home tonight: 4PRIS 1830. Brian had tried very hard to decipher the license plate of the car following him this afternoon, but without success. The car had not been very close. The driver seemed to know what he was doing and was mostly hanging back. Brian was sure that the car had followed him all the way home from work to his condo in Sunnyvale. He had not traveled just main routes but had also taken several side roads. What were the chances of somebody taking the very same route he was on? Sure, it was possible. Could it have been the same car he remembered seeing on the night of the murder? He definitely believed it was a Camaro, and it was black. And it had fancy trim . . .

Now what? Brian was at a loss. Only hours ago he had been convinced that Dona had overreacted, yet now he no longer found her to be irrational. He understood. Brian knew he wouldn't be able to fall asleep tonight. His first thought had been to call Brigitte. What a silly thought! It would make him feel even more foolish as well as childish. The second thought had been to call the police. Brian began to debate the merits of such a step. What could it all mean? Why would somebody follow him? Who would know that he was trying to investigate Jeff's files? At least it seemed to Brian that being followed was a direct result of the investigation Dona and he had undertaken. What if he was totally wrong? What if he was just being paranoid?!

Brian was sure that Dona had been careful in her investigation. He couldn't imagine that she would have talked to anybody about looking through Jeff's files. What about the system administrator? Had Dona spoken with her? What was her name again? Now he remembered—it was Cathie. Michelle seemed to know Cathie rather well. Maybe the two of them had talked. That had to be it.

If this had been the case, where did the information go from there? To Loren? It just had to be Loren. Michelle could have told Loren that Brian was suspicious of him. Ridiculous! Brian had never even mentioned his thoughts to Michelle. Maybe he should talk to Cathie. No, he didn't like that idea either. He didn't really know her well enough to ask such questions.

Brian realized that he wanted Loren to be the murderer. He felt guilty about it, yet, his hunches had been telling him for a while that something strange was going on, even before Jeff's murder. However, one of Brian's rules in life was to classify hunches as foolishness unless they could be substantiated. Mostly hunches could not be proven; that's why they're called hunches! Questions, questions, and no answers. What was he supposed to conclude now? Did this mean that he now believed in hunches? Recent events made Brian question what process would work best to ascertain truth. Yet, wasn't it also true that nothing could be proven logically or rationally about Jeff, his work, his murder? Brian had to admit that he had simply lost it—just like Dona. He couldn't really blame Dona for pulling out. To be honest, he wanted to do the same now! Brian wanted to escape, flee from whatever it was that might be lurking in the background. This desire for an escape had preoccupied all of his thinking while at work. Finally Brian had to leave work, totally disgusted with himself about his failure to regain control. Since meeting Dona he had been utterly useless at work, unable to concentrate or focus. He went home at 8 p.m., something rather unheard of!

Could all this fear have made Brian imagine that he had been followed? How could that person following him in the car have known that Brian would leave work early, unless the individual had already been waiting and was prepared to wait till he would leave?

By now Brian was convinced that this mystery person had something to do with Jeff's murder. To call the police and share his conclusion was simply out of the question. He could almost hear Lieutenant Woodraw's cool and, most likely, disdainful response to such a foolish suggestion. Anybody would be able to see that he was just scared stiff and most likely imaging things. What proof was there? None, really.

Besides Brian really didn't like Lieutenant Woodraw. That was a pretty stupid feeling as well, but it was the truth. Brian started swearing out loud and couldn't remember the last time he had found it necessary to resort to this kind of language. He hated feeling this way.

Who could help Brian now? Dona was out of the picture. The question looming in the background was why had Jeff changed his report? This was leading nowhere. Brian figured that he would have to contact Jeff's friend at Santa Fe University. He could only hope that Jeff's friend would trust Brian enough to talk about what Jeff might have been up to. What if Jeff had not told anybody about his personal work? It all didn't seem to make sense. Something was missing here. Brian just couldn't figure out what. All Jeff had ever told Brian was that he was excited about digital life, had done some work on it, and had a buddy at Santa Fe University who did similar research. Brian concluded that he would have to contact this person.

And why had Dona not followed the trail she had highlighted in her e-mail to Brian? She had written that she would try to contact the system administrator. Why hadn't she? He certainly had lost his marbles when talking to her! He had failed to ask her about that specific.

Maybe it was time to bail out, to stop being silly and forget about playing scary detective games. Then Brian realized that bailing out wouldn't help at all anymore if he had been followed. It would be too late. He already was involved, by definition. How was he going to convince whoever it was that he had abandoned the whole stupid idea of finding the murderer? He was trapped like a wounded animal looking for shelter. There was no way out.

Suddenly the phone rang again. Startled and dazed, Brian checked his watch. It was 10:15 p.m. Where was he? What had happened? Then he realized he had fallen asleep and had probably slept for about twenty minutes. The ringing phone had awakened him. This couldn't be his mother again—no, definitely not. This time it had to be Brigitte. Brian finally picked up the phone on the sixth ring.

"Hello."

No sound, nothing. No response. It was dead quiet. Too quiet—it was unnerving. Brian found himself just waiting, receiver in hand, motionless and unable to move. This didn't feel good at all. Then, as if somebody had either waited or possibly turned on a tape, Brian heard the following words: "You are warned! Give up! We know what you are doing! Don't be stupid! We will stop you!"

Then a click, and the line was dead.

Brian sank back onto the sofa as if in a trance, receiver still in hand. Then he heard the phone company's recording telling him to hang up. He finally did, unaware of what he was doing. So here it was. The big "it" had revealed itself, the unknown of which he had been so afraid. The force that had been chasing him was real and existed. Worse yet, Brian was its next target.

There was no longer any doubt in Brian's mind that he had been followed. It meant that he was close to something, closer than he had thought. So close indeed that somebody had found it necessary to threaten him. No way—he was *not* going to be bullied! Absolutely not! Brian could hardly believe his own determination. Somehow this phone call had changed everything. An intense energy surge fueled by rage over the injustice of it all raced through his entire body, mind, and soul. Totally aware and conscious that he was facing a real, tangible threat, Brian now knew exactly what he had to do. He would fight this injustice—yes, indeed, he would!

Chapter 11

A Productive Day

Tuesday October 10, 1995

This morning, shortly after getting to work, Brian had ventured to take a closer look around Jeff's cube. He had actually stepped inside. He wasn't sure what had prompted this, or what he could possibly be looking for. On Monday night, trying to go to sleep, Brian had this silly recurring thought about whether the bloodstains were still on the carpet. That was probably what had prompted his desire to look around. No, nobody had touched anything as far as he could tell, and the bloodstains were still there. Somehow they really seemed to jump out at him. He had stepped around them. It would probably take a while to get the carpet cleaned. Possibly, the police still didn't want anything touched. No, the police seemed to be done. Somebody had taken down the yellow "keep off" tape that had been up since Wednesday night. This must have been done before Brian had made it to work on Monday morning. The tape had still been up on Saturday when he had been in the office. That meant the police were done with whatever they had investigated. He wondered what had caused the blow on Jeff's head. No sharp object of any kind was in Jeff's cube. Nothing that could have had such a severe impact. Would Lieutenant Woodraw tell him if he asked? Brian didn't think so.

After staring at the blood for just a couple of seconds, Brian quickly gave up the idea of looking around Jeff's cube for more clues. No, no way, he couldn't deal with any of this right now. Today his focus was on his work and *not* on the murder. He wanted no murder business today. He needed a break. He was behind on several commitments he had made on his project, and he had received a reminder from his boss. Conceivably by now Brian was holding up the entire project. His work was needed for others to continue.

But before focusing on work, Brian decided to send off an e-mail to Ray Beachwood, Jeff's friend at Santa Fe University. Luckily the note with Ray's e-mail address was still stuck to Brian's monitor. Brian had jotted it down last Thursday afternoon when taking a first quick glance at Jeff's files. Today he wished Michelle hadn't interrupted him at that very moment, or that he would have been willing to continue his investigation afterward. He might have been able to find out a lot more before somebody had deleted Jeff's mailbox and files.

Brian didn't expect a response from Ray Beachwood before tomorrow or the day after. Brian's name wouldn't ring a bell, and thus his e-mail would be buried in a long queue of messages. Ray would have to read the e-mail before knowing that it was about his friend Jeff. Brian had not wanted to put Jeff's name in the header of the message. Maybe it wouldn't make a difference, anyway. If the murderer wanted to check Brian's e-mail messages, he could, but only if she or he had access to the company server. It was a risk Brian had been willing to take.

Since writing that e-mail Brian had been totally engrossed in his work. He found a leftover sandwich when walking into the break room around 1:30 p.m. to get a soda, so there had been no need to go out for lunch. Groups who held meetings over the lunch hour frequently ordered catered meals, and leftovers were set out for anybody to grab and enjoy. Except for that short break he had been working nonstop, unaware of the passing of time.

Yet even while intensely focused on his work, Brian had still been plagued by concerns about what had happened to Jeff's files. It was like his mind was working on two levels simultaneously; Brian was working and worrying, all at the same time. Brian and Dona had seen the files on Saturday afternoon, and by Sunday, when Dona looked again, the files were gone. Of course, somebody might have copied them over to another system or onto a tape before deleting them. Jeff's manager, Scott Jones, might have decided to save Jeff's work. To Brian the timing seemed unusual, though, since the files disappeared between Saturday afternoon and Sunday morning. Surely, nobody from system administration would work over the weekend on such a task?

Yet despite these recurring concerns Brian was definitely calmer today, and all in all he felt more balanced. Monday night's resolve to fight the injustice of Jeff's murder had made him sharper, keener, and more alert. It appeared that taking a stand and resolving to act had made a difference in how he felt. He couldn't be sure, but those gripping and numbing anxiety attacks so rampant since last Wednesday seemed to have subsided. Being busy and being able to focus again also contributed to his improved good spirits. Brian found it hard to believe that almost a week had passed since his life had taken such a sudden and unexpected turn.

Since receiving the threatening phone call Brian had abandoned the idea of talking to others at the company about Jeff's work. Over the last couple of days Brian had become increasingly suspicious and therefore avoided going into the lab today. He didn't want to have to talk to anybody and wanted to avoid having to answer questions.

Usually the lab served as a place to hang out and congregate. During little breaks engineers engaged in hot discussions about the latest stock price of Atlas and how Atlas's stock fared when compared with that of competitors. The engineers also enjoyed talking about what was going on inside Atlas—how far along a certain project was, what worked, what didn't, which engineering group was behind and struggling to make a deadline, and so on. Someone might bring up an article from the *Mercury News* that talked about their industry, and it could lead to a fiery debate about how "idiotic" the press was and why they always seemed to get everything wrong! Being precise, correct, and knowing technology better than the next person, in other words, playing "one-upsmanship games," was one of their favorite pastimes. They all found it extremely important to correct mistakes and incorrect assumptions! Even Brian, who rarely stepped outside of his shell, sometimes felt it necessary to participate, showing great intensity and enthusiasm.

Some of the guys were especially prone to grandiose posturing about how well they did in the stock market in general. They also liked to brag about their Atlas options and about how good they were at selling them whenever the Atlas stock price peaked. Brian found this behavior quite irritating and unsettling. He never participated in any of those discussions. Instead he would leave the room. He was proud of his Atlas options. To him these options represented a pinnacle of achievement. Yet, Brian avoided facing the reality that they also represented a lot of financial value. Unconsciously Brian was even a little embarrassed by how wealthy he actually was. He often reminded himself that so far it was paper value only. He wasn't really wealthy—these were just options. Until he exercised his options and bought shares at the option value and immediately sold those shares, there was no real gain. His mother frequently chastised him for not having exercised any of his options yet. He was angry at himself for ever having explained to her how the whole process worked. The result had been question after question.

"How many options do you have? Why won't you tell me? Why can't you sell them all at the same time? What does vesting mean?"

To put a stop to his mother's repeated interrogations, Brian finally told her that if he sold all vested options as well as the shares he had purchased through Atlas's employee stock purchase plan and after paying taxes on the profit, he would probably have in the neighborhood of $300,000 net, possibly even more if the stock price kept going up. What a fool he had been to tell her his yet unrealized net worth! Learning about the real value had only added fuel to his mother's pursuit. He still fumed each time she brought up the subject!

Now, instead of prying about his options, his mother would ask why Brian didn't use some of his options or shares or whatever they were to buy himself a house, or at least a condo. But what for? What was the point? Such a step would be the end of his current lifestyle. No, Brian liked to keep things the way they were. No attachments to anything. No obligations. Brian felt awkward about wealth in general. It made him feel uncomfortable, never mind why. He liked the status quo. Why complicate everything?

Suddenly Brian noticed that his mind had been wandering off. He came to and checked his watch. It was 3:43 p.m. Yet in spite of all the difficulties surrounding him, he had accomplished a lot today. As a result he felt pretty good. Throughout the day there had been moments of intense introspection. It was Brian's way of coping with the world of uncertainty around him, an attempt to reconcile what seemed amiss.

Actually, now that he thought about it, Brian realized he had avoided going to the lab ever since Jeff's body had been found. Strangely enough, nobody had really tried to make contact with him either, except, of course, Michelle. But Michelle was different. Was everybody avoiding him on purpose? Probably. Did they think he knew something? Did they wonder just how much he knew? Brian seemed to have become an outcast. Strange. Was there a specific reason why everybody was avoiding him?

They were probably just avoiding him because, under similar circumstances, each of them would want to be left alone, too. That's what it was. They also knew that Brian didn't like to talk about certain subjects when he was upset. A couple of the engineers had said hello in the hallway and the break room, but rather than talking to him, they had waited for Brian to take the initiative. Since Brian had not tried to talk to them, they had left him alone. Just as well, Brian concluded. He would not have been able to talk to them about the murder, or anything else he felt emotional about. What if one of them was the murderer? It was a horrifying thought and best left alone.

Nevertheless, all things considered, today was the first time in what seemed such a long time that he had actually felt okay. Brian was pretty caught up with his project and had satisfied those who had been waiting for his input. Could this be a good omen for things to come, or was that too much to hope for?

Chapter 12

Sudden Bad News

Tuesday, October 10, 1995, 4:05 p.m.

Only moments ago Brian had felt good about the accomplishments of his day. No more. Now nagging thoughts were plaguing him again. He didn't realize that these unwanted thoughts and feelings surfaced each time he began to relax his intense concentration or when something outside of his control interrupted his focus.

"Brian, I got some horrible news! You won't believe it! Wait till you hear this!"

Oh, no, Michelle again. Brian was still in his gopher mood and liked being inside his burrow. What could he say that would stop her? But she was unstoppable. As usual she would just roll right over him.

"Cathie had a very serious car accident!" Michelle sounded quite upset, and her usually cheerful face expressed horror.

"Cathie, Cathie who?"

Brian was stunned. He had no idea what or who Michelle was talking about now. It took a while to leave the burrow . . .

"You know, Cathie Hughes, the system admin!"

"Oh, that Cathie." Brian froze and went pale.

"What's the matter, Brian? You look like you just saw a ghost!"

Nothing ever seemed to escape Michelle. Even while scared herself she didn't miss a beat. Brian's body language had given him away. She could read him like a book!

"Evidently Cathie had an accident on the way to work this morning some time between 8:30 and 9:30. Cathie has this horrible commute, you know. She actually lives in Santa Cruz and has to take 17 to get to work. Well, of course, at first I thought that's where the accident took place. I mean on 17. There are accidents all the time on 17. I am glad I don't have that commute. Anyway, the accident wasn't even on 17. Instead it happened not too far from here. She had left 85 and was on 237. The accident occurred shortly after exiting from 237 near Fair Oaks. All I know is that she was seriously injured. The police contacted her husband, who works in Santa Cruz, and he called Cathie's manager. Actually, since the manager wasn't around, the admin of their group, Judy, took the message. And I, of course, heard it from Judy. According to the husband, Cathie is in critical condition. Can you believe all of this? Isn't this horrible? More and more bad news every day!"

Brian couldn't respond, even if he had wanted to. His mind's eye still saw the car following him Monday night, and since Michelle started talking he had visibly tensed up and was back in super-alert mode. He experienced the same sensations of imminent danger he had experienced when receiving the threatening phone call on Monday night. He had to act now. To ignore these warning signals would be foolish. He would call Lieutenant Woodraw. What had he done with her business card? Or should he call Brigitte first? No, the police! He would call Brigitte this evening from home.

Michelle chatted away for a couple of more minutes, but Brian didn't really hear anything else. Her words were totally drowned out by his intense anxiety. He knew she would try to get more details about Cathie's accident, and then she would be back. And so it was. Michelle left as suddenly as she had appeared only a couple of minutes ago. Before leaving she turned around to say, "I'll be back as soon as I know more. See you then!"

Now, what had Brian done with that card? He spent the next couple of minutes going through the various stacks and piles on his desk. Most of the time he tried to keep up with all the information flow and made order every other day or so. But since last week things had just piled up . . .

Finally, there it was. Good.

Knowing that he would be tempted *not* to call, Brian forced himself to pick up the phone and dial the number of the Sunnyvale police department. The phone rang three times before the distinctly cool voice of Lieutenant Woodraw answered by saying, "Hello, Woodraw here."

Brian almost put the receiver down again. Instead he heard himself stuttering: "This, um, this is Brian, Brian Smelzer, um, remember . . .?"

"Yes, of course I do. How have you been?"

Brian suddenly broke out in cold sweat. He didn't feel good at all. His stomach was doing flip-flops. How was he going to tell this all-together woman about his irrational fears? She would simply consider them silly and childish. But it had to be done. He just had to get it over with.

Brian finally managed, "When we talked the last time you said to call you in case I had more information." He was regaining some control.

"Yes, indeed. I'm very interested in any additional information."

"Well, I don't really have any facts, but . . ." Brian's voice got tentative and trailed off. Feelings of insecurity hit hard.

The lieutenant waited a moment for Brian to continue. When he didn't, she said, "We still don't really have much to go on, so, I'm very interested in anything you might have come across or thought about. Every possible lead could be of vital importance."

The lieutenant's voice actually sounded sincere and not the way Brian remembered it from that first meeting. The apparent change encouraged him to share what he had been doing, or, to be precise, what he had tried to do. At first he thought he would get chewed out for 'playing detective', yet there was no reprimand at all. Lieutenant Woodraw proved to be an expert listener.

"I really cared about Jeff and had hoped to find reasons why somebody had wanted to kill him. So I asked Dona for some assistance. She was friendly with Jeff and worked with him on the same team. Dona agreed to look through Jeff's computer files, but before she had an opportunity for a more detailed review, the files were deleted from Jeff's computer. This happened during a specific time frame between Saturday and Sunday. Dona also showed me how the latest product report Jeff had sent through interoffice mail differed from the one previously sent by e-mail. Dona believes this to be significant, and after talking with her, seeing the two reports, and in light of the fact that somebody deleted Jeff's files, I would have to agree with her."

Brian paused for a moment, struggling to regain his breath. His sentences had tumbled out at high speed. He wanted to get them out fast, before he changed his mind. He expected the lieutenant to respond, but she did not. Instead she seemed to be waiting for him to go on, and so he did.

"I don't know how much you know about system administration within a UNIX network. Only a system administrator can delete somebody's e-mail address. Of course, probably others in the information services department know the password to the mail server. This mail server backs up all incoming and outgoing e-mail messages. I wonder if some of Jeff's messages are still on this server. However, it's important to note that the average employee does *not* have access to this mail server. Therefore, it seems significant to me that Jeff's mailbox and e-mail address have been deleted only a few days after his murder. Of course, it's possible that his former manager, Scott Jones, asked for this to be done. The fact that Jeff's files have been deleted from his computer system is another issue. All somebody would have had to do is figure out Jeff's password, which is not impossible, and then this person would have been able to do anything with Jeff's files.

"In addition there's something else I wanted to tell you about, and it's kind of personal, and maybe I was just a little paranoid. Anyway, on my way home from work yesterday evening I was under the impression that somebody was following me. At first I didn't give it too much thought, though it upset me, but later that evening I received a phone call, and somebody threatened me."

The lieutenant spoke up immediately, and her voice was crisp, alert, and fast. "At what time did you receive this phone call, and what exactly was said?"

"The phone rang at 10:15 p.m. I remember checking my watch. I had dozed off. I almost hung up because the person, a male, well, I should say it sounded very much like a male voice, did not speak right away. Later I was wondering if the message had been taped because of that initial pause and the peculiar sound of the voice. Just as I was about to hang up the phone, the voice said, 'You are warned! Give up! We know what you are doing! Don't be stupid! We will stop you!'"

"I can most certainly understand your concern. Calling me was the right thing to do. We have to give serious consideration to such calls. The tone does seem to suggest that whoever is behind this, at least so far, seems to mostly want to scare you off. Has anything else happened since then?"

"Well yes, and that's why I called you. I learned that the system administrator, a young woman named Cathie Hughes, had a car accident this morning. Dona had intended to contact Cathie on Monday morning. Cathie does system administration for our building, and she would have known who might have deleted Jeff's mailbox or might have asked for it to be done. Well, anyway, to me it seems important in light of what I explained earlier. Dona and I looked through Jeff's files for just a couple of minutes on Saturday afternoon. Jeff's mailbox was still there at that time. Dona had planned to look more closely on Sunday morning. When she realized on Sunday that files and a mailbox no longer existed on Jeff's system, she got scared. Neither of us contacted Cathie. Therefore I'm very concerned about the nature of Cathie's accident. I mean, I don't want to sound paranoid and read too much into a possible cause for Cathie's accident, but that threatening phone call has made me edgy."

"Calling me definitely was the right thing to do. I'll have somebody check out today's accident reports. As I said before, all leads are very important. Due to the threatening phone call, I believe it will be best to give you police protection. We have to take this phone call seriously. I need to make the necessary arrangements for protection. You'll get a call from us as to when it will kick in, okay?

"We also need to get access to those files you mentioned, in case they still exist. I'll contact information services at Atlas. We need to get permission from your company. Jeff's files might be considered important product information. I'd also like to look at those last two reports Jeff sent out. We'll start with the manager of Jeff's group, Scott Jones. I interviewed him last week."

Brian had protested several times, maintaining he really didn't need police protection, but his protests had been to no avail. The lieutenant had insisted, and Brian had yielded to the authority in charge.

It was only after hanging up the phone that Brian became aware of the implications of being under actual police protection. Agreed, it might make him feel safer, but it also implied that he was in real danger. Furthermore, his personal freedom would be heavily constrained. How was he going to deal with that?

"Brian, Brian, I have the most incredible news!"

Brian almost jumped out of his chair. Michelle again . . . What else could have happened?

"You won't believe what I just heard from Suzanne who works for Helen Archer in human resources. An Angel Blank called all the way from Africa and wanted to talk to Jeff, and Helen had to tell her that Jeff is dead! That must have been horrible! How must this Angel have felt? Angel, what kind of name is that anyway? I tried to get more details, but that's all Suzanne knew. We think Angel is, well, I mean was, well, you know what I mean, she was a really close friend of Jeff's."

Brian was stunned and speechless.

Chapter 13

Dinner with Brigitte

Tuesday October 10, 1995, 6:30 p.m.

About twenty minutes after Brian's phone call with Lieutenant Woodraw, Brigitte had called. She had been very excited. Evidently she had quite a story to tell about Loren Grimm and events that had preceded his departure from his former employer. Brigitte wanted to discuss everything over dinner. Could he make it?

Another sudden change. Brian actually felt a deep sense of loss. He so much longed for life to be again the way it used to be. He had liked and therefore missed his reflective and deliberate way of life. Would he ever regain control again? Brian wished he could stop thinking all together. Maybe that would help. But he couldn't. It was impossible, and as a result his mind was spinning out of control!

At first Brian had felt hesitant about meeting Brigitte for dinner, but being with her certainly beat staying around at work until the wee hours, especially since he could no longer focus or concentrate. The news about Cathie had wiped him out. Would spending time with Brigitte make him feel better? He just couldn't tell anymore what worked and what didn't.

When Brigitte had called around 5 p.m. Brian told her he needed to finish one more important segment of his work. They had agreed to meet at 6:30 for dinner.

Now Brian was on the way to the restaurant. The engine's steady rhythm and even pitch lulled Brian into a false sense of security. The Thing was made of metal and had nothing on the inside that could muffle the engine's noise. Suddenly it occurred to Brian that he had acted rather impulsively. As a result he started feeling guilty and quite uneasy. He admonished himself to relax and to stop fretting. However, it was rather unheard of for him to leave work early to go out for dinner. This was the second time within a week! Nothing was the same anymore. What was he to do? Brian felt like a pawn in somebody's game. But whose game was being played?

Brigitte had been rushed on the phone, so Brian hadn't mentioned anything about Dona's findings, nor had he talked about his telephone conversation with Lieutenant Woodraw. They had simply taken care of the logistics of where to meet and when. To be honest, he hadn't really been very involved in that decision. Within split seconds Brigitte had proposed three to five choices while, as usual, Brian was still mulling over a number of options and possibilities. Over time he had learned to just agree and go along for the ride. Actually, he preferred it that way. Experience had shown that he always enjoyed Brigitte's choices. This applied to place or event. Brigitte had picked a place—he had agreed. They would meet at one of the new restaurants just one block south of University Avenue in Palo Alto.

Brian noticed that his mood was improving the closer he got to the restaurant. Also, by now he felt less out of control. Brigitte had sounded rather thrilled about her news about—what was the name of that company again? He couldn't remember right now.

A couple of minutes ago Brian had exited 101 and was now approaching University Avenue. He expected to arrive in plenty of time. Just a couple more blocks, and it was only 6:20. Brigitte had mentioned the location of a small parking garage in case he wouldn't be able to find free parking spots in the streets. They had really seen each other a lot since Jeff's murder. Usually they only met once a week and maybe talked on the phone once or twice each week. Everything in Brian's life seemed to have changed since the murder. These thoughts brought on a renewed wave of concern.

There, that must be it! Sure enough, there was Brigitte, waving madly. While Brigitte waited at the entrance to the garage, Brian parked the car before joining her.

"Hey, you got here early, too. That's great!" Brigitte exclaimed while she gave him a quick hug. She knew Brian felt uncomfortable about public displays of affection.

"Yes. I'm glad I got out of there when I did. A lot has happened since Sunday." Brian's face looked relaxed and happy. Brigitte had quite an influence on his mood and feelings.

"Oh, I'm dying to hear about it! I almost called you last night." Brigitte looked him over carefully, having become aware that something had happened that had touched Brian deeply. She decided to wait till they were seated before asking him any questions.

"Actually, I wished you had." Brian's response was quite spontaneous and surprised them both.

They had crossed the street and had entered the restaurant and were now waiting for the hostess to seat them.
"I just love the decor in here, don't you?" Brigitte exclaimed as she looked around approvingly.

"Oh, I hadn't really noticed. I guess it is pretty unusual." Brian scanned the restaurant. Parts of the place seemed dark because of the color of the wooden furniture. Yet the room gave an airy and open impression due to its size. There was a balcony above with additional seating. At one time the balcony had probably been a closed-off second story. Maybe they could sit up there? It looked interesting. No, he figured Brigitte would want to sit outside. Though it was October, it was still warm enough to enjoy the outdoors. Brian noticed little heaters above the outdoor tables. He wouldn't be too cold. Picking up on Brigitte's comment, he said, "So what do you like best about the place?"

"Oh, lots of things! Mostly the ambiance and the New Orleans music."

Brian decided to drop the subject. He had never been able to understand what ambiance meant to certain people. He also remembered that Brigitte could get quite excited when he didn't understand those subtle nuances she valued so much and found so important.

"Brian, how are you doing today? Have you recovered a little bit, or do you still feel like you're in shock?"

Since the questions referred to his feelings, Brian immediately became uncomfortable and unsure how to answer, even though he knew that Brigitte was genuine in her concern.

After hesitating Brian finally said, "Oh, I'm not sure. I can't really tell. It's, like, I don't really know how to describe it . . ." His voice trailed off.

Brigitte had found out what she had wanted to know. Brian was pretty lost and couldn't describe how he felt. That's what she had tried to get at. It was better to determine first how Brian was feeling before engaging in a long talk about something he didn't want to get into.

"Well," Brigitte said, "let's order a nice glass of wine first, or would you rather have a beer? And then, let's talk, okay?"

"Wine is fine. You pick it."

Brigitte knew a lot more about wines than Brian did, and he was glad that he didn't have to make an additional decision. Actually, he decided to just order what she ordered. Somehow he always liked her menu choices better than his own. Her choices always looked more appealing.

After ordering two glasses of Mirassou Chardonnay, they each studied their menu. It wasn't long before Brigitte announced, "I think I'll have the ahi tuna. What are you going to have?"

Brian was taken back by Brigitte's choice. Now what? "Oh, I see, well, let's see, what comes with that ahi tuna . . .?"

Brian was no longer sure he would like Brigitte's choice. Was this the tuna they served all raw? Was he really in the mood for experiments? Hmm . . .

Brigitte was only too aware of Brian's indecision and tried to be helpful. "Why don't you try the pork chops? You told me once you really like dishes like pork chops, and look what else you get with it, scalloped potatoes and a corn dish. What do you think?"

Brian was in a quandary and simply didn't know what he wanted. "Is the tuna raw?"

"No, they actually sear it a little on the grill, but it is raw inside."

"Okay, I'll have that, too."

"Really?"

"Yes."

Brigitte was sure Brian wouldn't like his dish but left him alone.

"So, are you all set now, and can you listen to my story?" Brigitte had learned that it was best to start with a preliminary question that would set the stage. If she just burst out spontaneously with what was on her mind, she couldn't count on Brian really listening and paying attention. It was as if he had to first turn a switch to be able to get engaged in a discussion. But she didn't mind too much. She had gotten used to it by now.

Brian nodded as he carefully put the menu to the side of the table, wondering what his food would be like.

"Remember when I called you last Friday night and told you about the company Loren worked for?"

"Yes, yes, I remember. You said the company was called Safe Systems. And I meant to tell you that when I was in the lab on Saturday two guys were talking about Loren and his former employer. According to them Loren had been one of the founders."

"Oh, now you ruined my big surprise! Why didn't you tell me about this on Sunday night?"

"I honestly didn't think that it was all that important. Plus a lot has happened to me since then. I'll tell you about it after you're done with your story."

"Okay. Anyway, the fact that Loren Grimm was one of the founders is quite important. So let me tell you the rest of the scoop."

As far as Brian was concerned, it suited him just fine to listen to Brigitte's story first rather than get into his own. His own story still felt almost unreal, and it would take a lot of energy to put the events of the last days into words. Besides he so much enjoyed listening to her. He loved to look at her when she got this excited. Her cheeks were slightly flushed, either from excitement or from the first sips of wine or possibly both. He loved her short hair. It suited her well, since it highlighted her oval facial features while emphasizing well-outlined lips. Her sparkling eyes were a mixture of brown and green. When she got excited and/or emotional, which happened a lot and quite easily, her eyes would flash with an extra zest of green. She was again dressed rather smartly in an olive-colored silk blouse with short sleeves and a V-neck, and as usual she wore stunning silver jewelry, this time a choker shaped in a very unusual design. The rustic brown skirt had small patterns in olive matching the color of the blouse, thus creating an overall symmetry of lines and colors. Brian liked what he saw.

Brigitte was in her element. She loved telling stories.

"Through various contacts, one of my managers, you know, Alan, was able to piece together what seems to have happened at Loren's previous employer and learned who the key players were who launched Safe Systems. According to Alan, many in the Valley had been surprised that their idea even got funded. Apparently Safe Systems recently filed with the SEC—the Securities and Exchange Commission, you know—and they're ready to go public very soon, possibly this month. The investment bankers are being very careful in picking a date to make sure the IPO—initial public offering—is well received by Wall Street. All IPOs representing Internet-related products have been going through the roof on opening day, and most are still going strong. Safe Systems seems to have an Internet security product, and the stock is therefore expected to do well. However, so far, Alan couldn't find out any specifics about the product. He might have some more information later on.

"Alan has a good friend who knows the founders of Safe Systems. Loren Grimm was indeed one of the founders. I don't know yet when Safe Systems was launched, and so I don't know how long Loren was there before he left in January 1995, as you told me. Loren had a big tiff with the other founders over something. According to Alan's source, it was product related. As a result their split was quite nasty. Actually, from what Alan could gather, Loren got fired. Alan wondered how the split might have effected Loren's stock options. The usual rule of thumb is that options get vested for four or five years, which means you have to stay with the company that long to realize all your options. Loren seems to have only been with them for about a year. This might mean that only one-fourth to one-fifth of his options would have been vested. But all of this is sheer speculation. If it turns out to be true, Loren would have to be more than ticked! But who knows, Loren might have been smart and negotiated a better deal, one that did not require a long vesting period."

"You certainly know a lot about options, and you explain it so well. At first, when I got my first options from Atlas, I was quite confused."

"Well, to me options are like the blood that pumps the heart of the Valley and keeps it going! You could say options are like the drums we're all marching to. I'm sure you're only too aware of the value of your own option package, aren't you?"

Brian had become irritated. What was Brigitte driving at? What could options possibly have to do with pumping blood to the heart of Silicon Valley? Sometimes Brigitte could be so extreme in her metaphors. Uncertain how to respond but only too aware that she had also spoken about his own option package, he ventured, "Well, yes, I do understand my option package. But I don't see what that has to do with what you were talking about."

"Well, isn't it obvious? You were excited about being a part of a startup! You wanted to be part of the 'scene.' I'd better explain this because I can see you're looking at me strangely! The Valley is the heart, and the Valley's heartbeat is represented by the Valley's innovation, excitement, and breakthrough technologies. Engineers want to be a part of that heartbeat. Their endless efforts are the blood that keeps the system going and the heart alive. What motivates the engineers? There have to be incentives to keep the engineers going, right? Engineers like the concept of getting rewarded in the form of options because owning options or shares means they own part of the company. They don't just labor for the future value of the options. It's much more than that. They're working to bring about technological change, and this in turn makes them feel more alive. But that's not all. They also love challenges; actually, they can't live without challenges. Bringing about technological changes in today's world is as big a challenge as one could find, don't you think? It's like trying to tackle Mount Everest again and again! The fascinating part, for me at least, is, that they don't perceive the inherent risks. For instance, the company could flop and not be successful, or any of a number of negative scenarios could take place. Instead they've convinced themselves that if they give it their all the venture *will be* successful!

"When you joined Atlas you had no idea whether Atlas would succeed or whether they'd go under after a couple of years. Your hard work could have been wasted, and your options would have been worthless, right?"

Brian was not at all sure how to respond. He hadn't really been able to follow Brigitte's strange-sounding discourse. What did she mean by "challenge" and "changing the world"? It sounded so farfetched, and she had nothing to support her position. He didn't want to talk about that part, but he could answer her last question about his decision to join Atlas. So he said, "Sure, when you put it that way, you're right. It might have been risky joining Atlas. But I didn't see it that way."

"But you should have been thinking about that when making your decision! Here you were, right out of college, joining a more or less obscure, small company, a startup, and basically you had no idea how it would turn out, right? That means you took a risk!"

Brian started to feel quite uneasy and restlessly moved around on his chair. Brigitte had a way of forcing issues. He had never even remotely thought about any of this. He was not a risk taker. He was sure he wasn't. He failed to see her point. It just didn't add up and made no sense.

Undaunted, though aware of his restlessness and uneasiness, Brigitte continued. She was on a roll now. Brian could tell. Most likely she could teach a course on this, or something . . . To Brian it felt like she was taking him apart bit by bit and he didn't like it at all. He began to resent her implications.

"So you joined Atlas five years ago?"

Brian just nodded. What would stop her? Nothing, probably.

"How big was Atlas then?"

"Roughly 160 people." He started to feel like a first-grader.

"So you see, it was kind of risky. I bet you could have gotten a better salary somewhere else, right?" Again Brian just nodded. Maybe he could get up and excuse himself . . .

"You most likely were compensated for being paid less in salary by receiving a more generous stock option package, right? And furthermore, since options take four to five years to vest, the company also enticed you to stay that long."

Brian definitely didn't like where this conversation was going. Brigitte was beginning to sound like his mother. Why did it seem so important to discuss his options and their worth, especially right now? It made him feel terribly uncomfortable. But Brigitte continued.

"Those who joined later definitely didn't get what you got, right? You see, they took much less of a risk. Well, I've followed the Atlas stock over time. There was a two-for-one stock split about eighteen months after they went public, and a second two-for-one stock split about a year ago. So whatever amount you were granted when you joined has quadrupled by now, and, of course, the stock price has been climbing ever since. I bet you're also in their employee stock purchase program. Hey, you must be worth quite a bit by now, right?!"

Brian wished the ground would open up so he could hide. This was so embarrassing. Before he could say anything at all, Brigitte exclaimed, "And I bet you feel uncomfortable about all of this!"

A miracle happened! He was saved from further torture by the waitress, who stopped and asked if they needed more time to choose. This caused Brigitte to slow down for a moment, and Brian had some time to recover a little. They ordered their food. Then the onslaught continued.

"Wasn't this 'being-a-part-of-a-technology-breakthrough-company' a kind of dream you had before you joined Atlas? And wasn't it this dream that influenced your decision making?"

"I've never dreamt about anything like that."

"I know, I know. I'm sure you weren't aware of this. But that doesn't mean that it was not so.

"My four-year stint at Alan and Steve's small marketing consulting company has given me an opportunity to learn a lot about the goings-on in the Valley. I've concluded that what excites people in Silicon Valley is the feeling of being associated with creating a new world based on the invention of technological breakthroughs. People also like to be associated with the inherent glory attributed by our society at large to these innovative new ideas. I believe that unknowingly many people want the glory more than anything else. If they can't have their *own* inventions, they can at least participate in the inventions of their company. It's like a cult following. In my opinion their behavior is similar to those who like to identify with famous people, like movie stars, sports stars, or any other celebrities. By getting to know these movers and shakers and by believing what they say, or by actively identifying with them, by that I mean by vicariously living through them, mimicking their styles, fashions, cars, homes, or whatever, the admirers hope to become like those they admire. You see, the admirers end up believing in the illusion that identification with a desired object enhances their sense of being. That's what I'm trying to say. The sad part is that no illusion will ever satisfy this inner longing to 'be somebody.' So instead of focusing on their own inner longing, people are preoccupied with chasing an illusion. You see, this means that they're really cheating themselves. They live a life that's not their own. Sometimes I get really depressed about our pitiful struggles with our inherent humanity."

Brigitte had visibly changed the deeper she got into her subject. There was a touch of sadness in her appearance. Then quite suddenly she straightened herself up and continued, "Every new invention is believed to increase the value of all who are associated with the work. The greater the invention and innovation, the greater the value of each person. It sounds so silly when you analyze it, but trust me, that's what it feels like for many people caught up in the 'heartbeat of the Valley,' as I call it. I've talked to a lot of people and seen how it affected them.

"You see, high technology has brought about a lot of changes in our culture. The appeal to be a part of the 'in scene' is tempting and strong. I'm not saying it's wrong. It's just that we seem to lose ourselves in its lure. When I took German in college I came across the poem by Heinrich Heine about the Lorelei, and I was extremely struck by its meaning, so much so that I still think about its message today. The poem is based on the legend of the Lorelei. The Lorelei is a high rock beside the Rhine River near where the Rhine meets the Moselle. Legend says that the rock's remarkable echo was the voice of a beautiful but wicked siren, who lured mariners to their destruction. Enticed by the echo, they would get too close and would crash on the rock. There was nothing wrong with the rock itself. It just happened to have a beautiful echo. But the rock also spelled danger and caused the boats to crash if you got too close. My point is that the world of technology is just as enticing as the Lorelei's echo was, and many of us can get lost in its appeal! I wonder, though, what will become of us? What will represent our 'destruction,' the loss of our real identity? I'd consider this loss a high price to pay for attributes that aren't even real, wouldn't you?"

Brian's mind was spinning out of control. What was this crazy stuff about the Lorelei, and what did it supposedly have to do with him and Silicon Valley? Brigitte had lost him right at the beginning when she had started to extrapolate meaning from metaphors that represented—what, really? He had no idea. Brigitte could be so overpowering when she got caught up in her favorite subject of trying to discuss the meaning of life. She should stick to facts that could be supported. Having an identity—what did that mean, anyway? Who would want to know? Well, Brigitte did. Sometimes he forgot that she had majored in psychology and had also taken philosophy classes. Brian preferred to remain a fence sitter and observe what was going on. Life was a lot safer and simpler that way.

Hoping that Brigitte would get back to Loren and Safe Systems, Brian hesitantly offered, "I never really think about what you just talked about, and I find it rather confusing."

"I know. But maybe you should think about what makes you tick and why you work here in the Valley, and why you work so hard. Anyway, I didn't mean to embarrass you or give you a hard time. I do understand. Sometimes I'm just so strongly in touch with how lost everybody seems to be that I get carried away when I talk about this subject. So, back to the story about Loren and Safe Systems. I know I got off the main point."

Brigitte closed her eyes for a moment as if to refocus and then continued. But her voice had changed. She had lost her zeal.

"Other contacts Alan spoke with hinted that at the time of Loren's departure from Safe Systems it was rumored that Loren had used somebody else's design and that he might have actually stolen it. This design had been incorporated into one of Safe Systems' new products. Evidently the president of Safe Systems found out about it, and that was the end of Loren's association with the company. The question is, how and in what way was this issue resolved? And whose design had been stolen, if indeed it had been stolen?

"I told Alan that Jeff also used to work at Safe Systems. Now Alan is trying to find out if there might be a link between Jeff and Loren. It would be interesting to find out whether they worked together on a project. Another important point is, when exactly did Loren Grimm work at Safe Systems? What was his start date? What was the date of his departure? And the same goes for Jeff. I have a hunch that this might be very important."

Brian was terribly relieved that Brigitte had abandoned her philosophical discourse. Talking about Loren and Safe Systems felt safe. He had no trouble at all following Brigitte's current analysis.

"I agree, Brigitte. We actually touched on one of these points last Thursday over lunch, remember? Jeff joined Atlas after the Fourth of July weekend. What I haven't told you yet is that I now also know how long Loren has been at Atlas. When Michelle, Loren's admin, talked to me about a missing appointment book, she mentioned that in the nine months she had worked with Loren, he'd never taken the appointment book with him."

"Great! We definitely know when Loren left Safe Systems. Why was Michelle talking about the appointment book, anyway?"

"Well, according to Michelle, Loren was not around at all the morning after the murder. Concerned about possible missed meetings and not having heard from him, she checked whether his appointment book was on his desk, hoping it might provide clues as to his whereabouts. She discovered that it was not in its usual place on the desk or anywhere else in his office. Michelle believes this to be of importance."

"I agree with her. It could indeed be important. But let's get back to the timeline. We know for a fact that Loren left Safe Systems in January 1995. We also know that Jeff joined Atlas in July 1995. So when did Jeff leave Safe Systems, and who hired him at Atlas?"

"Well, you see, I need to talk to Michelle about that. I always thought that Loren had hired Jeff. That's what I always assumed. But I don't really know. Michelle should know."

"Yes, I'm sure this point is important and linked to the murder." Brigitte paused for a moment, thinking.

"Well, I guess that's all for now. Alan should know more by tomorrow, Wednesday, or the latest by Thursday. "Brian, now tell me about you and what's been going on."

Brian wondered what he should talk about first. What was more scary, the threatening phone call or that he might have been followed? He decided to start with the fact that he was under police protection now, which meant that he was exposed to less real danger. Once that part was out in the open, he could slowly work his way into the scary parts. To his surprise Brigitte handled the news better than he had expected.

"Brian, I've really been worried about you! I had bad feelings the last couple of days. Well, let's forget about it now. I'm very relieved that you're under police protection! It makes me feel less worried."

When Brian related why Dona seemed to have gotten so upset and that the system administrator had been in an accident, Brigitte exclaimed, "I knew it! I just knew it all along! Jeff was up to something! This proves it! It also means that he had concluded that he might be in some kind of danger. I wish he'd talked to somebody or left behind more than a changed product report. A note expressing why he had changed his report would be really helpful. Who were his close friends?"

"He has an old buddy from MIT who's now at Santa Fe University. I sent him an e-mail this morning telling him about Jeff and asking what he might know about Jeff's work. And, wait a minute, I just remembered, Michelle said that somebody called Angel tried to reach Jeff by phone and instead talked to human resources. Michelle thinks she's his, well, really close friend."

"Really, well, that's a surprise! Did Jeff ever mention her?" Brigitte could hardly believe that Jeff had a girl friend. Well, she thought, at least there was one engineer who thought about more than just work!

"No, never." Brian still couldn't get used to the fact that there was this person who seemed to have been close to Jeff.

By this time their food had been served and they had started to eat. Brian didn't like the ahi tuna very much but decided not to fuss about it. It was too strange, too different, a real disappointment. Lately nothing he touched, did, or decided seemed to turn out well. His mood could swing quite suddenly, and little incidents like not liking the food could get him down. Brigitte could tell he was upset but decided not to address his mood. After all, she had asked him several times whether he really wanted the ahi and had made other suggestions.

As their meal was winding down they summarized the open issues one more time. Brigitte was convinced that Cathie's car accident was no coincidence. Brian thought he might learn more details about Cathie's car accident from Michelle by tomorrow morning.

By Wednesday or Thursday Brian expected to hear from Jeff's old friend at Santa Fe University. They decided that Brian should call Lieutenant Woodraw to tell her about Safe Systems and how it related to Loren and Jeff. Of course, it all depended on whether Lieutenant Woodraw considered this information important. The police could decide whether they should talk to the founders of Safe Systems and/or to Loren Grimm. Brian and Brigitte would rely on Alan, Brigitte's manager, for more information about Loren, Jeff, and Safe Systems.

They lingered a while longer after finishing their dinner and even ordered a second glass of wine. When Brian started to feel lightheaded he realized this had been a bad idea. He generally didn't drink much alcohol. Brigitte had wanted to follow him home because she could alert the police if something unusual occurred, but he had talked her out of it. What was she thinking? After all, he wasn't a child! Fortunately she pulled back when she realized that he was getting upset. However, she insisted that she would call him at home around 9:30. It was 9:00. She lived only ten minutes away from the restaurant in Palo Alto. It would take Brian about twenty minutes to get home to Mountain View. He was very tired by now. He hadn't slept much last night. His eyes were burning. He needed sleep.

They paid their bill and walked back to the garage. While hugging Brigitte for his good-bye, he had the sensation that he would feel safer if he could just hang on and not let go of her, ever . . . But without revealing his emotions he turned and headed for his car.

Not now. This wasn't the time to bring about changes in his relationship with Brigitte. They were friends, close friends. Romance hadn't really come up yet. Sometimes Brian wondered where she really stood and whether she was at all interested in him romantically. What a foolish thing to think about right now. He certainly had enough going on already.

Brian quickly focused all of his attention and energy on what lay ahead. First he needed to get a good night's sleep. Then it was back to work tomorrow, hopefully re-energized. That was all there was to it! He would just have to wait and see what the next day would bring. Easier said than done, and he knew it. But he made himself believe that he could tackle whatever lay ahead.

On the drive home Brian caught himself again and again scanning the roads for black Camaros while frequently checking his rearview mirror. But, if somebody was indeed following him, that person could use a totally different car. Who knew for sure? Tonight things seemed to be calm, at least for now. As far as Brian could tell, nobody was following him.

Chapter 14

News from Santa Fe

Wednesday Morning, October 11, 1995

"Michelle, do you have a second? I wanted to ask you about something."

"Brian, gee, what a surprise! You never come to see me anymore."

"Oh boy," Brian thought, "this is not going to be easy." But Michelle's face looked friendly.

"I'm sorry. I didn't mean to, well, anyway . . ." He looked kind of lost.

"Oh, don't worry. I was just teasing you! So what's up?" Michelle was cheerful, bright, and no-nonsense. She knew Brian would come around if she gave him time to recover.

"I'm going to get my coffee now. Do you think you could stop by whenever you find the time? That way we could talk in my cubicle, away from everything."

"Oh, sure, I'll be there shortly. I just have to make one more phone call, okay?" Having said that, she picked up the phone. Brian left the upstairs as fast as he could. He didn't want to run into Loren Grimm.

Brian was glad he had acted right away this morning without wasting too much time thinking about what he had dreaded so much. Who would think it could be so difficult, actually almost painful, to ask somebody a couple of questions? Well, he certainly did! Ever since he had left his apartment about twenty minutes ago he had been rehearsing what to say to Michelle and how. What might be the best moment to approach her? How would she react in response? What if she thought he was just a snoop? In fact, Brian had been so preoccupied with all his concerns and worries that he hadn't even checked his rearview mirror to see if he might be followed, this time by somebody from the police.

Something must have gone wrong at the police department. Nobody had called Brian to let him know that he was now under police protection. He was sure he had understood correctly that he would be alerted. After talking to Michelle he should probably contact Lieutenant Woodraw to inquire about the status. He felt uncomfortable not knowing. Every time Brian thought about Lieutenant Woodraw something was triggered inside of him. She still made him feel so darn uncomfortable. He had hoped he would have gotten over it by now. He agreed with Brigitte that somebody should tell the police about Safe Systems. But why did it have to be him?

Calling Lieutenant Woodraw would take care of two issues. Asking about the police protection was a good cover to also bring up Safe Systems. That should make the whole situation a lot easier for him to handle. Yet Brian still felt rather stupid. How could he possibly pull this off without sounding like a busybody? But a promise was a promise. He didn't even want to speculate what Brigitte might say if he wouldn't call. Okay, he would do it. However, his nagging and lingering concerns simply wouldn't go away. He had never really stepped out of his self-imposed comfort zone. Would it even be worth it?

First Brian would talk to Michelle about what she might know about Loren and Jeff. Had they really worked at Safe Systems during the same time period?

A couple of seconds after Brian settled himself down with his cafe latte and his e-mail, Michelle bounced into his cubicle, lifted a pile of papers from the extra chair, set them onto the far corner of Brian's work space, and sat down.

"What happened to your cube? I've never seen it like this before. You usually don't have this much stuff lying around!"

"Oh, oh, yes, I guess you're right. I hadn't really noticed it. Yes, it's true, I haven't been able to catch up with things in here since . . ." Brian stopped in midsentence, feeling rather stupid.

"Hey, no problem. None of us can be perfect all the time, right? What's up?"

Brian cleared his throat and for a split second thought he wouldn't be able to get any words out at all. Afraid he might change his mind, he acted immediately, reminding himself it was just Michelle and she had always been nice to him. Her comment about his cube had triggered another wave of insecurity.

"I guess you know that I talked some more with Lieutenant Woodraw about Jeff and what I might know about his background. And by the way, if you don't want to, you certainly don't have to talk to me about this."

"I'm confused. What are you driving at?" Michelle looked puzzled. Sometimes Brian just didn't make any sense at all!

"Well, it's just that I wanted to find out certain information about Loren, and, well, you know, I wouldn't want you to feel like you're betraying Loren or something by answering my questions."

Now Michelle understood and immediately exclaimed, "Oh, Brian, don't be silly! I've been friends with you for a long time. You should know that! If anything my loyalties are more with you than with Loren. After all, Loren is my boss. I'd never be able to talk to him like I talk to you. Really, Brian."

Brian was overwhelmed by her expression of friendship. Oh, wow, now what? He concluded he'd better get the whole thing over with fast before he changed his mind. Suddenly he felt very exposed.

"Well, I kind of had a thought and was wondering if you knew something about the company where Loren used to work because that's where Jeff used to work as well. And so . . ."

Before Brian could say more Michelle jumped in, "Oh, Brian, just go ahead! Ask me anything. I'm not married to Loren! I'll be glad to tell you whatever it is I know. If I don't know, I'm sure there's a way for me to find out!"

"Oh, good, because I really would hate to see . . ."

"Brian, stop it! It's no problem."

For the next couple of minutes Brian explained why it might be important to know whether Loren and Jeff had been with Safe Systems during the same time period and why finding out whether they worked on the same product back then could possibly shed light on Jeff's murder. Michelle couldn't contain her excitement when Brian mentioned the possibility that Loren had left Safe Systems on less than friendly terms and might have been involved in a "little" scandal, as she called it.

"You know," Michelle said, absolutely thrilled and visibly bubbling over with excitement, "I've been convinced for a long time that something fishy was going on way back then. Right after I started working for Loren there were an awful lot of phone calls from people at Safe Systems as well as from several lawyers. Loren was very hush-hush about it all. I sensed that right away. That's why I would have never talked to him about it. But I was curious and still am. I remember him being very angry after some of those phone calls and I learned to avoid him at certain times so he wouldn't yell at me about something silly only to let out his frustration and anger. He has quite a bad temper, you know. It was a new job for me at the time, a promotion. I didn't want to blow it. So I just felt him out at first. And after a couple of weeks, things definitely cooled down. But I never really forgot those early incidents."

As far as Michelle was concerned, she and Brian had now signed up for a little "pact," all of their own. This refueled Brian's earlier hesitation and uneasiness, but all in all he figured that he had accomplished more than he could have asked for. After all, they did mean well. And it was a serious matter, right? Jeff had been murdered.

Michelle continued, "Remember last Thursday, the day after the murder? We talked about it then. I told you that Loren mentioned only a couple of weeks ago that he and Jeff used to work together at Safe Systems. Let me think if I can remember the discussion. Oh, yes, I do remember now. It was early in the morning, and Loren had just gone to get his coffee. He was sitting at his desk looking through the *San Jose Mercury News* business section. He must have been reading something that got him excited, because like out of the blue he told me that he and Jeff had worked on something really exciting at a previous company and that it had been considered a breakthrough. He then explained that that's why he had wanted Jeff to join Atlas.

"Boy, can you believe it? We really are up to something, aren't we?"

But right now Michelle had only a vague idea as to when exactly Loren and Jeff had worked at Safe Systems. However, she confirmed that Loren had been with Atlas for nine months. She knew the exact date because it was the day she had gotten her promotion to executive secretary, January 18, 1995. Before working for Loren, Michelle had worked for Brian's boss, Bob Laidlaw, as well as all of Bob's engineering team, including Brian. Back then she and Brian used to talk more.

"So the idea is to figure out how long Loren was at Safe Systems. Hmm, let me think . . . Human resources would have his resume on file. No good. They wouldn't let us look at it. It's considered part of the personnel files and thus confidential. Well, let's see. There must be another way. You know, I always keep the old phone message books. It's an old habit, considered old-fashioned, but I like it. Anyway, phone messages come in a sort of book. Each message gets copied, and this copy remains in the book. You have no idea how handy these old books are sometimes. Like when Loren loses a contact, or something like that. So in this case all I have to do is go back to the very first book I ever had when Loren started back in January, and I should find names and phone numbers of those early contacts. I remember I frequently spoke with somebody's administrator at Safe Systems. I can't remember her name right now. But the information will be in the book. I think it would be easy to call and ask her a couple of questions. She and I hit it off very well. I'm sure she could tell me how long Loren had been there, and if we're lucky, she might have known Jeff as well. If not, she might be able to tell me who would know. I could get a contact.

"Now the other point is Jeff. We want to know how long Jeff was at Safe Systems, and we want to know who hired him at Atlas. I just remembered that I might have a copy of Jeff's resume. As a rule of thumb I make copies of all resumes of the people Loren interviews or comes across. You wouldn't believe how many resumes he has to handle! Anyway, I like to keep track of each one. I just thought about something else. Loren had a meeting with Jeff before Jeff started working here. I always assumed it was a formal interview. But now, looking back, I'm not convinced any-more. Maybe they met because of what happened at Safe Systems. Who knows? At least it's a possibility, right?"

Since Michelle actually paused for a moment in her ongoing monologue, Brian managed to nod and say, "Yes, that's true."

Michelle went on as if he hadn't said anything at all.

"So, either they talked about the past, or it was an informal kind of interview, since they already knew each other. If it was an interview, it doesn't necessarily mean that Loren initiated the process of hiring Jeff. Though, as I told you before, Loren did tell me that he used to work with Jeff before. He didn't hide this fact. But that's all he said, and it doesn't really prove anything in particular. I also remember now that Jeff did not work for an agency like most contractors do. No, we had to do all the paperwork with him directly. We had to set up our own little process. I helped Sarah with it. She was fairly new at the time. She supports your group and Scott Jones' group, as you know. Anyway, what I meant to say is that every invoice Jeff billed to Atlas gets approved by Scott Jones, who is—I should say was—Jeff's immediate boss. After that the invoices get passed on to accounts payable.

"I think I'll also have a little chat with Sarah. She should know whether it was Scott Jones who hired Jeff. She's kind of slow and doesn't pay much attention to what's going on, but you never know, I might just get something out of her. If not, I'll just ask Scott myself. Why not? That should work!"

Suddenly Brian's phone rang, and as usual he ignored it.

"Aren't you going to get that?" Michelle was surprised Brian wouldn't pick up the phone.

"Well, I don't really want to right now . . ."

The phone stopped ringing. It had rolled over to voicemail.

"I'll get it later," Brian said sheepishly.

"Boy, you guys are so bad! No wonder I never can get any of you on the phone! I gave up long ago. That's why I always come by in person. I know, you guys like to use e-mail. But I don't. It's too tedious!"

"I know." Brian wasn't about to say more for fear of making her angry.

"So, where were we? I guess I said I would find out how long Jeff was at Safe Systems. Is there anything else we should find out?"

"Well, the other point I was wondering about is, have you heard anything else about Cathie's car accident?"

"Oh, yes, that's right. I've been meaning to tell you. She's in very critical condition, and the doctors said she was lucky. Somebody slammed into her car on the driver's side. That's why her injuries are so bad, even though she was wearing her seatbelt. They think she might have seen the car coming and braked really hard so the impact was less severe. The driver of the other car suffered only minor bruises, since it was the passenger side of his car that collided with Cathie's. At least that's what I've heard. You can't always trust those stories you hear, if you know what I mean. The whole thing is bad enough as it is. Cathie seems to have internal and severe head injuries, but supposedly she's conscious. She's not paralyzed or suffering from anything really severe. These days everyone thinks about Christopher Reeve and what it's like to be paralyzed—well, that was the first thing that came to my mind, anyway. Nevertheless, it sounds quite critical."

"I'm relieved to hear that it wasn't worse." Brian was thinking to himself, "I thought she might have been killed," but didn't want to talk to Michelle about it. He also didn't want to ask what kind of car it was that had hit Cathie's car. Maybe Lieutenant Woodraw would tell him. Well, probably not . . .

Michelle continued, "I have been thinking that ever since Jeff's murder, Loren has acted rather strangely. It hit me even more so while we were talking just now. Also, since last week, he's barely around. Remember, I told you last week that I didn't see him at all last Thursday, and I never figured out whether he came by early in the morning or possibly later that night. I actually doubt it, and I told the police this as well. But I don't think I told you yet that he also was a no show on Friday. I'm convinced that it was unplanned because several people looked for him during the day, and he had left me no special instructions except to say that he had to attend to something personal that had suddenly come up and I was to call Barbara, John's secretary, since evidently John had left him a rather upset voicemail about some issue."

"Barbara? I can't remember. Who is Barbara?"

"Oh, yes, you know. I told you several times. She's John's administrator. Remember when I told you on Monday morning that executives, including John, the president, had been getting a lot of phone calls because of that rumor about the joint venture? Anyway, Barbara is John's secretary."

"Oh, yes, I remember now."

"Well, anyway, Loren was in on Monday and Tuesday. Especially on Monday he was in a terribly grumpy mood. But that's probably because he had a meeting with John scheduled for later that day. The meeting was at 4:30 p.m., so I didn't see him again, because I go home around 5:30. When I left he was not back yet."

"It's really none of my business, but did he meet with Lieutenant Woodraw?" It had taken a lot of courage for Brian to ask that question.

"Oh, I forgot to tell you. Yes, I found out that he met with her on Thursday afternoon at the Sunnyvale police station. I was so curious about it that I asked him yesterday. Well, he got irritated, grunted, and mumbled something like, 'I don't see why you have to know.' He implied that he had had no choice *but* to meet with the police, whom he considers to be a 'darn nuisance.' That's a direct quote, by the way."

"Gee, I wouldn't want to talk to him when he's in that kind of mood."

"Oh, I'm used to it. It comes with the territory. All managers have something 'wrong' with them, if you know what I mean. You'll never find the 'perfect' boss. The way to deal with it is to find a way to make it work for me. I mean, if he really got to me, then I would look around for something else. But so far it's working out okay. Down the road, maybe, after I've worked for him for a year and I've proven myself, I think I'll try for something else. Actually, I'm always looking around and keeping my ears open, in case I hear about an opening somewhere inside the company. I don't really want to leave Atlas. I like it here. Did you know they now have job listings online? I always look through those. Before they published the job listings online it was a nuisance to find out about new openings. But now it's really easy. As you know, John wants us to be the kind of company where employees feel encouraged to apply for internal job openings and to be able to grow within the company. In the end you're on your own, though, and you have to make the system work for you. Nobody gives you a job or a promotion just because they like you. No way! In order to get ahead you have to prove yourself first. That's life!

"Well, I better mosey on along now. I know, I can get kind of longwinded and start telling all sorts of stories. When I started working for Bob Laidlaw about two years ago he told me once that I really confused him at times. Well, you guys don't always make sense to people like me either! But I better stop now. I can tell you're getting antsy, and I have things to do."

Brian was horrified that she had identified his restlessness so easily and was about to say something. Before he could, Michelle continued, "Oh, don't look so embarrassed! I understand. You engineers just can't handle conversations that go on and on unless they have to do with something technical or relate to your specific job somehow. I'm not upset at all. See you later! I'll be in touch. Or is there anything else you have on your mind?" Michelle had noticed a frown on Brian's forehead.

"Actually, I just remembered one other question I'd wanted to ask you. Does Loren still drive his black BMW convertible? I'm asking because there was a car I didn't recognize in the parking lot the other night. It was a black Camaro with fancy gold trim."

"Yes, he still drives that BMW. A black Camaro, hmm. I've never seen a car like that around. Is it important?"

"Oh, probably not." Brian didn't want to say more.

"Well, I guess I'll see you later, then." And off she went.

Brian's entire body started to relax, and he felt better once Michelle was gone. It was true that he had become increasingly restless toward the end of their conversation. Too many details, too many reference points, too much of everything that he liked to avoid. At least he had kept his promise to Brigitte and had acted on something about which he had felt quite uneasy.

Now, what next? Back to the e-mail. Were there any from his team?

After spending about twenty minutes carefully making his way through the first thirty of a total of over seventy e-mail messages, Brian suddenly realized that the next message he was going to look at was from Santa Fe University. He almost stopped breathing because he got so excited about what he might learn, or hoped to learn.

It looked like Ray Beachwood had answered right away. Yes, indeed, he sent the message late last night.

Date: Tues, Oct 10, 1995 10:46 PM MST
To: brian@cicero.atlas.com
From: beach@santa.fe.edu
Subject: My friend Jeff

   I was devastated and terribly upset after receiving
your e-mail and learning about Jeff's death. I do want to
address your questions hoping that the answers might
shed light on Jeff's murder. First of all, I am stunned by the
news. To tell you the truth, I don't think that the cold facts
have really hit me yet. Jeff and I were close friends at MIT.
We roomed together for three years. Though this was a
number of years ago, we always kept up contact and
managed to see each other at least once a year.
   Your assumption was correct. Jeff kept me abreast
about his latest work. However, this work had nothing to
do with Atlas; rather it relates to what he had been inventing on his own. Jeff was a special guy with unique concerns and interests. He was quite talented in his field of
networking, system administration, and security. Actually,
he was obsessed with security stuff. Not knowing how
much you know about digital life, and respecting how
much Jeff wanted his invention kept under wraps, I will just
provide you with a conceptual summary, which will not
compromise Jeff's invention. Though, come to think of it,
this is probably totally irrelevant now.
   Jeff had used digital organism/life technology (a form
of digital intelligence) to design a security software tool he
called "digital security defender." The software tool is
always on the alert (by taking on a life of its own, so to
speak) and is looking out for any possible system break-
ins. Thus it works like an early warning system.
   A second part of the program (another form of digital
life) plays the role of a system administrator who would or

could abort any break-in before it can be executed. This program would identify the pattern of attack and use this knowledge to abort the attack. Of course, all of these tasks are being executed in code, hidden from the user. The instance the digital security defender identifies a break-in, it is called upon to abort the attempt (in the role of the system administrator). To jazz up his program, as well as add additional functionality, Jeff designed the tool in such a way that the digital defender will also provide a visual onscreen snapshot of where the break-in is taking place, meaning which computer, which file, etc. while simultaneously revealing the system name and location of the computer initiating the break-in. Therefore, even an aborted break-in can still provide vital and important facts and information about the attempt since the process has been captured and saved in a snapshot. It is all rather fascinating and exciting, and I am sure the tool would be of great interest to most companies.

Jeff had been working on his project for quite some time. I would say he started about one to two years ago. Back then he was not working at Atlas, and I can't remember what company he was with. I do know, however, that he had a very bad experience there. Evidently somebody he was working with, or for, had more or less stolen his early code, combined it with some of his own crop, and then declared the final result his own. He didn't use Jeff's code for a digital intelligence design though, but rather incorporated the code with his own for a security software application the company had been working on. When Jeff found out that somebody had stolen some code, though I don't know how, he went to the president of that company with his design and was able to get the guy to believe him. I don't know how he pulled that off! I think Jeff struck some deal with them. I remember some lawyers were involved, but I don't know any details. Jeff didn't like to talk about the incident. I think he was simply too upset about what had happened and possibly still angry as well.

The other part which was unclear to me at the time was how the other person had found out about Jeff's design in the first place. Jeff wasn't the type to brag or even talk about his invention. Since that time, I guess it was last January, Jeff greatly enhanced his design. I believe he was pretty close to finishing it. He seemed to be interested in selling it or possibly starting his own company. And now it all ended this way and we don't even know whether his code is lost forever.

I wonder what will happen to his invention now? Who will carry on where he left off? It would be such a waste to have all of it disappear. Even though Jeff shared some details with me I would never be able to reproduce his work. That's why I am so saddened by the events. The invention had so much potential!

I can't remember when Jeff left that company and was rather surprised when I learned that he had joined Atlas. I didn't think Atlas was interested in any of the kind of work he was really good at and specialized in. But I don't really know Atlas that well either.

I don't know whether any of this information is helpful to you. I hope it is.

I also thought about something else. You might be able to make contact with the following person. Jeff was close friends with a gal whom he met way back during the college days. She is quite a character. Well, you could even say she is a little crazy. Though Jeff really cared a lot for her, she didn't seem to want to tie herself down to anybody. She was even more of a free spirit than Jeff himself was. But the two kept up with each other all these years, even though it's been seven years since Jeff and I graduated from MIT. Her name is Angela, but everybody called her Angel although she was no Angel in the sense of the word. That's probably how she got that nickname, kind of as a joke. Angel dropped out of college during her junior year, while we were in our senior year. She got bored, she said. I seem to recall that Angel showed up out of the blue in the San Francisco area sometime earlier this year and contacted Jeff. She wanted to know if he would go on a four-week trip with her through Alaska. And he did. I was really surprised and concluded she probably still meant a lot to him. But after the trip he never told me anything about how things worked out and I didn't pry. If Jeff didn't want to tell you anything, he just didn't! Then again, maybe he was just too busy with his own project, or with his work at Atlas.

I wish I could tell you how to contact Angel. But I have no idea. Her last name is Blank. You could possibly check phone listings in your area. Angel might be able to shed some light on Jeff's personal life. I am convinced that he shared more with her than with me. That's just the kind of relationship they had.

If you have any other questions that I might be able to address, just e-mail me. And please keep me posted. I would really like to understand why somebody killed Jeff and whether the police will be able to resolve the case and find the murderer.

Ray Beachwood
Computer Science Dept.
University of Santa Fe

Chapter 15

On the Way to Alaska

Saturday Morning, June 3, 1995

"Jeff, hurry up! Let's go! I *don't* want to miss the plane! Come on, the taxi is waiting! Let's go, let's go!"

No response from Jeff. Why didn't he answer? Surely he must have heard her. Angel was annoyed and irritated. Why did it always take him so long? What was he still doing in his bedroom? Wasn't he done packing? Probably not! Well, standing around waiting didn't do any good. She'd better go and take a look. After storming down the little hallway she positioned herself right in front of Jeff's room. Her face was flushed. She was intense and ready to attack at a moment's notice. What would send her over the edge? Jeff was safe. He didn't see her!

"I just *hate* it when you don't respond!" Angel was exasperated!

Oblivious to the scene around him and totally preoccupied with his tasks, Jeff finally emerged from his room, carrying two duffel bags. The hallway was narrow, and Angel decided to walk backward, ahead of Jeff, toward the front door. Staring first at Jeff, then his duffel bags, her face mimicking true horror and disbelief, she exclaimed, "Oh, no! You have *got* to be kidding! That's it? You mean to tell me that all you need for four weeks is in these two duffel bags? Good grief— really, Jeff. What *were* you thinking? Never mind, never mind! I get it. You don't want *me* telling *you* how to live! That's fair. I wouldn't like that either. My lips are sealed! Well, let's say, I'll work on it. But don't count on it! All I can promise is that I'll do my best, if I remember . . ."

"What? What's the matter?" Jeff looked up at her, truly confused by Angel's outburst.

After reaching the front door, Angel stopped for a moment before continuing. Her voice was strained and expressed great incredulity.

"You ask, 'what's the matter?' Well, isn't it obvious? How can anybody live out of two duffel bags for four long weeks? But that's not the real issue here, is it? What is the matter is that I have a terrible urge to tell you how to live. Oh, well, you know what I mean. I can't even find the right words! This is going to be so-o-o hard! I'm not sure I know *how* to let others be themselves. And then, considering that I'm the one who invited *you* on this trip, I feel like I have to, well, I don't know what. I guess I'm wondering if I have to, let's see, I'm looking for a word, how about, accommodate you in return? I don't like the sound of that at all! Jeff, *say* something! This is important to me! Ask me: "What do *you* expect from *me*?" If I have to make sacrifices, does that mean that you would also be willing to make sacrifices? That probably wouldn't work because unless I told you, how would you know *when* I make sacrifices? I don't even like thinking about all of this. No, it feels horrible. I don't like this at all!"

To demonstrate her utter frustration, Angel threw her hands up in the air before stepping outside into the stairway of the condo building.

"Angel, remember, you were worried about getting to the airport on time. I don't think now is the time to get into this." Jeff was fishing for the keys to lock the front door. He was as calm as could be. He was used to these kinds of theatrics. It was just "Angel talk" and it didn't bother him too much most of the time.

"Fine, fine. You're probably right! Let's forget about it for now. I agree, this is neither the time nor the place to solve major personal problems. And believe me, this is a major problem! I can feel it in my bones. Something about this is *really* bugging me! I can tell. Okay, let's get going first, and then we can worry about sacrifices and stuff like that later on. Agreed?"

Jeff didn't want to get into a hot discussion about something that hadn't been defined but rather seemed to be a figment of Angel's imagination. Sometimes she was more than a challenge. But wanting to strike a conciliatory note he said, "Yes, let's talk about it some other time."

Angel started to walk down the stairs to the ground floor. Jeff followed, wondering how two duffel bags could lead to so much commotion. It took only a couple of minutes to load his bags, climb into the taxi, and take off. Their adventure had begun!

"Jeff, isn't it great to get going! I am so-o-o excited! If only you knew! Are you excited?" Gone were the earlier feelings. Angel was in a totally different mood by now.

"Yes, I am." Jeff knew that Angel got over her excitement pretty fast most of the time.

Angel had cuddled up next to Jeff and seemed quite content saying nothing for a while. Jeff was used to her sudden mood swings. Just to be here and feel her body warmth and energy next to his felt so right. Why tell Angel that sometimes he just liked to listen to the rhythm of her voice even if he didn't understand what she was really talking about? He had registered that she had seemed quite intense and excited about something earlier on in the condo. That was enough for now.

To Jeff, Angel appeared to be free and exuberant, especially when she was all caught up in some emotional outburst. He liked her that way. Suddenly he remembered how Angel's mother had chided her for always talking too much and too fast. From what Jeff had been able to observe and based on the stories he had heard, Angel's mother criticized Angel for, well, just "being Angel." That's at least how Jeff felt about the mother's criticism.

Reflecting back on the past, Jeff remembered how again and again he had wanted to protect Angel, but he didn't know from what. To him she seemed fragile, in spite of, or maybe because of, her insistence that she needed nobody at all. She made a big deal of demonstrating her independence by flashing her flamboyance and belligerence. Jeff was sure it was an act, a way for her to protect herself.

Why did it seem so hard for her to admit that, like all people, she sometimes needed support and loving care? At least that's what Jeff believed.

Jeff also wondered about Angel's current relationship with her parents. Though she had visited out east back in February, she had been unusually taciturn upon her return. Jeff had attributed her behavior to the sorrow she must have felt over the death of her grandfather, whom she had adored and idolized. Angle's grandfather had made up for an unhappy family life at home. Her parents' marriage never seemed to have been a happy one right from the start. Even back in 1985 Jeff had figured that Angel's parents were heading for divorce. Sure enough, divorce proceedings had started in 1991, but the settlement wasn't finalized till spring 1995.

Jeff was interrupted in his daydreams when Angel suddenly started to sort through her purse. She seemed to be making sure that the tickets were handy. The tickets made Jeff think about the trip. He was looking forward to being with Angel. It had been quite a while since he and Angel had spent any length of time together. But he was also cautious and had taken a wait-and-see attitude, remembering that every previous attempt to make a go at a good and lasting relationship had failed. He was baffled by the fact that even though they truly enjoyed each other immensely, they each nevertheless found it necessary to doggedly defend themselves when they felt attacked by the other. What qualified as a personal attack and what didn't? Where were the boundaries? He wished he knew. All he knew was that after a couple of bad fights over feeling misunderstood, they both couldn't handle the pain of rejection. Why did they choose to separate from each other again and again even though later on the fights appeared to have been over insignificant differences that seemed of utmost importance at the time of each fight. Jeff didn't really want to get caught up again in the clutch of those earlier power struggles. Why was he going on this trip? Did he really believe it would be different this time around? No, he did not. There was no reason to believe anything had changed. Ah, but there were feelings. It was much harder to explain feelings. Besides, right now he was looking for a refuge. He needed to escape for a while. He needed to momentarily put his life on hold in order to recover from the stress and disappointments of the last couple of months.

Angel had badgered Jeff since the end of April with this trip idea, and in the end he had succumbed. Somehow the timing had worked out. He had left Safe Systems middle March 1995 after his legal settlement. Since then he had worked at home fine-tuning the second part of his invention. Everything in life seemed to be timing. Angel had brought up the Alaska trip right after he decided to work at Atlas as a contractor. Considering what had just happened at Safe Systems, this move to Atlas could be risky. But he had a plan; well, maybe it was more a desire. He wanted to get even, which really meant he wanted revenge. Jeff believed it was necessary. Loren Grimm had stolen his design, and all Safe Systems had done about it was fire Loren! Sure, Jeff had understood that they didn't want to get into a lengthy and tedious legal fight in the courts. But did they really believe that this would be the end of Loren's shady practices? Jeff held to the belief once a crook, always a crook! That's why an act such as Loren's had to be purged for good. Loren had to be stopped from ever taking advantage of other people again. Jeff wanted to be at Atlas to stay on top of any move Loren might make. Financial and legal settlements did *not* address what was really at stake here. Jeff wanted to catch Loren in the act, so to speak, and hopefully this time around Loren would have to pay more dearly. Jeff was totally convinced that Loren would be up to his old tricks again!

Jeff had been shocked and dismayed upon learning that Loren had been hired by Atlas. He had considered warning somebody at Atlas about Loren, but that was not Jeff's style. It would be much better to actually be there.

Jeff's contacts in the technical "underground" community of the Valley were extensive, and it had not taken him long to get linked up with Scott Jones, who later became his boss. Jeff had exactly the kind of experience and expertise Atlas needed for one of their products, a new security application.

Jeff vaguely sensed that he was obsessed with plotting revenge and that this obsession prevented him from pursuing his own invention as much as he wanted to. When Angel invited him to travel the Alaskan Highway to the Yukon Territory, with Anchorage as their final destination, Jeff figured that it would be a great way to trade in his stressful life for a four-week adventure. Jeff knew that he had been strongly impacted by what Loren had done. Ever since then his world had been in chaos, and Jeff found himself groping for something to hang on to. He needed a break. Not the kind of break to do a lot of thinking. He had already done that, and it only made him feel like he was going crazy. No, what he needed right now was an "Angel adventure," as he called it. She could be such fun to be with! Also, somehow, Angel always seemed to understand his longings, his hopes, his dreams. He needed a friend. He had never needed a friend more than right now!

"Jeff, Jeff! You're not listening to me!"

Jeff had been so caught up in his thoughts that he been unaware of Angel's voice.

"Angel, I'm just doing some thinking. I'm thinking about us and the trip. That's what you want me to do, isn't it?"

"Oh, aren't you sneaky! You know *just* what I want to hear!" Angel laughed, but she wasn't quite content to leave it there yet. It was important to make one more point. "Don't you agree it was best for me to pick you up to make sure we're on time?"

Jeff just nodded, and Angel seemed satisfied.

Deep down Jeff still believed that it would have been much more efficient to just meet at the airport. This had been a bone of contention earlier on when Jeff felt it necessary to point out that Angel was wasting at least $100. She lived in San Francisco and had taken a taxi to pick him up in Menlo Park, and now they were partially retracing half of the distance to get to the airport. Jeff had suggested she stay overnight at his place. Horrified, she had replied, "And repack everything once more? No way! Rather I'd spend $100 or whatever it takes to avoid that. And besides, you have a problem with being on time!"

Neither of them had wanted to allude to the fact that they hadn't really spent any nights together since Angel had reappeared in January. They were both afraid of getting close again.

Jeff had yielded to Angel's plan. After all, it was her money, not his. Angel had never experienced a lack of money. She simply couldn't relate to how somebody else felt about uselessly spending $100. Similar issues had come up plenty of times since he had known her, and Jeff had concluded that the subject of money was better left alone on this trip. Jeff also had to admit that she was probably right about the possibility of him showing up late at the airport.

Again Jeff's thoughts drifted to the past. He recalled how he and Angel had met in the fall of 1985. By now they had known each other for almost ten years. Back in 1985 Jeff had been a sophomore at MIT and Angel a freshman at Smith College. MIT and Wellesley College always organized social exchanges put on by the fraternities in the frat houses along the James River. Since Angel's good friend Maggie went to Wellesley, the two of them had attended a party put on by one of the fraternities. Angel had come to spend the weekend with her friend at Wellesley. Whenever Angel had to "get away from the country" (by this she meant Smith College, in Northampton), she would visit Maggie at Wellesley, just outside of Boston. The ride to Wellesley took about two hours. On this particular Friday night in early October 1985, a time Jeff would never forget, he had met Angel for the first time.

According to Angel, she hadn't been very interested in Jeff when they met. He belonged to the category of "one of those guys who is only into computers and not much else." Actually, at first she had not even wanted to join Maggie to attend this MIT event. She hated fraternities. She would rather have gone bar hopping in Boston. Maggie was quite opposed to going bar hopping, however. They were not yet twenty-one and Maggie didn't like it when Angel fudged about their age or manipulated those wanting to see their IDs. It was amazing what Angel could come up with to charm her way into any place that struck her fancy. Angel, in contrast, frequently wondered why she even bothered with Maggie. Maggie always worried about something, even when the situation was pretty harmless according to Angel's value system. However, they had been friends since kindergarten, and old childhood ties such as theirs can become very close over time. They were so used to each other. They had grown up in the same neighborhood and shared a similar family background. But that's where the similarities ended. The choice of college had almost sent them off in different directions. Angel had wanted to go to Berkeley, in California. She had based her perception of Berkeley on the student protests of the late sixties. It seemed like the perfect place to her, away from the constraints of the traditional East Coast values. Her parents had simply refused, and after a prolonged fight

Angel seemingly gave up. Later on it became apparent that this standoff was only temporary.

One of the first things Angel asked Jeff on the night they met was whether he belonged to one of those "awful" fraternities. Since he didn't, she was at least willing to talk to him. Jeff had been dumbfounded by her questioning.

Jeff had noticed Angel from the moment she had entered and had not let her out of his sight. Intrigued and totally mesmerized he observed her for about fifteen minutes. Before she showed up, he had toyed with the idea of leaving pretty soon. He regretted having tagged along with his roommate, Ray, who belonged to the fraternity that was throwing the party.

Angel had been talking nonstop to several people. Jeff had had to wait to catch her alone. She seemed to be a magnet to whom others were drawn. Granted, she did stick out from the more subdued conservative crowd around her. And it wasn't just because of her tight black leather pants, black leather boots, and big mohair sweater in bright canary yellow. Why in the world did she die her hair that black? It couldn't possibly be her own color. And there was a lot of hair, either frizzed or naturally curly all the way down to her shoulder blades. She wore huge dangling earrings matching the yellow of the sweater. Big dark eyes accentuated by heavy charcoal eyeliner seemed to penetrate and challenge whoever or whatever entered their scope. Angel's outfit and makeup made her look like—a gypsy. Yes, that was the word Jeff had been looking for!

Before Jeff quite realized how this had come about, he found himself involved in a heated debate over the purpose of life. He felt dazed at first and never really understood what had hit him. He had never really spent much time discussing the purpose of life with anybody. The whole discussion seemed to have started when Angel asked him if he had seen the Live Aid telecast in July 1985 on TV. Of course, she had attended the event in person and felt everybody who really cared about the suffering in the world should have attended as well! He wondered at the time if she was even aware of the fact that some people had neither the time nor the money for such an undertaking. The fact that Jeff knew nothing about the event meant, at least according to Angel, that Jeff also didn't care about the plight of the starving people in Africa. She was very impressed with how Bob Geldof had risen to the occasion a year earlier and had brought together a bunch of British recording stars, resulting in the record "Do They Know It's Christmas Time at All?" Suddenly Jeff found himself in the strange position of having to defend himself for not being involved enough in the kind of issues that really mattered in life. She had started shooting off a barrage of questions about whether he didn't care at all about what happened to mankind and didn't he know how many people suffered, and on and on.

Jeff began to wonder if Angel could be for real. He soon learned she was. She meant every word she said, and she said plenty of them! He concluded that it was Angel's energy that had drawn him and the others like bees to nectar.

Or maybe they were more like moths who, while exploring the light, got sucked up and burnt in its heat and energy source? How close could one get to her and still be safe? She was so alive—yes, that was the word he was looking for to describe her—so very alive! But could that also spell danger for him?

Even today, ten years later, Angel still had this impact on Jeff and she probably always would, in spite of the fact that they had broken off their relationship several times over the years and had mutually agreed two years ago, in January 1993 to be exact, that they should just be "best friends."

This thought brought Jeff back to the reality of today. He looked at Angel, still snuggled up next to him. It felt good. Could it really be that in spite of everything they had experienced before they were now embarking on the first leg of their upcoming adventure? Upon arrival in Vancouver, BC, Canada, they would pick up an RV and head for the Yukon Territory and Alaska. Angel's idea was to "just drive and stop wherever they wanted to and for however long it suited their fancy"! Maybe this trip was just the kind of medicine Jeff needed to calm the demons in his heart and soul, and so he had agreed to go. It was easy! Angel had made the flight and RV reservations. Jeff was assigned to get a good map of Canada and Alaska and a good guide with campgrounds. He hadn't, however, been allowed to discuss the content of his guide books. She insisted that she wanted to be surprised and just live for the moment. Her exact words had been, "After all, Jeff, how many times in life can you allow yourself to just be and not suffer possible negative consequences!" She had a point there. There wasn't any risk involved once you got over the kind of thinking that required you to see certain places and make sure you didn't miss out on specific destinations within a certain time frame. The way Angel wanted to handle the return was to be able to say, "Now we have to calculate the time and figure out what it would take to just drive straight through to get to Anchorage." The return flights were booked from Anchorage to Vancouver, where they would change planes to return to San Francisco.

Jeff was ready to be surprised by whatever came their way. Or was he? Sometimes he wondered a little, yet so far it hadn't really been too difficult to adapt himself to Angel's "way of doing things." He actually felt excited. Sitting next to Angel in the taxi, he concluded that it wasn't at all scary to embrace and accept her energy. He remembered Angel telling him about the fields of red poppies she had come to love in Europe. She was ecstatic about them! According to Angel the orange California poppies shouldn't even be compared to this red variety. They simply weren't in the same league! Angel's red poppies could transform green tranquil meadows into wild fields pulsating with life and intensity. Orange poppies, in contrast, were simply too subdued and lacked vibrancy.

To Jeff, at this very moment, in the taxi on the way to the airport, Angel seemed to be like this red wildflower, independent, vibrant, seemingly changing everything with which she came into contact. In a sudden flash of insight Jeff knew and understood just how important it was for her to remain untamed and wild, just like the red poppy. The wild poppy fields were her playground. Nature and the elements seemed to embrace her! Jeff wanted to protect her, wanted to make sure that she would not get plucked from her field. After coming to California a couple of years ago and remembering Angel's love for poppies, he had picked some once along the wayside where he had lived. What a shock it had been when those beautiful orange flowers had shriveled up and died shortly afterward. That's why Jeff wanted Angel to be free, why he wanted to go on this adventure with her!

Chapter 16

Thanksgiving 1985

Wednesday, November 27, 1985, 3:25 p.m. at the New Canaan Train Station

"Jeff, Jeff, over here!"

Jeff turned his head, following the sound of Angel's voice. He would have recognized her voice anywhere! There was a big grin on his face and a sparkle in his eyes. He lifted his left hand to his dark green baseball cap, formally saluting her. With big bouncing steps he headed toward Angel, who was standing next to her car in the parking lot.

Angel watched Jeff intently. Her heart beat madly, full of anticipation and excitement. Suddenly she realized that her mother would be shocked by Jeff's appearance. His jeans looked quite worn and seemed a tad too long, but not long enough to hide his raggedy-looking sneakers. At least his navy blue sweatshirt looked fairly new. The dark gray ski jacket, tied nonchalantly around his waist, seemed okay. But the athletic bag that evidently substituted as an overnight bag had definitely seen better days. "Never mind about my mother," Angel told herself. Immediately her focus shifted, and it was back to her own reference points. She scanned Jeff's entire appearance more like an artist would, looking for color, texture, and symmetry. All Jeff really lacked was some color to brighten up his overall appearance. Never mind about her mother's opinion! It didn't really matter. Angel would take Jeff on a shopping spree and splurge. She relished the idea. Her body responded with a surge of titillating sensation. She felt entranced! Oh, love felt so good! Of course, Jeff, would bark at her idea, but so what? People could be so fickle and get so hung up on silly integrity issues! Angel was determined to fix that.

Angel's focus shifted again, and this time her mind's eye tried out what colors and styles might look best on Jeff. His hair was neither black nor brown. He might have been blond once. Strands of uncombed hair hid his forehead and partially covered penetrating steel gray eyes, sparkling intensely at times. Jeff would look good in just about any bright color, especially greens and reds. Colors that either matched or contrasted his eyes would be great choices. To Angel there was something quite special about Jeff's eyes. Once she had read somewhere that eyes were the door to a person's soul. When she looked into Jeff's eyes she did feel transported to his very soul, the eyes being the conduit. However, it was equally exciting, or possibly even more so, to lock her eyes with his and experience the sensation of two masses of intensity clashing in one immense power surge. At times, when their eyes interlocked, they were like clashing swords, setting off sparks created by the sudden impact of two equally strong forces. Angel loved that feeling!

Angel continued studying Jeff's face. His look was open, friendly, and inviting. Well-defined, balanced, and smooth face features softened the force and intensity of the steel gray eyes. And she thought he looked absolutely wonderful when he grinned from ear to ear! Jeff was lanky, slim and quite tall, just a little shy of six feet. He always seemed partially hunched over, maybe to make up for his height. Angel's mind's eye saw Jeff in a navy blue overcoat, made of light wool, possibly reaching down to his knees, maybe with a hood. He could keep the jeans, but he needed a colorful, bulky sweater to liven up his appearance. Yes, indeed, Angel concluded, he would look smashing once she fixed him up a bit!

If Jeff had known what Angel was thinking he would have been terrified. Jeff's thoughts were more along the line of trying to understand why Angel was interested in him at all. He had been puzzled by this thought ever since meeting her that fateful night in early October at the frat party. She could have had any guy she wanted, looking the way she did! Walking toward Angel right now, he intently felt her eyes on him, touching him and holding him. Her eyes were so alive and expressive. Her hair seemed to be a couple of inches shorter than the last time he saw her and was less frizzy. A lavender-colored headband tried to hold her mass of hair in check. Lavender seemed to be the color of the day, repeated by a lavender sweater, socks, and jewelry. Jeff had noted that Angel wore colors as themes, yet she always wore black jeans. He had never seen her in blue jeans. She didn't wear a coat. She had probably left it in the car. The sun was out, and it wasn't too cold today, probably in the high forties. Jeff had never seen Angel wear a skirt or a dress. He wondered whether she would dress differently for Thanksgiving. That wasn't the only thing he was wondering about.

Jeff surveyed his immediate surroundings. The train station looked a lot smaller than he had anticipated. Just one building and a parking lot. Angel had parked her red Porsche Carrera on the left side of the parking lot, next to the building. Jeff had pictured New Canaan as an important place, since he knew that a lot of wealthy people lived around here. Instead the train station looked like it had been left behind, a relic from some long-forgotten era. He felt like a country bumpkin. He wondered what it had been like growing up in these surroundings. He was quite curious, and that was probably why he had finally yielded and agreed to spend Thanksgiving with Angel and her family.

Jeff's demeanor suddenly changed. A worried frown appeared on his forehead. Thoughts about Angel's family had brought about acute tension. He started to feel uncomfortable and awkward. He didn't belong here. He should have never come! Once again he had fallen victim to Angel's power of persuasion. But that wasn't his only problem. The announcement that he would not spend Thanksgiving with his own family had led to arguments with his mother who had been hurt, yet why should she be? Sooner or later all children had to leave home. Once his mother had left home as well. But somehow parents never seemed to consider realities. Jeff had nothing really against his parents, but he also didn't feel like he had all that much in common with them. Trying to cheer up his mother and hoping it would relieve the guilt he felt over wanting to do his own thing, he had promised to come home for at least two weeks during the Christmas break. Now he wondered if he could survive two weeks at home.

"It was stupid to take the train. It takes forever! I should have picked you up in Boston," Angel exclaimed as Jeff got within earshot.

With a truly horrified expression on his face, Jeff responded, "No, no way! Definitely not! I wanted to take the train." He didn't own a car, and thus he had to rely on public transportation.

"Yeah, yeah, I know, you told me. But what's the big deal?"

It was a big deal to Jeff, and Angel knew it. Now he looked crushed. Angel sighed. He could be so sensitive at times. She just didn't get it. But if she had insisted on picking him up, they would have ended up "splitting hairs" again, as she called it, and by now she had learned the hard way that he didn't really understand what she meant by "splitting hairs." Jeff was convinced that he was just trying to differentiate between alternate perceptions. Angel believed that they were both just stubborn. That was all! Headstrong and stubborn, and, to make matters worse, they had grown up in very different worlds. Deep inside of her Angel knew that this was causing problems, but she didn't want to pay any attention to her feelings.

After a rather embarrassing passionate kiss and embrace, initiated by Angel, in front of a number of people in the parking lot, Jeff sat down in her car, overcome by all sorts of conflicting emotions. What spell did she hold over him? It had to be a major one, of that much he was sure. Whenever he was near her it felt like he was walking on clouds, never touching the ground. Nobody had ever made him feel this way before!

Jeff and Angel had seen each other every weekend since they first met. He would never forget how after just talking for a couple of minutes she suddenly asked him if he wanted to get out of there and just drive around a while. That's when it had started. Ever since then he had been saying "yes" to just about every crazy idea she had proposed. It was like magic. And he would never forget that ride in her Porsche. How could he? What an experience! She was a madwoman behind the wheel! Jeff had been scared to death! He wondered if her parents had any idea about her driving habits and whether her mother was in a perpetual state of worry. Well, this was the weekend he would find out what her family was like. Then again, maybe it would be better not to find out. His concerns and worries increased.

What had made the ride even scarier on that fateful night was the fact that it had been raining quite heavily at times. Jeff had finally been able to coax Angel into finding a coffee place, where they had spent several hours just talking. When they got kicked out at 1 a.m., closing time, they just sat in the car in front of his dorm until 4 a.m. and talked and talked and talked. The streets and scenery of Boston, the James River, the row of dorms, perched next to each other, didn't even seem to exist. Angel and Jeff noticed only each other. All that mattered were Jeff and Angel and their moments together. By 4 a.m. Jeff really wanted to call it a night. He was tired. Angel wasn't tired at all and protested at first, but finally yielded.

Overwhelmed, taken aback, surprised, confused were some of the words that came to mind when Jeff tried to describe what it felt like being with Angel. But nobody would be able to call her boring! She had a different take on just about every aspect of life, and it seemed like his head started spinning every time he tried to figure out what she talked about.

So far they had seen each other eight weekends in a row. Angel had always stayed with her friend Maggie in Wellesley but had spent most waking hours with Jeff. He needed to tell her that he was way behind in his studies. They had to cut down on the time they spent together. But how? Angel didn't take college seriously and believed he studied too much. Though she was taking art design and art history classes, she didn't study for any of them. She was mostly interested in "doing her own thing," as she called it. Jeff was confused. What did going to college have to do with "doing one's own thing?" College was meant to get you equipped to ultimately make a living in some profession or field of interest. Why did she even bother with college? Obviously she was disinterested and kept complaining about the attitude of the professors.

However, Jeff had observed one recurring obsession in Angel. Every one of her discussions seemed to be geared toward figuring out what made life worthwhile in the first place. She was dismayed that college offered nothing really to contribute to such an important pursuit. As far as he could tell, she had no good answers to her favorite riddle. Until he started talking to her, it had never even occurred to him to ponder all the philosophical questions she raised almost incessantly. Life just was, no more and no less than that! But not for Angel. She pondered why she was born, why her parents were the way they were, why human beings hated each other so much, why there was so much pain in the world, why people didn't really care about other people. And on and on it went. Nobody could do anything about it, so why get all worked up about things you couldn't change? Somehow, he didn't quite know how, she got him wondering about her obsession. Lately he had frequently found himself thinking about the purpose of his own life. It wasn't very satisfying, though. Rather, life appeared a lot more disconcerting now. There seemed to be no real tangible answers that could explain the purpose of life. Maybe he should look into taking a philosophy class, just to form a more educated opinion. No, he didn't really have the time.

Jeff wanted to believe that his frequent clashes and power struggles with Angel were mostly due to their different backgrounds. He came from a middle-class family and had grown up in Hartford, Connecticut. His father worked in the insurance industry, Hartford's main business. His mother went back to work when the third child started kindergarten. She was an elementary school teacher and would probably work till retirement age. Without his mother's income, life would have been a little too tight on his dad's salary. Jeff's parents had always been concerned about saving up money for the three boys to go to college some day. Jeff had two brothers, Chris who was two years younger and would be graduating from high school next year, and Hank who was four years younger and was a junior in high school. Jeff had no idea how his mother felt about her work. Did she like it, or did she work because her husband expected her to chip in? Lately, since thinking about the purpose of life, he wondered if she worked for the financial security her work provided in the form of a teacher's pension once she would retire.

Jeff was twenty years old and glad to be away from home and into his second year at college. He rarely visited his family, though Hartford certainly wasn't that far from Boston. It's not that life at home had been bad, but he just hadn't enjoyed it very much. He had often wondered whether his parents were really happy together. They never really talked much about anything that seemed to interest or concern them. His dad was a very quiet guy and pretty withdrawn. Only the middle boy, Chris used to be able to get him to come out of his shell more. But now Chris, was into his own life and had started to ignore his father, just like Jeff before him. Hank, the youngest son, was close to his mom. Jeff felt they were way too close and thus Hank lacked independence and confidence. He was her "baby." Oh, well, it was not Jeff's life and shouldn't be his concern. They could do as they pleased! Once Jeff had discovered computers he had avoided the family as much as possible and the computers became the center of his life and still were. He remembered how he had had to plead his case with his father to get his first computer, an Apple II when he was thirteen in junior high back in 1978. Without his mother putting in good words for Jeff, his father would have never agreed to pay half of the purchase price. Jeff had worked a number of odd jobs throughout his high school years and thus had been able to contribute half of the cost of the computer himself. Jeff's working so hard for his share had convinced his father to contribute the other half of the purchase.

Since arriving at MIT Jeff had focused mainly on Sun workstations. Jeff was absolutely taken by the networking and system administration concepts. To Jeff it was a world full of magic and possibilities which he desired to explore and longed to master. His dream was to add his own spin to it some day.

Angel's next question brought Jeff out of his reverie and back to the demands of the moment. She had highlighted what he could expect this weekend. It was Wednesday, and he was to stay through Saturday of this Thanksgiving weekend.

"Now listen up. Don't you let anybody at my house intimidate you! They're snobs, that's all. They don't know any better, okay?"

Jeff felt a sudden cold grip around his heart. The shock made him feel numb. His worst fears were now confirmed.

He also felt anger rising inside of him because somehow he felt betrayed by Angel. She should have told him earlier. Then he wouldn't have come! She must have known this. She had tricked him!

"Man, now you tell me! I should have known."

Angel in contrast didn't show any signs of concern, and in her opinion Jeff was just overreacting.

"Oh, stop fussing. I hate it when you get this way! That's life. You can't change it. They're snobs and that's all! It's stupid to take them seriously. They have no idea what life is really like."

Still overcome with nagging fears, Jeff was not about to be swayed by this kind of logic. Actually, it made him even more angry at Angel. With a tinge of cynicism in his voice, he remarked, "That does seem to be your favorite phrase— they have no idea what life is really like! I've never yet heard you talk about anybody who 'knows what life is really all about.' Why do you always say that?"

Angel was not at all impacted by Jeff's cynicism.

"So, you got a problem with that? That's a fact! Trust me. They don't know, and they aren't looking! They're real zombies, that's all. You see, my father didn't even make all the money he now has. Well, some of it he earned himself, granted. But mostly he inherited all the money from his father. My grandfather made the money. So what does that make my father? Nothing, in my opinion. He doesn't matter. I only care about my grandfather, and the two of us get along really well. He's an old rebel! You'll meet him. He's coming tomorrow. My grandmother died two years ago, but he's still going strong and living in the same old apartment on Park Avenue, which he bought a long time ago. A driver will bring him from New York City. He also has a great housekeeper and many good old friends. He's never bored and still very active at age seventy-six! You know, he started his own investment company, all from scratch. He's really clever and has a special knack for making something out of nothing, if you know what I mean. All my father knows how to do well is not make any waves and keep everything the way it always has been. He is so-o-o boring."

Angel stopped for a moment, overcome by anger toward her father. She simply couldn't stand him! Then she continued, "Anyway, I love this story I'm going to tell you now. Back in 1898 my great-grandfather, who was only eighteen at the time, immigrated to this country from Chernovtsy in Bucovina, which is now part of the Ukraine. Till 1918 it belonged to the Austrian Hungarian Empire and was called Czernowitz. After World War One Czernowitz became part of Romania. Then, after World War Two Bucovina was split into two parts. The northern part, and that includes Czernowitz, became part of the Soviet Union, and the southern part went to Romania. According to my grandfather's stories, and he loves to talk about all of this, Czernowitz had been a thriving Jewish community. It seems they identified themselves with the Austrian Empire and the German culture. That might explain my great-grandfather's name, Simon Blank. Blank is a German word and means bright, polished, but it can also mean 'bare.' My grandfather says the authorities in the Austrian Hungarian Empire assigned names to many of the Jewish families who came from surrounding parts to live in Bucovina, and these authorities purposely chose demeaning names. They wanted to declare the family as being 'bare,' 'worthless.' I get really upset about such things. I bet you are surprised that I even care about all this stuff, right?"

Jeff looked at Angel and was indeed surprised. There was a seriousness in her face that he had never really seen before. Unsure what to say in response, he commented, hoping not to upset her, "You really do seem very interested in the family background. And it's quite a story!"

Angel's mood had already changed again. She was back to being upbeat and energetic. Yet now there was a certain inflection in her voice that had not been there before.

"Well, I've given all of this a lot of thought, though I'm not quite sure why. It seems important to me. I have this odd feeling inside that I should find out more about my great-grandfather. I would have loved to meet him. Old man Simon seems to have been quite a character. In a strange and peculiar way I've always identified with him. Maybe that's why I'm so much into clothes and styles. Who knows? From what I heard he was pretty good at what he did. I mean his sewing.

"Rather than getting an education, something my great-grandfather Simon had wanted, my grandfather Max, who was born in 1909, insisted on doing his own thing. This must run in the family."

Angel grinned, quite pleased with her point. She took delight in believing that at least some members in her family's past wouldn't consider it strange and unusual when she chose to randomly pursue whatever struck her momentary fancy.

"My grandfather Max was a real entrepreneur and did very well for himself, especially when you consider that he didn't even finish high school. He started with absolutely nothing, but worked hard and in the end managed to make quite a fortune by opening a chain of general stores all along New England. He used the proceeds from his business to invest in the stock market and finally sold off the chain and started an investment company of his own. This was way after the crash of 1929. My father, his name is Paul, is the social climber, the one who felt compelled to prove that his family was no longer built on self-made success but 'sophisticated' success, as he likes to call it. You know, my family even has all these little expressions for everything, and minute differences are extremely important as well. So, anyway, my father wanted to tackle Wall Street the right way, with the perfect lily-white credentials. He got accepted at Harvard for his MBA back in the fifties. That was a big deal to him. Of course, another point on his agenda was to marry a 'society girl,' my mother. And I can't stand her! She comes from a family of lawyers, old money, and believe it or not, she's not even Jewish! I've never understood why she married a Jewish upstart, and no matter how hard I've tried, I can't get anything out of her.

"We do not have much contact with her side of the family, especially since both of her parents died a couple of years ago and she was an only child. She inherited a fortune of her own, believe you me! My maternal grandmother set up trust funds for my brother Michael and I. I just never pay any attention to that kind of stuff, and besides, I can't touch the money till I'm twenty-five. When you're nineteen, twenty-five seems a long way off! I'm convinced that marrying my father was an act of revenge by my mother toward her parents. She's very much into the revenge game and quite good at it, too. That's why we don't get along. We're always trying to do it to each other in this underhanded kind of way. Sometimes I think it bothers me that I'm half Jewish and half whatever, American, Anglo Saxon, or what? What am I really? Our immediate family has no roots. Nobody cares about things the way they used to in the old days. My grandfather Max is still very much into his Jewish roots, and he always tries to convince me to follow the Jewish traditions. But how can I, really, unless I know why I would want to, right? And shouldn't I at least first learn how Judaism differs from Christianity? I just don't know anything about either one. My mother has an Episcopalian background. Her background is mostly English. But I was not baptized by the Episcopalian church either. So, you figure! What am I?"

Angel paused for a moment. Her voice reflected a slight trace of sadness, a general sense of feeling lost, somehow abandoned. But by what and whom?

Jeff's head was spinning from trying to keep up with all the family stories. Before he could say anything, luckily, Angel continued.

"Well, that about sums it all up. I get rather disgusted every time I think about my family. Why couldn't they at least just be themselves and be happy? Why all this striving for social acceptance?"

Now Jeff was even more worried about meeting Angel's family. He pleaded, "Please, don't say any more. It's more than I can handle! I should have never come. I don't belong here! Why, please tell me, why did you want me here?"

Angel was only too eager to do away with such nonsense. Jeff's fussing was simply ridiculous.

"You wonder why I want you here? Isn't it obvious? I like you. I even love you! I want to be with you! And besides, how many more times do I have to tell you that I hate being with them? I can't stand them. Actually, I despise them! With you there it will be fun because you and I can have fun together!" Angel had slowed down. She wanted to hide how she really felt. She didn't want Jeff to know how lonely she sometimes felt at home . . . But Jeff didn't detect any change in her behavior. He was too preoccupied with his own worries.

After a couple of moments of silence Jeff said, "What would be different with me here? Most likely it will make things worse for you, won't it, since they'll consider me to be a bum, or hick, or whatever they will label me?"

Angel sat up like a bolt. She was not going to listen to any of this!

"No, they won't say anything or do anything. That wouldn't be proper, and they know if they start fussing, I'll create a 'situation' as they call it. And mind you, you can't have a 'situation' at the Thanksgiving dinner table! So, as far as I'm concerned, I can control the whole event, especially if I don't care how they feel about me—and I don't!"

Angel was working very hard to convince herself, and yet there was this numbing feeling inside that didn't want to go away. Why was there always so much unknown sadness inside of her when she spoke about her family?

Jeff thought for a moment and finally said, "I don't know, but listening to you talk about them, and you actually talk about them quite frequently this way, I wonder whether deep down you don't care after all!"

Jeff had to duck fast, knowing that this kind of statement would provoke a physical reaction. Angel loved to exhibit her disgust by pounding on his arm or body. Only one of her arms was still on the steering wheel. The other one was moving madly, trying to deliver some punches. The car responded by moving around and swaying off course. Jeff concluded that it definitely wasn't safe being with her!

With renewed vigor and putting the sadness and loneliness she had felt a moment ago out of her mind, Angel said, "Aren't you getting smart, ducking as I try to get you for what you said?" She used these kind of physical exchanges to mask her real feelings.

Angel continued with a couple of more attempts to deliver some punches. Jeff in turn defended himself by deftly moving out of her reach. The farther he moved away, the harder she tried, and Jeff finally stopped, since she kept taking her eyes off the road. Angel also stopped. They both felt better.

The physical exchange had been a good way to let off some steam. Jeff was less anxious now.

It was a twenty-five-minute drive to Angel's house located in the back woods of New Canaan. The family owned fifteen acres of land and had ten horses. Angel had moved from the scary part of the family story to just some facts that would come in handy, as she called it. She informed Jeff about mealtimes, when Angel and Jeff would have to join the family, when they could ignore them, and so on. It looked like they would have the rest of the afternoon to themselves, and her idea was to go horseback riding. All protests on Jeff's part that he had never sat on a horse and that he had no proper attire were useless. She would fix it all. He would just have to go along for the ride. Jeff concluded that it was sink or swim now!

Dinner tonight would be spent with some of the family. Angel's mother, Penny, would of course be there. Angel's dad might show up really late and eat by himself. Angel's younger brother, Michael, would be there as well. She had no other siblings. Jeff was looking forward to meeting Michael. According to Angel, Michael was also into computers. He was a junior in high school.

"Angel, please, please slow down!" Jeff was reacting to getting bounced around because Angel hardly slowed down while maneuvering through some nasty turns in the road.

Angel had no intention of slowing down. Indignantly she declared, "Having a sports car is no fun if you can't go fast! Don't worry, I know what I'm doing! I think you worry way too much about all sorts of things."

Jeff gave up. He had learned by now that, according to Angel, everybody who didn't enjoy taking risks the way she did was just a worrywart.

"Oh, by the way, one last point. I think my father is having an affair."

Jeff detected something close to gleam in her voice, yet he was too shocked to think about it or try to make sense out of it. Instead he felt totally overwhelmed again, and with real dread in his voice he said, "Okay, that's it! I think this is where I get off." Jeff slumped into his seat and wished he could somehow disappear.

"Oh, shut up! I think it's fascinating in a way. At least my father is showing his true colors. I hope he gets found out sooner or later. I'm dying to see what my mother will do."

Angel was definitely enjoying this!

"Angel, really . . ."

"Well, we all have to try to amuse ourselves when life is so boring. I figure if I have to spend the entire Thanksgiving weekend with them, I might as well make the most of it by exposing what might be going on behind their conventional masks. Otherwise I'll be bored to tears! And besides, you know that I invited you because it will be so much more fun having you around to share all this with, right?"

Jeff recognized that she was joking and having fun. He decided to joke a little himself.

"So, now I am a toy?"

"Yeah, don't you like it?"

Jeff knew Angel was just teasing him, yet he also realized that he would have to do some deep thinking to determine why he had come along for this very scary ride and experience. What did Angel represent to him?

Jeff was totally unprepared for Angel's next move.

"Anyway, I just want to have fun with you and also go into New York City on Friday to do some shopping."

"Shopping, on the day after Thanksgiving, when the crowds are at their worst?"

"So, what's the big deal? When else would you have time to go shopping with me?"

"Who says I want to go shopping with you?" Jeff was almost speechless.

"I didn't say you wanted to. I said we were going shopping."

"I see. There certainly is a difference." Jeff knew there was more to come.

"You have to promise me to agree to something that is very, very important to me!"

"Like what?" Jeff started to feel quite uncomfortable again.

"I want you to promise me that I can treat you to something special on Friday."

"I don't understand. What do you mean by that?" Jeff's confusion grew.

"Oh, you dummy! I want to buy you something *fun*!"

"*Fun*, like what?"

"Anything and everything! You'll see!"

Jeff was dumbfounded and unable to respond. What was he to do?

They spent the remaining ten minute drive arguing over Angel wanting to spend money on Jeff. To his horror, he found himself giving in—again. Jeff was beginning to wonder if he was going to lose himself completely. That's what it felt like. He had no better words at the moment. How about this for an irony? Being with her and giving in to her outrageous ideas was bringing about what she wanted most—a conceived need to ask himself what "life was all about," or more specifically, who he was, what he was all about, and why he did what he did. He'd better not mention this to her. Who knew how she would react and what else might be in store for him if she found out? She was rubbing off on him. That much he knew for sure.

Suddenly Angel pulled up into a driveway. Jeff's face froze in utter horror. He felt numb and cold all over.

Oh, dear God, look at that driveway and that house! The only other time he had seen a house like that was in some fancy estate magazine in a doctor's office a couple of years ago. He was going to die here this weekend. For the first time since meeting Angel it dawned on Jeff what her life might have been like, growing up in this environment. There just couldn't be a future for the two of them. It was impossible!

Chapter 17

Leaving Vancouver

Sunday, June 4, 1995, 10:35 a.m.

"Maybe we should have picked up the RV yesterday afternoon after all. This is such a hassle!" Jeff looked upset and frustrated.

Angel felt great, and nothing Jeff said would change this. "Oh, come on, Jeff. Get off it! We already talked about this. It's over and done with! At least the RV place turned out to be only ten minutes from our hotel. And besides, I just didn't feel like it yesterday and wanted to have some fun walking around downtown Vancouver. Didn't you have fun last night?" There was a mischievous tone in her voice.

Jeff realized that he was overreacting to the circumstances. He felt irritated and disconnected and didn't quite know why. This bothered him. And now Angel wanted to discuss last night. That's probably what brought about his strange mood in the first place! He had to be careful. She could get quite sensitive about these matters. Trying to sound positive and upbeat, he ventured, "Yes, I *did* have fun last night. You're right. It's just that I hate to waste time, and we wasted plenty of it this morning!"

But nothing was bothering Angel this morning. "Well, so what? We don't really have to be anywhere by a certain time, or do we? So why should it matter how much time we do or don't waste, anyway? Look at the bright side of things. Didn't we have the most wonderful breakfast you can imagine?"

Angel closed her eyes as if reliving the experience before continuing with a voice filled with awe and wonder, "I just loved that wide open breakfast lounge in the hotel and all those windows revealing the most glorious, panoramic view of the harbor. How breathtaking! Even the weather has been perfect. I think we've been pretty lucky so far, and I can only hope that it's a really good omen for our trip. I've been told it rains a lot around here. So here we are, gorgeous surroundings, sun shining, not a cloud in the sky—and you're fussing just because things didn't go as perfectly and as smoothly as you'd hoped or expected!

"As for myself, I feel great anyway, even if you can't share my elation. What else do you want or need right now? You wait and see. Just because you're so miserable and downbeat, dark and ominous clouds will come as if from nowhere and cause the sun to go into hiding and put a damper on everything. Then even I will get down, for sure!"

Angel paused for a moment and then continued, her voice very soft and halting, "When I close my eyes I still see that view from this morning. You could see all the way from the harbor into the wide, unrestricted openness of the Pacific Ocean. Something about it all touched me deeply. It made me shiver. It was speaking to me."

Jeff didn't catch the touch of melancholy in Angel's voice. He was too focused on the heavy traffic they had encountered.

"Did you pay any attention to the view this morning? Did you look out toward the ocean? The view just went on and on. There seemed to be no end to it. Though I can't see myself enjoying being on a cruise ship, I think I would love being on a boat, imagining moving ever so slowly toward this great all-embracing void. I would become one with the void, suspended in time and space. It would be an existence without limits and restraints. The illusion would be that there is a final destination after all and that I do not have to worry. Yet, in reality, I would never reach this destination. Instead, I would just be on a wonderful, never-ending journey. It feels scary and wonderful at the same time. That's why the view seemed so mystical to me. I felt like I was really close to some mysterious force, and yet at the same time I didn't seem to be able to ever get hold of it. It kept slipping away, if you know what I mean. And that's why the joy is tempered by apprehension and uncertainty. Joy should just be joy, always! Yet somehow the void seemed to imply that no joy is just joy. That still makes me sad."

Suddenly sadness and a touch of weariness had marred the beautiful picture Angel had described so eloquently. Trying to dispel the gloom and doom that had dampened her earlier joy and elation, she tried laughing off its effects, but her laugh had a metallic ring and sounded contrived. Angel didn't really feel like laughing. What had happened? Why did she suddenly feel so anxious?

Forcefully Angel declared, "You know, taking off like that into the mystical unknowns would be like a Christopher Columbus experience, don't you think? He took off not knowing where he would really end up. Judging by the kind of luck I've had so far in life, I would most likely drop off the earth! And yes, I know that I've been indulging myself in rambling metaphors, something you're not too fond of. I know! So don't get excited, and don't give me a lecture about how my feelings make no sense at all!"

This isn't good, Jeff thought to himself. Pretty soon Angel will be severely depressed. It always happened, though he didn't understand why. It started with a declaration of elation and ended with a description of life being an empty void. What was she trying to say? What was she feeling at times like this? It just didn't make any sense to Jeff. Still trying to ward off the inevitable, he hoped to snap her out of her mood by saying, "Oh, Angel, don't get into one of those moods again. You know how depressed you can get if you keep dwelling on these feelings of yours."

With a stubborn look on her face Angel declared, "Yes, I know, but I just can't help myself. This is what's going on inside of me all the time, whether you like it or not!"

Angel decided to change the subject. It was tough to get Jeff interested in talks about the mysteries of life. It seemed to irritate him. Why? When they had met ten years ago,

Jeff had been more open, at least generally speaking. Now he didn't want to deal with these 'Angel issues' anymore. Something had happened since then. What had changed? She missed his openness from years ago.

Jeff was still listening when she shared her crazy feelings. At least Angel could tell that. Also, he always seemed to be able to keep up with her when she went on and on talking about subjects to which he himself seemed to have trouble relating. So maybe he was still interested, at least a tiny bit. Or was this just wishful thinking? Recently she had experienced recurring doubts. Sometimes, during very clear and conscious moments, Angel's intuition told her that Jeff did *not* understand, but she chose not to pay attention to those sudden flashes of insight. Was she just kidding herself? But if so, why and what for? What was she avoiding or running away from? And it was true. He was right, unfortunately. If she let her feelings take over, something she simultaneously longed for and feared, she did indeed get depressed, terribly depressed.

Brushing the dark thoughts aside, Angel became solicitous, hoping to engage Jeff, knowing it would dispel some of the loneliness she felt. She wanted to hear him say something that made her feel good. "So, are you still cross about the slow start, or was I able to distract you with all my chitchat?"

"You know, you can always distract me!" Jeff smiled.

"Well, that's good to know. At least I now know for sure that I can still cast a spell over you!" Angel grinned mischievously.

"You just can't help yourself, can you? You always have to tease me, right?" But Jeff didn't mind at all. He was quite relieved. Angel seemed to be snapping out of her gloom.

"Well, I read somewhere in one of my many psychological books, as you call them, that when one teases others one really likes them. So shouldn't you feel flattered when I tease you?" She was having fun!

"Yes, I am, if you don't go overboard. Mostly I'm really excited about going on this trip with you!"

Angel needed more validation and continued. "Does that mean that you've forgiven me for choosing the expensive Pan Pacific Hotel for our stay last night?"

A slight frown appeared on Jeff's forehead. He was still a little upset. "Well, I wished you had given me some warning! I was certainly not prepared for anything of the kind."

But Angel was on a roll now. "If I had told you beforehand, it would have ruined the entire experience, don't you think? I had wanted to surprise you and used the frivolity of the digs to show you that I was still interested in *all* of you! So look at last night as my way of seducing you!"

Jeff became quite uncomfortable. Angel had a way of getting right to his feelings, and he always got scared when she did. Trying to stop her, he said, "Really, Angel, you can get quite carried away."

"Are you saying you *didn't* like last night?" Angel was not about to give up so soon. She wanted to hear Jeff say that he loved sharing all of himself with her as much as she did!

Jeff began to feel embarrassed, and there was sincere fear in his voice as he pleaded, "Please, it's all just too much for me. Give me time. I need time to get used to being 'reunited with you,' as you call it."

Angel realized that this was the point where she had to stop. "Okay, okay, you're right. I am overdoing it! Besides, I was afraid that you would make me change the reservation at the hotel if I had told you beforehand. Not only did we have that incredible view this morning over breakfast, but we were also in close proximity to the entire downtown area. I just loved that little bistro we found on Robson Street last night. I really had fun with you last night—not just the dinner! Okay, okay, don't wince! I'll stop talking about it now."

Angel didn't realize how much she wanted Jeff to say that he had liked their lovemaking as much as she had. That he had enjoyed being with her again, sharing himself with her. It was so hard to tell what he really felt at such moments.

Jeff seemed to have sensed what Angel wanted to hear and said, "Yes, I liked everything as much as you did. I'd better say it now. Otherwise you'll try to get me to make a statement for the rest of the day, right? Furthermore, I guess one could say that you finally fulfilled your old wish of having me join you on one of your bohemian, or should I call it existential, outings."

Angel threw a quick glance at Jeff, wondering if he really meant it. And he did. She was thrilled and felt warm and fuzzy all over. "Gee, Jeff, I am really touched! Do you mean it? So there is hope that these experiences might grow on you?" Her voice was carefully controlled. She was still afraid of being disappointed and finding out that she had hoped for too much.

Jeff felt like his feet were back on safer ground. This he could discuss. "You have to be patient with me. It will take some getting used to. Like this morning when I got antsy about wanting to get going and all of that stuff. But generally speaking I can say that I am behind the whole idea of the trip. Well, let me qualify this. I'm behind what I so far perceive this trip to be about. I'm sure you have more surprises in store for me, just like the hotel and your renewed interest in me, which, you have to admit, you really kind of sprang on me without giving me any advance clue. I think I did well, considering how unprepared I was. And at the same time I always get apprehensive that I'll just let you down again, like so many times before." The ground was not so safe anymore. Could he ever be on safe ground with her?

Angel was surprised and taken aback. She had never considered that Jeff might feel responsible for her moods and feelings. That was all wrong! She didn't want that! He had to understand. "No Jeff, I don't think that. I have come around. Or, I should say, I've calmed down a lot. For now I just want to say that I am simply thrilled about being with you! You'll see. You'll get the hang of it sooner or later. After all, we have four weeks. Maybe by week number four you'll allow yourself to be more spontaneous.

"Oh, and by the way, thanks for being willing to drive the RV all through downtown, just so that I could take one more last look, this time right from the bridge, out into the harbor and into my 'mystical nothingness.' I simply loved it! And I do know that we're kind of driving around in a circle!"

Jeff grunted but didn't say anything else. He had to pay close attention to the traffic, which had gotten quite heavy ever since they had left the bridge leading from Stanley Park near downtown Vancouver across the First Narrows to north Vancouver. Pretty soon they would connect to Highway 1, which they would take east. Later Highway 1 would change directions and go south, leaving north Vancouver and, using another bridge, this time crossing the Second Narrows, return to Vancouver. In effect, they were almost going back to where they had started out. But the second bridge was a short distance south of the hotel, so they weren't quite completing a full circle.

Also, to be exact Jeff should inform Angel that the view she loved so much was a panorama of the Georgia Strait. The entire Vancouver Island was situated between Vancouver and the Pacific, and then there were still the Charlotte Islands before the Pacific came into view. The open ocean Angel found so mystical was much farther away than it appeared. But he knew from experience that such specifics wouldn't matter to her. Such a remark would only upset her and would not change her feelings. As far as she was concerned she had seen the ocean, which reminded her of a mystical nothingness. Why would "nothingness" be appealing to her? Nothingness sounded rather ominous to him. But she wasn't interested in his viewpoint unless he happened to agree with hers! However, he was sure that she would make this trip a very special one. She seemed to have a real knack for pulling off seemingly impossible adventures.

Angel had been looking around at the immediate scenery, checking the map, and then asked, "How high are these mountains? They remind me of the mountains around the Bay Area."

Not wanting to take his focus off the heavy traffic, Jeff said, "If you want to find out, you'll have to read the map and the AAA book I brought along."

"Oh never mind. I'm not yet in the mood for studying specifics. Maybe later. But I do want to see where we'll be going next."

Angel picked up the road map of British Columbia. Studying the map, she said, "So, had you planned to stay on Highway 1? How about if we stay on this side of the Fraser River and drive along the foot of the mountains of Route 7?"

"That's okay by me. But we have to cross over here and get back to Vancouver first, right?"

"Yes, that's true. But then we can take 6, a tiny connection from 1 to 7, and then we're back on the northern side again. Later on 7 connects back to 1, so we won't have a problem getting to Highway 1."

"Okay, I'm game!" Jeff was content to just go along with Angel's plan.

Angel folded up the map and looked around for something to do. "I think I'll get acquainted with our new digs, here. I'm referring to the camper. Let's see what we have to work with. I didn't want to bring this up earlier, but we also have to stop and buy food and other supplies."

"I know, I know. That's why earlier this morning I got so impatient."

Angel didn't like it that he brought up the earlier conflict again. Sometimes he just kept going at it again and again. It seemed to take him so long to forget certain issues. "Oh, let's just make a fun thing out of it all. I'll look for a little supermarket on the way. And then, after that, we can stop somewhere, and I'll fix us a kind of picnic lunch."

Jeff visibly cheered up. "Wow! You will?"

Angel's face expressed utter dismay. Why did people always draw these strange conclusions about her? Why was Jeff surprised? Disdainfully she declared, "Just because I usually eat out doesn't mean that I'm not good at preparing sandwiches! And believe it or not, I can actually cook!"

"I'm not saying that you can't. I'm just surprised that you will."

Jeff wondered what other surprises Angel might have in store for him. He wasn't one to turn down good food. Knowing how much Angel enjoyed good and expensive restaurants, he figured she might also be able to cook well. He would soon find out!

Angel had gotten up from her front seat to take a close look at the inside of the camper. After a couple of moments she said, "You know, I really like the setup. It's very compact and functional, though of course pretty small. But it's all quite attractive. You know, this is the first time I've seen the inside of a camper."

Right behind the driver's seat was a little table with two benches that could seat four quite comfortably. Right next to it was a small window with a cute little checkered red-and-white curtain. Across from the table was a door to the outside. To the right of the door, looking from the inside, were a stove, a sink, and, across from the sink, next to the table, a refrigerator.

"Boy, look at the size of that fridge! I can't believe it! It's really much bigger than I had expected!"

Jeff mumbled something she couldn't understand and kept his eyes on traffic.

Next to the fridge was the door to the bathroom. Angel opened it and looked inside. "Hey, the bathroom is not bad either!"

No response from Jeff this time, but it didn't bother Angel. She had proceeded to the back of the camper. "Wow, some bed! I had no idea how comfortable these campers can be! Did you know?"

This time Jeff responded. "I didn't know much about campers either. But I inspected the unit this morning when you were haggling with the poor guy over the paperwork and got him all confused."

"Oh, be quiet. I don't want to hear about that again! Where are the additional beds? They said it sleeps four."

"You see those cabinets above on the right and left sides of the queen-size bed? They fold out, and each of them is a bed. And, of course, you can also fold away the queen-size bed."

Angel took a close look and concluded, "Gee, if you were a family, you certainly wouldn't have much privacy, would you? What if we fight and one of us wants to withdraw and sulk? What then?"

"Oh, Angel, don't talk about those things. Besides, I think you're teasing me again." Jeff tried to look at Angel through the rearview mirror, but couldn't tell what mood she was in now. Was she really teasing?

A thoughtful look had settled on Angel's face. She seemed preoccupied with something and said, "Yeah, you're right. I am bad! I'm going to try out the bed now and lie down for a while. Then again, maybe that isn't a good idea. I think I might get carsick lying down."

Jeff was confused again. Now Angel suddenly wanted to lie down! To him she appeared to be continuously changing her mind about everything. "I thought you wanted to see the scenery we are driving through. That is why we're driving on this side of the river, right? You know it would have been faster if we'd taken Highway 1 right after leaving the hotel."

"I know, I know. You're right. I'm coming back up front. It's just that I didn't sleep well last night. I had a bad dream."

Angel was definitely getting depressed again. Jeff could tell. Trying to encourage her somehow, he asked, "What was it about this time?" Every so often Angel got quite disturbed by her dreams. Jeff didn't really understand this about her, nor did he pay much attention to dreams in general. What meaning could they possibly have?

But Angel didn't seem to want to talk about her dream and got quite evasive. "Oh, let's just forget about it. It was all quite confusing, and I don't think I really want to talk about it right now."

"Okay, suit yourself, but you know I am always interested." In a way Jeff felt relieved. The entire conversation so far this morning had been draining his energies. Too many unknowns, too much uncertainty. What had really been going on?

Still thinking about dreams, Angel added, "My dreams are often very weird. Sometimes I also get foreboding feelings out of nowhere And not just in dreams. I hate those feelings. They really get me down."

Jeff said nothing for a while but focused on the road ahead. Unless Angel was ready to talk about something, it was useless to prod her. He decided to change the subject. "So, are you satisfied with our living quarters back there? I think it's a pretty neat unit. For the next four weeks we'll live within the confines of this camper. Hard to believe, really!" Jeff felt on safe grounds talking about the camper. "This seems to be a fairly new unit. If they ever rented it out before, it must not have been for a long trip. The speedometer said roughly 1,500 miles. Before we left for the trip I did some planning and calculated about how long it would take us and what might be worthwhile to see along the way. You want to talk about the plan?"

Angel looked gloomy. "Not really. I'm sorry, Jeff. I just got really cranky all of a sudden. Only a moment ago I felt so great! Sometimes this happens to me. It was just because looking at the bed I was reminded of last night, and then I remembered the dream. Just give me some time, and I think

I'll be okay. How about you take a break and I do some driving? That way I would have to focus on the road, and it might just take my mind off what's bugging me inside."

Jeff was concerned, but there was really nothing he could do. "Okay, that sounds good. We'll stop when we see a little supermarket to do our shopping, and you can take over the driving from there, okay?"

"Okay."

For the next fifteen minutes Angel remained quiet, and Jeff was left to his own thoughts, but he didn't mind at all. He thought about the trip. Hard to believe that pretty soon they would be in the wide open spaces of British Columbia. No hectic schedules, and so far no stress. In the end Angel's moods seemed to work themselves out, even if he got apprehensive at times. In his opinion she needed her space more than she realized. He gladly obliged. Usually he was the one who asked for time alone. It was more unusual for her to do so. Maybe the last couple of years had taught her how to take more time to think things over. At least he hoped so, for her sake. He did wonder what was going on in her head, though. Ultimately she would spill the beans. He had never yet experienced her not sharing what was going on inside of her. Something must be really bothering her to be this quiet. He looked around at the scenery. Angel was right. Everything looked great in this glorious sunshine. The temperature was perfect, not too hot, not too cold. He loved the mountain ranges on the left side of the road. Actually, he loved the whole idea of the trip and had gotten more and more excited as the departure time drew near.

Was it possible for Angel and Jeff to develop a lasting relationship after all? Or was this just going to be another failed attempt, like all the other times before? Jeff wished he could figure out what always seemed to derail their relationship. He guessed that a lot had to do with plain stubbornness on both of their parts as well as an unwillingness to let the other one be. To Jeff it seemed like they tried to control each other too much. He was sure of that. It was easy now to say that he believed he could improve and handle the relationship better this time around, but he had believed that many times before, and yet somehow, it had never worked. What unknown force kept tearing them apart?

Jeff went down memory lane.

He could still remember the first breakup as if it had been yesterday. He had been so hurt by it. It came out of the blue. Just like that, everything changed. Angel called him on the phone from her parents' home in New Canaan the second week in January of 1988 and announced that she would not be coming back to Smith College, but rather that she was about to leave for a trip to Europe with some family friends. They would be going skiing in Switzerland and Austria, and she was going to stay in Europe for a couple of months. That was that. Distraught, frustrated, unwilling to explain herself, she finally hung up the phone, crying. There had been real fear in her voice when she exclaimed that she couldn't handle talking about it any longer. Jeff had been devastated.

To this day he did not understand her past actions and decisions. Stunned and overcome by despair, he had hung up the phone. It had taken him three long months to recover. Even today he still wanted her to explain why she had left and was actually afraid to breach the subject with her. With four long weeks ahead of them, Jeff hoped he could finally put this bad memory to rest. He hoped to have an opportunity to talk about what had really happened back then. He needed to understand. How else could he come to grips with the hurt of the past?

Chapter 18

Somewhere in Alaska

Tuesday, June 11 1995, 9:48 a.m.

"Angel, are you all set now? I want to get going!" Jeff's voice sounded irritated and impatient.

Angel called out from the back of the camper. "Yeah, hang on a sec! I can't find my favorite Strauss tapes!"

Jeff moaned, but Angel couldn't hear him. He was sitting in the driver's seat of the RV studying the roadmap. They had camped about 100 miles west of Watson Lake. It would have been easy to get to Rancheria last night. But Angel had stubbornly refused, insisting she couldn't stay one more minute on this utterly boring highway, and therefore they had to stop! Jeff had yielded because he had not been very keen on getting into another head-on collision with Angel. He had been tired and had wanted some peace. Also, he had been very hungry.

Jeff hoped that Whitehorse might offer the kind of amenities and fun adventures that could snap Angel out of her current slump. Over the last couple of days he had been wondering whether he shouldn't have just stayed home. She had complained incessantly about how boring it was to drive day after day while nothing ever seemed to change or happen and the landscape always looked the same. Two days ago they had discussed this dilemma at length while taking a breather from the endless driving she had complained about. It had given Jeff a chance to do some fishing, and he had looked forward to the adventure. But during their stopover Angel had declared that wasting a whole day on fishing was even worse than driving around in the middle of nowhere, yet she had no idea what it was she wanted to do instead of fishing! When driving at least one was moving forward, toward a goal, a target. What exactly did that mean? It had left Jeff clueless. When asked about what she had expected from the trip, Angel only replied, "Definitely not this!"

Jeff looked out toward the horizon. Another storm seemed to be heading their way. Far in the distance he could see a thick curtain of a dark ominous mass reaching from the depth of the sky all the way to the earth below. That had to be pouring rain, Jeff concluded. The clouds were letting off some of their heavy load before climbing the next mountain range.

Jeff turned his attention back to the map. His look was brooding and forlorn. It was 275 miles from Watson Lake to Whitehorse, and they were about 100 miles west of Watson Lake. They could be in Whitehorse around 2 p.m. Jeff's spirits picked up a little as he considered the possibility of stopping in Whitehorse. Maybe they could stay a couple of days and explore the entire surrounding area.

Time was no problem. They had been on the road for a week and had traveled roughly 1,400 miles. The distance from Whitehorse to Anchorage was only about another 800 miles. Jeff had already checked that out last night. He wondered whether Angel was ignoring the fact that they had planned to be on the road for four weeks. At their current pace they would be in Anchorage in three days. And then what? Of course, they could go to Fairbanks and stop at McKinley Park. He very much wanted to do that. It would certainly be helpful to discuss their options.

Jeff sighed. He was sure Angel would blow up if he suggested they explore Whitehorse over the next couple of days. He had learned the hard way that planning was definitely out and spontaneous responses were in. It's just that he still hadn't figured out how to adapt himself and put up with her impetuous ways. Why couldn't two intelligent people put their heads together and hatch out a plan that both parties liked? He didn't get it. But today was not the day to try and fail again! He had sensed tension in Angel's voice. He wanted no blow-ups today. He felt tired and weary.

"I found them!" Angel exclaimed from the back of the camper.

With a bunch of tapes and her Walkman in one hand and her favorite mug of coffee in the other, Angel made her way to the front of the RV and sat down.

Jeff was so annoyed and felt so out of sorts that he said, "Do you realize that you're always dragging your feet in the morning and it takes you forever to get set?"

Angel checked Jeff's face, looking for clues as to why he sounded so upset. He definitely looked down, yet she was cranky herself and felt feisty. She declared, "What is that supposed to mean? Are you upset about something? If so, just say so, but don't pick on me!"

Jeff's look softened a little as he replied, "I wasn't picking on you. I was just making a statement."

Angel wanted to make her position quite clear. Her voice was forceful and challenging. "Well, I don't want to hear about it, okay? What kind of crack was that, anyway?" His anger had made her defensive, and whenever she felt defensive, she responded by attacking.

Jeff was stubbornly pursuing what could only lead to more trouble. But why should he always give in? "Well, it is true, though, isn't it? You're in a bad mood again, aren't you?"

Angel's voice was rising. "No, I was not! But now I am! I hate it when you get this way!"

Jeff felt like saying "What way?" but decided to let it go. Instead he started the engine. This morning, while Angel was still asleep, he had taken a little walk into the fields next to the highway and had witnessed the most awesome sunrise. What a wonderful experience it had been! He had felt so good then. And now—just a couple of words and bang, the good feelings were gone. Just like that. He was angry at himself for not having acted upon his desire to wake Angel to experience the sunrise with him. He had missed her. He was convinced that if he had awakened her, the whole day would have been off to a better start for both of them.

But this argument was not over yet. Angel had more to get off her chest. "Well, if you have to know, yes, I *am* cranky! Actually, I'm bored to death! I'm sick of seeing nothing but this godforsaken hinterland!"

By now Jeff was determined to hold his own. "Why do you call it a hinterland? It's the Yukon Territory."

Angrily, Angel yelled, "Don't split hairs with me! To me it's a hinterland, okay! It's a hinterland because it feels like all civilized life as we know it has come to an end!"

Jeff paused for a moment. There was no turning back now. He had been here before. It was like getting on a carousel that kept going and going and didn't stop anymore. One lost all sense of being. Something took over. He heard himself saying, knowing this was *not* a wise response, "I see. So you're cranky because we're in the hinterland, and the hinterland makes you feel bored."

And here came the onslaught. The carousel was out of control again! "I didn't say 'bored.' Forget it, Jeff! And besides, by now hinterland has lost all its true meaning. And yes, if you have to know, you guessed right—I am *also* bored!"

Yet, Jeff kept going. He simply couldn't stop himself. "I thought we already discussed your boredom attacks two days ago."

By now hostility had crept into Angel's voice. "Don't you start again! I can't stand it! Yes, indeed, we did discuss my 'boredom attacks' *already*, as you put it! But who says that discussing something stops a feeling? I still *feel* bored—okay?!"

"So, what do you want me to do about it?" Jeff asked, and to himself he thought. "I'm an idiot, why can't I stop?"

"Why do you men always have to assume that just because women complain or get emotional, they want *you* to fix their lives? Who died and made you men king, anyway? I'd really like to know. What a ludicrous and ridiculous assumption, really!" Angel looked totally disgusted.

"What's that supposed to mean? Are you saying you hate all men?" Now Jeff was confused. Angel seemed to have switched tracks somewhere. This was way too abstract for him. Why couldn't she say what she meant?

"No, stop it! Don't always jump to conclusions! Remember, this discussion started when I said, 'I feel bored'! All I'm saying is that sometimes I just say something because I feel that way. That's all!"

"I don't get it. Are you bored, or aren't you?" Jeff was desperately looking for a way to reconnect.

Angel was exasperated by now, and with her voice rising even more, she exclaimed, "Jeff, stop it! This is going nowhere fast!" But her voice sounded less hostile and more resigned.

Now Jeff's face looked controlled and rigid. He was unable to sort out what he was really feeling, but he couldn't stop either and said, "So what else do you want to talk about?" His voice sounded bitter and full of resentment.

"Well, nothing really. That's why I brought my favorite tapes to the front. I want to drown myself in Johann Strauss music."

"Why?"

"Because!"

"Does that mean you don't know or you don't want to tell me?" Jeff felt abandoned. There was a pang of pain in his heart.

"Well, both, kind of." Angel had paid no attention to Jeff's feelings even though she could feel that he was quite upset. She was way too preoccupied with her own misery.

"Does that mean that I can't discuss Strauss music with you?" Jeff was looking for an opening. He was pleading now.

"No, it does not mean that!" Now Angel wished this discussion had never started in the first place.

"Then what does it mean?" Jeff's voice was very sad.

Angel felt Jeff's pain. She could no longer numb herself to it. But she didn't want to acquiesce, either. "It means that I just want to 'feel' for a while and not talk to you about my 'feelings.'"

"What's the difference?"

"Jeff, *you are driving me nuts!*"

Jeff stopped talking. He was too emotional to continue. Angel closed her eyes and listened to her music.

Jeff felt rejected and was deeply hurt. Why wouldn't Angel talk to him about how she really felt? Why did she always withdraw into her private sanctuary? He felt abandoned and misunderstood and believed that somehow he had failed.

Angel was far away—somewhere, transcended to a secret place of her own by her beloved music. Jeff was alone with his painful thoughts. He felt acute pain inside. He loved her;

he wanted to be with her. He wanted to share *everything* with her. He felt like she had closed the door on him and wouldn't let him in.

What if Angel decided to leave him again? Why was running away always her favorite response to her inability to cope with her emotions? After all, this trip had been her idea. Didn't that mean that she had made a commitment?

Jeff considered the pros and cons of their current dilemma. He had to be fair. There had been fantastic times as well. Angel was a lot of fun to be with, especially when she was in a good mood. Her energy was infectious. But loving her was like being stuck on a roller coaster ride that had never really been tested and could easily topple and crash into a whole array of unknowns. During those moments it felt like darkness was settling in all around him with all hope gone—forever. Jeff hated moments like these.

They had taken it easy and had never gone more than 350 miles in a day. It was true that some days had been kind of boring, with nothing much to see but the same old scenery all over again. Angel was right. They had made one-day stops in three locations. Jeff had done some fishing—and Angel had done her complaining. That's when her boredom attacks had started to impact their relationship. She also hated all the mosquitoes. Well, Jeff thought angrily, that's what the wilderness was all about, right?

Only two days ago Angel and Jeff had discussed what was "real" wilderness and what wasn't. Jeff still didn't understand what kind of wilderness Angel was looking for. Why was she always looking for something that didn't seem to exist? And why did she love Johann Strauss music so much and why wouldn't she share with him what the music meant to her?

About thirty minutes went by, and neither of them had said anything at all.

Suddenly, "Hey, Jeff! I got a great idea!"

Jeff's first reaction was deep concern and apprehension. Angel would want to find the next airport, he was sure. No, maybe not. Her voice was upbeat and excited. Her face seemed to be glowing; her eyes were sparkling. Is this how the music could transform her? It couldn't be. Or could it?

"When I was in Innsbruck I met a gal, her name is Connie, who used to work on one of the cruise liners. You know the ones that sail the Inside Passage to Alaska. When I met her she was visiting family in Austria. She was about to start her new job in Skagway, doing special tours for the tourists from the cruise ships. Anyway, the job involves showing them around, dressed in historical costumes of the Gold Rush days, stuff like that. She said they act out certain scenes from the past. Exciting, don't you think? Anyway, I want to look her up. Let's stop in Skagway! How much farther till Skagway? It's not too far from here, is it?"

What about my ideas about Whitehorse, Jeff thought? "But you don't even know for sure whether she took that job, do you? Wouldn't we be wasting our time trying to find her?"

"So what if she isn't there? It would still be fun looking for her. And besides, we could explore Skagway. Don't you want to? Skagway is famous because of the Klondike Gold Rush. I am sure you know when that was. I never try to remember specifics."

Jeff felt on safer ground again. "The Klondike Gold Rush was around the turn of the century. But Skagway is not on our route. And besides, since when are you interested in anything that has to do with history?"

"Who says I'm not interested in history? It all depends on whether I get curious about a specific subject. Like, what does it trigger inside of me, what does it remind me of. Stuff like that. Then I get really excited about history! And why wouldn't Skagway be on our route? What is? Nothing really, unless we decide we want to see it, right?"

Oh, no, here we go again, Jeff thought. "I see. Does that mean that I have the same rights you claim for yourself? Let's say I get curious or excited about a place. Would you go with me?"

"Well, it all depends. Not if I think it's boring!" Angel was convinced that hers was *not* a selfish attitude. Because, after all, boredom was the worst thing that could happy to any human being, right?

"But doesn't that mean that you have a double standard?" How could anybody be so selfish, Jeff wondered.

"Gee, Jeff, really! Don't you get it yet? I just want to have fun! Don't you want to have fun? Going off the beaten track and trying to find somebody sounds like a lot of fun to me. That's all."

Jeff decided that this was definitely *not* the time to bring up Whitehorse and why he would consider it fun to stop there for a couple of days. Instead he stayed on the

Skagway track. "How could it be fun if you don't know for sure whether your friend is in Skagway? And how good a friend is she? You never really get close to anybody because you always insist on 'doing your own thing.'"

"Jeff, stop it. I can't stand this anymore!" Angel looked quite angry again. After looking at Jeff's face she softened a little, "Jeff, please . . . don't sulk again. I can't stand it when you get this way!"

Jeff's face looked tense. His jaws were tightly clenched. Anger was slowly rising inside of him. "Well, Angel, what do you expect? Is there anything about me that doesn't bother and irritate you? What's wrong with asking questions when I don't understand something?"

Angel's face looked sad and gentle. Her emotions could change very rapidly. She hadn't meant to hurt Jeff. She didn't understand why he always got so hurt when she behaved in a certain way. Now her voice was intense, imploring, soliciting, and pleading for understanding. "It's just that I don't like to give an account of why I feel a certain way and why I don't want to talk about it. That's all it is. Not more than that. It's just scary. It has nothing to do with you." There seemed to be a faint tremble in her voice.

But Jeff was stuck on his course. "And here I thought that we had decided before the trip that we wanted to learn how to get closer to each other. How can we if you won't even tell me how you feel?"

Angel had turned off her tape. Suddenly her face looked distraught and full of anguish. Her eyes had a dull and blank look, as if seeing nothing at all. Jeff could only guess at what might be going on inside of her. He had seen her like this before. She was in pain. Now he felt even worse. It was all his fault! Why hadn't he been able to stop before it got to this point?

"Angel, I love you! Doesn't that count for anything?" Jeff's voice was very soft and anxious. He couldn't stand the thought of losing her again.

Angel was still staring straight ahead, focusing her blank stare down the long forlorn highway. The words came slowly and hesitantly. She seemed to be groping for a way to express herself. "Yes, I know you do. But this doesn't have anything to do with you. It's all about me. I don't like to share those feelings. And I know that I'm not being fair, and it does mean that I'm not giving my all to the relationship. I want to, but something always seems to hold me back. I'm trying, I really am. Couldn't we just leave it at that, please?" Her face expressed great anxiety and tension.

Jeff thought for a couple of minutes. He felt great sadness and pain emanating from Angel. A cold mysterious vapor, possibly even poisonous, seemed to have enveloped her entire being. Could this vapor kill their relationship, their love? This was a do-or-die situation. Jeff felt it. While keeping an eye on the road, he intently watched her face for any outside signs of her inner feelings of despair. "Is it because of this 'feeling' you just described that you always chose to run away from me before?"

"Yes." Angel's voice was so low that Jeff had trouble hearing her over the noise of the engine. Her face was an expressionless, lifeless mask. This lifelessness was intensified by a voice void of intonation and inflection. "I love the Strauss operettas and Beethoven's Fifth because the music is so intense that it becomes a bridge to my own intense emotions. When the two forces merge I feel free, released, bursting forth, liberated from all constraints and restrictions, transported to a special place in time and space. I long to share this feeling with you, Jeff, I really do. But I just don't know how, at least not yet. Does that make any sense?"

"Is it okay if I say not really?" Jeff ventured.

Angel's voice was becoming more lifelike again, but still lacked hopefulness. She continued, "Yes, it's okay, because I know that it doesn't make sense to you. Of all the people I have known, you're the only one I've ever longed to share these kind of feelings with. I'm sure to you it seems like I don't want to."

Jeff was stunned and totally speechless. Angel finally shared herself and he felt even more confused. Why did life have to be so complicated?

"It's okay, Jeff. I have to work this out on my own. I can't really expect you to understand my innermost feelings. I myself struggle to describe them and, more importantly, understand them or make sense out of them. Over time I'll get better at sharing myself. I know I will. Just give me time! In the meantime I won't give up trying to share myself, okay? And that's a promise! Do you believe me? Can you wait and be patient?" Now Angel was pleading.

Jeff was too overwhelmed to say anything. He was frightened, too, though he didn't understand why.

Now Angel's voice was almost back to normal, though Jeff was convinced that it was a little bit of an act on her part. "How about I share my music with you? Like, instead of listening to it on my earphones, I'll put it into the tape recorder. That would be a good start, don't you think?"

Angel unbuckled her seatbelt, raised herself halfway out of her seat, bending way over to the driver's seat. She somehow managed to put her arms around Jeff, hugging him without causing him to lose control of the steering wheel.

"Angel, I told you before, doing this could be dangerous!" Jeff stiffened up. Maybe he was not really ready to be hugged. There was still too much pain.

"I know. And I don't care! I'm showing my feelings!"

The old zest was back in Angel's voice, but Jeff still wondered a little bit if it was real, or whether she was trying to convince herself that everything was just fine. Next thing he knew the music of Strauss was blasting at full force throughout the RV while Angel was singing along, in German, at the top of her lungs. He had forgotten that she was fluent in German since staying in Austria for several years.

A couple of minutes later, interrupting her singing and pointing toward the oncoming storm, Angel exclaimed, "Wow, look at those storm clouds moving toward us. I bet the storm will be on us any moment now. Did you feel that gust of wind? It even shook the RV! And look, there, there! Can you see it? There's a beautiful rainbow! Wow, look at those colors! I love rainbows, don't you? They seem like a promise, a glorious promise of things to come . . ."

Jeff nodded. He had been aware of the weather changes. They could be in for another one of those sudden downpours. Weather seemed to change fast around these parts.

"Stop, stop! Right here! *Now!*" Angel exclaimed.

Jeff did, more a reflex than a conscious act.

Without waiting for the RV to come to a full and safe stop, Angel had jumped out and started to run. Suddenly she turned around, just as Jeff had safely parked the camper and was about to follow her.

With a voice full of exuberance and ecstasy Angel declared, "If you want to know what the Johann Strauss music means to me, it's this!"

Angel spread out her arms as far as they would go, swaying from side to side as if wanting to embrace the drama around her. "Can you feel it? It's right here, all around us! I'm one with the elements, the wind is taking me, and I no longer have a will of my own! It feels wonderful! I'm *free!*"

A sudden gust caused Angel to lose her balance, and she almost fell to the ground but was able to catch herself. Turning her back to Jeff, she ran into the wind. Jeff suddenly had the curious notion that the wind was embracing her, welcoming her. A flash of insight told him, "The wind has been waiting for her, to release her of what has been holding her back."

Angel turned once more. "See that rainbow? I'm running into the rainbow, and when I get there I'll let myself fall into it."

Jeff watched and felt far away. He was cut off from Angel, lonely, isolated, abandoned. He wanted to join her, be with her now. He wanted to feel what she felt, experience what she experienced. He stepped into the open field and suddenly cried out with pain. He had stepped into a small ditch and had lost his footing! His right ankle really hurt. He hoped he hadn't sprained it. In the field beyond he could hardly recognize Angel, who was still moving forward as fast as the strong currents of the wind allowed. Suddenly the rain intensified. It was pouring now. Angel didn't seem to notice.

Uttering a long and lonely wail, Jeff let himself fall down into the ditch. A cold, clammy wetness slowly penetrated his sweatshirt.

Full of despair and grief, Jeff wondered, "Why can't I join Angel?"

Chapter 19

A Weekend in Seattle

Sunday Evening, July 2, 1995, at the Inn at the Market

"I just loved that place we just ate at, didn't you?" Angel was upbeat and excited as she threw down her jacket and headed for the cozy sofa in their suite.

"You know, I have to hand it to you. You've been a really good sport about all the things I've put you through."

Jeff grinned. He, too, was in a good mood. "That's for sure," he replied, sitting down in the chair next to the sofa. Angel had stretched herself out, and there was no room left for him next to her.

Looking content and happy, Angel asked, "So what do you want to do tomorrow, before we fly back to San Francisco on the Fourth?"

"If you think I'm going to say anything at all after all the outrageous surprises you've sprung on me during this trip, you're quite mistaken." Jeff pretended to be all serious and made his voice sound stern and strict. Just as Angel was about to open her mouth to ward off his apparent criticism, a broad grin appeared on his face.

"Oh, now I see! You're just giving me a hard time! Okay, okay, you're right. I can't blame you for wanting to pay me back for what I've done to you! There you were, at the airport in Anchorage, expecting to fly directly to San Francisco, and instead I wheel you off to Seattle!

"And that was only the beginning. I should really pity you! You should have seen the look on your face when you walked in this afternoon, as the bellboy opened the door to the suite. What a shock it must have been for you! For a second there I thought that you were going to have a fit! So what happened? Why didn't you fuss and lecture me about my foolish ways of lavishly spending my money on you?"

"Oh, I realized that this is your way of showing me that you care and that you just want to have a good time with me and, most importantly, that you love to celebrate. And I do feel like celebrating myself. In spite of some of the rough times we had, I really enjoyed this trip!"

"Really? You mean it? You're not just saying that?"

"Yes, I mean it."

"Oh, Jeff." With that Angel got up and threw herself onto Jeff's lap and kissed his face all over in a flood of unrestrained affection. Jeff played along, feigning suffocation by desperately moving his arms and legs in the air. She finally stopped. Jeff laughed happily. He loved to see her happy like this. He thought, "If only we could have been this happy all the time during the trip."

Unfortunately this had not been the case. Sometimes it had taken a while to work through respective depressed moods· caused by each of them feeling rejected by the other. A whole day would go by when one or both of them withdrew and sulked for a while, licking their wounds. Angel had usually been the one ready to make up and let bygones be bygones. Jeff was thankful for this characteristic of hers. It was a lot harder for him to do so. He didn't know why. It just was.

All in all, though, it had been a good trip. They certainly knew more about each other now than ever before. It had also been a time of bonding. The toughest part had been Angel's boredom attacks, as Jeff called them. In the end he let her deal with her boredom on her own and tried hard not to feel responsible for her moods. But it helped to be open to whatever she wanted to do next and to not question her sudden spontaneous ideas or ask for reasons for them. The experience of spraining his ankle and falling in the ditch, as Angel ran off into the rainbow, had taught him a lot. It had taken him days to get over feeling rejected and left out. He still didn't like thinking about that entire experience. He felt odd about it.

The other disappointment had been that Angel had not been receptive to exploring what Jeff defined as "unresolved issues of the past." He so much wanted to understand why she had run away so many times. He had been apprehensive about pressing the point. To be honest, he had been too chicken! He didn't want to deal with how she might react if he seriously pursued the past. Angel always said that what was gone was gone. To emphasize her point she would add, "No use crying over spilled milk." There was a lot of truth to this statement, yet sometimes he wondered if this wasn't just an excuse to ignore what she didn't want to be reminded of. She always talked about learning from past experiences. Didn't that mean that she thought about the past? He was certain that she was hiding or avoiding something she didn't want to deal with.

Jeff himself could never quite let go of the past until it was resolved. For him this meant open issues had to be addressed and examined, and one had to come to some kind of rational conclusion. There might be no good resolve, but at least there would be closure. Maybe their relationship could work itself out in the end, but somehow Jeff doubted it. Suddenly Jeff didn't feel so good anymore. Now there was a real ache inside of him.

Angel interrupted Jeff's gloomy thoughts by exclaiming, "I love you, love you, love you! You know that, don't you?" Again she covered his face with affectionate kisses.

"Yes, I do." Jeff tried to forget the gloominess he had felt a moment ago, but he couldn't quite shake it off.

"Oh, come on, let's curl up on the sofa. There's not enough room on the chair for both of us to be comfortable."

Jeff followed Angel to the sofa and sat down. She stretched out, using his lap as a pillow, looking up at him while talking. He ran his fingers through her curly hair.

"You know, I want to talk to you." Angel was examining Jeff closely.

"I figured that." The uneasiness inside of Jeff intensified.

"Before this trip is over I need to understand why you want to work at Atlas."

Jeff's entire body tensed up, and a pained look settled on his face. He thought, "Why couldn't she leave this alone?" They had been over this again and again, yet, Angel couldn't let it rest. Jeff didn't want to ruin this evening or their last two days together. He already felt sad each time he realized that pretty soon they would have to part and go their separate ways for a while. Talking about his upcoming job was going to ruin everything. He just knew it!

Though Jeff was quiet and had not responded, Angel didn't seem to want to pay attention to how he felt and continued, "The way I see it, you have this great invention, which you expect to finalize over the next couple of months. You even have enough money from the settlement with Safe Systems, which means you *don't* have to earn money while you work on your own invention. You could finish your invention sooner if you didn't work because you would have more time. Can you *please* tell me *why* you want to work at Atlas?"

Jeff sighed and then replied, "We've been through this before. You know my position. You disagree with it, and that's okay. I can understand that." Anger was rising inside of Jeff. Why couldn't she leave him alone? Why did she always have to pressure him? Losing control he said, "Oh, yeah, so you think I do dumb things? What about you? How do you explain having run off so many times in your life, leaving everybody and everything behind? How about that?" As soon as the words were out he regretted them. He had moved away from Angel to be alone at the other end of the sofa.

Angel remained calm. She had expected this. "That's a low blow, and you know it. But I deserve it. I asked for this discussion, and I'm a big girl now, and I can handle it. You're right. I, too, have done many foolish things, and to tell you the truth, if I had a chance to go back, I would *not* repeat many of my earlier choices and decisions. That's exactly my point, though. Today, in hindsight, I can see how it actually harmed me as well as those close to me. And that's why it hurts me so much to see you do this to yourself."

Jeff was not to be assuaged. There was still a lot of anger in his voice. "As you pointed out, you see that *now*, because you made those earlier choices, which you would not repeat today. Let's assume you're correct and my going to Atlas would turn out to be bad for me. Then, according to your logic, I wouldn't really know that till *after* I had made that choice and lived through it, right? I know that you mean well. However, *your* mistakes can't save *me*. I have to take my own lickings and beatings in life. All I know is that I just have to do this. That's all there is to it!"

There was a strong sense of finality in Jeff's voice, but Angel was not about to give up so soon.

"No, that's *not* the point! The real issue is that you're about to do something that's very stupid and won't lead to anything good. I just feel it."

"If we keep going on like this, you know that it will ruin the rest of our time together, don't you?"

"Yes, I *do* know that, but I also know that I can't live with myself if I don't bring it up. If you won't listen to me, then at least I need to understand *why* you've decided to work at Atlas. And I'm not interested in the rationale behind your decision. I want to know why you're out for revenge and most importantly, why you want to experience the satisfaction of having revenged yourself, because that's all it is. You know that, don't you?"

"There, you did what you do so frequently. You decided to generalize and as a result concluded that, according to your interpretation of my emotions, I'm just taking revenge. I'm willing to say that you believe this to be true. But your perception is not my perception. So I couldn't possibly come to the same conclusion, could I? That wouldn't be logical, would it? Because frankly I don't see the situation the way you do."

Now they were two fighters engaged in close combat. Totally exasperated, gesticulating madly with her arms, Angel had sat up. She no longer felt cozy and comfortable. Rather she was close to despair. She didn't quite know why, but she was full of bad premonitions about Jeff going to Atlas. Looking right at Jeff with a face full of pain and agony, she exclaimed, keeping her voice low and flat, sounding lifeless, "How can you *not* see it the way I do?"

"Angel, we keep talking in circles. It doesn't do any good."

Angel knew that it was useless to go on from here, yet the fear she felt inside made her heart beat rapidly and she felt so scared and lonely and abandoned. Why did she feel this cold naked fear inside? What was happening to them? Trying to get hold of herself, she finally said, "Fine, then please explain to me one more time, what are you trying to accomplish at Atlas?" She was hoping that Jeff might just add something else to his story, something that would convince her that everything was okay after all. She wanted to be convinced.

Jeff looked resigned. They had been over this again and again for the last week or so. It had started as the trip was winding down. The reality of life after the trip was encroaching and taking over. They simply could not see eye to eye, yet Angel would not leave it alone, in spite of what he had tried to explain.

"Will you promise me to listen and not interrupt all the time?"

"Gee, now you're even beginning to sound like my father." Angel momentarily turned her head away from Jeff, staring into empty space. Her face looked sad and very depressed.

"Angel, please . . ."

"Okay, okay! I *will* listen and *won't* interrupt!"

"Call me stupid, call me silly, call me revengeful. You're entitled to your opinion. But you need to understand how upset I am by what Loren Grimm has done to me. I know you believe that this was all settled a couple of months ago when Safe Systems paid me for my intellectual property.

And yes, $250,000 is a lot of money. But nobody ever stated clearly that Loren Grimm had stolen this code from me. As far as I'm concerned, the payoff did not settle the real issue. For me this is a question of justice, and as far as I'm concerned, justice was not served. I didn't want the money. I had wanted to take the matter to court. To me it means that I lost! I had wanted Loren Grimm convicted of his wrongdoing, in court, out in the open, in order to put an end to his shenanigans. He's a creep, and I'm convinced he's only too likely to steal somebody else's code again!

"Unfortunately, at the time Carl Walter, the president of Safe Systems, didn't find my evidence convincing enough, and most of all he didn't want the story to be publicized. The settlement was the only option I had that validated, at least within Safe Systems, that Loren Grimm had been involved in stealing intellectual property. According to Carl my proof would not have held up in the courts, so I gave in. There were moments when I actually felt humiliated. It was as if *I* had done something wrong, *not* Loren Grimm! Things were all upside down.

"I was also upset that Safe Systems simply paid me off and thought that payment would settle everything. How could it?" By now Jeff looked quite distraught.

"May I say something?" Angel asked carefully.

"Okay, but I wasn't done."

"Fine, go on then."

"So, you see, for me a lot is at stake here. Mostly it's a question of justice. I want to fight for what I believe in. That's all! And let's face it, you would fight, too. I have no proof, but I'm convinced that Loren Grimm will try to screw somebody else—again. He could do it at Atlas, or wherever else he might be in the future. He's always trying to get the most out of everything and always for himself. He exploits people. That's just the way Loren is. And I want to stop him, once and for all. I know that you believe that this is none of my business, and I can see why you believe that. But that's not how I look at it. Furthermore, I'm not joining Atlas just because of Loren. I'm also excited about the project they want me to work on. As you know, I haven't decided yet what to do with my invention. Maybe Atlas is the kind of company that would be interested in using my invention for the purposes I believe it should be used. So, you could say, I'm also testing the waters at Atlas. I want to get to know them, and I want to check out whether Atlas could make good use of my invention.

"So, call me stupid or paranoid, or whatever, but since Loren left Safe Systems last January I've been convinced that ultimately he will do to somebody else what he has done to me, and I just want to stop it. Okay? That's all there is to it! And—you can talk now!"

Angel had listened intently and patiently. This would be her last attempt. After this she would give up.

"Jeff, again and again you tell me that I'm just being emotional about this or that, and you're right. I frequently am quite emotional and let my emotions impact my decisions. My point is, if you're so good at assessing my behavior, then why can't you see that you're letting your emotions rule you as far as Loren Grimm is concerned?"

Jeff looked away and tensed up even more. Angel knew it was useless to go on. But she just had to find out how Jeff's time at Atlas might impact their life and their future together.

"Well, Angel, you of all people should know that it's a lot easier to see other people as they really are than it is to become aware of the truth about yourself. One of your favorite quotes is 'nobody can jump their own shadow.' Well, what it means, that I can't see what you see. I can't jump my own shadow. The shadow and I are one. I am not able to see my shadow separately. Every time I move, the shadow moves, so, it can't be jumped! That's just the way it is."

Angel knew that she had tried in vain. There was an iron-clad finality in Jeff's words. Numbness was settling in, and she was very scared. It felt like somebody was trying to pull the rug out from under her. Her attempt to stop Jeff had failed. But, no, she couldn't give up. She had to try something, anything. She had to get to some safe ground somehow. It was imperative! To give herself and Jeff time to recover from the intensity of their emotions, she switched the subject to the practical implications of Jeff's move to Atlas. She was hoping that her fear could be controlled by talking about facts and reality.

"So, basically you will stay at Atlas how long?" Angel's voice was shaking a little. She was trying very hard to gain control.

Jeff was too wrapped up in his own feelings to notice Angel's. "Well, I don't really know yet. It all depends on what's going on at Atlas and what Loren is involved in now."

"Please try to be a little more specific. It's very important to me, actually for both of us. A couple of months is how long? Till September, October, or what?"

"Oh, I figure till October or November, but I can't really tell."

"And once you leave Atlas you would be willing to explore our relationship more seriously, and I'm rephrasing what you told me a couple of nights ago when I told you that I would quit my job right now in order to just be with you, and I even suggested we should take the plunge and get married."

Now Jeff realized that this whole scene had been about them, about their future, about possibly getting married. Why couldn't women simply state what they really meant? This was so frustrating! Jeff responded, "Angel, I really can't deal with this subject of yours right now. You know that I love you. And yes, I want to get married down the road. I'm committed to that. But I can't really make that kind of a decision right now. Please give me a couple of months. Please understand, okay?"

"What else can I do? You've left me no other choice! Sure, I could run away again, but I don't want to do that anymore. I have learned that in the end I have to face what I am running away from, anyway and by that time it's often more of a mess than before. Also, somehow it hurts a lot more when you realize what an idiot you've been. Anyway, I think there is a perfectionist in all of us. We just hate to find out that we've been stupid and all wrong about our choices!"

Jeff was getting confused. He no longer understood what Angel was really talking about. He asked, "But aren't you running away again by taking this silly job at that travel agency, which will take you away from me and prevent us from being together for long stretches of time?"

"That hurts, really hurts, and you know it!" Despair had overtaken Angel by now, yet Jeff had no idea what was going on.

Jeff felt apprehensive and had become stubborn because Angel had insisted that he see his decision her way, but he hadn't meant to hurt her, and so he said, "Yes, you're right. I lashed out. But I'm feeling lousy right now."

By now Angel knew that she was fighting a lost cause and wished the conversation could just end without further repercussions. Yet she heard herself saying, "Feeling lousy does not entitle you to let your mood out on me and to get on my case again, does it? I'll tell you why I'm joining that 'silly travel agency,' as you call it, even though I don't really feel like explaining it anymore. I'm going because staying here and having to watch what you're doing to yourself is much worse. I wouldn't be able to handle that. So, strictly speaking, I'm running away from the frustration and pain I'm sure are going to come my way. You're right, I am running away again. But let's face it. You wouldn't have much time for me and our relationship anyway. For you it's all black and white. Right now, you don't want to deal with our relationship, so you want to put me on hold. Well, I don't like to be put on hold. I can't live that way. I am a breathing, living creature with many needs and hopes and dreams, and unlike you I'm not able to put all of those feelings on hold for a while."

Shocked, Jeff replied, "But I'm not asking you to put those feelings on hold." He was getting increasingly confused.

"I know that you don't see it that way, but for me, that's what it boils down to. That's what it feels like to me. You want me to wait till October or November before you seriously want to consider what I would like you to do now.

"It's probably just water under the bridge anyway and a waste of time. But I had another reason for wanting to stop over in Seattle. You always call me manipulative when I come up with such ideas, and you call my ideas schemes. However, to me they're not schemes. They are just ideas. Crazy ones maybe, but still, they are my ideas! Also, I don't think I'm being manipulative, because in the end I always let you in on my ideas. Granted, I try to persuade you to see it my way first before sharing my ideas. But I would never force you into anything you wouldn't want to do!

"Anyway, I'll just say it now and get it over with. Otherwise it's going to haunt me down the road. and I might blame myself for not having talked about it earlier. I wanted you to consider leaving Silicon Valley and moving with me to Seattle. It would be a totally new place for both of us. A great way to start all over, you and me, making a home, a life and a future for ourselves! Of course that would work only if you were content to just work on your invention. And you now told me you would not find that very appealing. So forget my stupid scheme."

Angel was terribly depressed by now. All life had gone out of her. There was no trace of the earlier joy and exuberance she had felt. There was no more hope.

Jeff was quiet. He felt boxed in. He could not do what Angel asked him to do.

Angel continued, her voice low and dull, seemingly without any feelings, "I know you can't see my point. And that's what's upsetting me the most. There's even more I want to get off my chest. Right now I feel like I have nothing to lose, even if you end up getting even more upset.

"Remember when we left Vancouver that morning, at the beginning of our trip, and I suddenly got all upset and said I had had a bad dream? Well, I've had this same dream several times during our trip, and I just don't seem to be able to shake it off. I know you don't really believe in intuition and dreams the way I do. But I do. I spend time trying to understand what the dreams might say. I've learned a lot from my dreams. They've helped me to work through some difficult situations, like the death of my grandfather. I start looking for clues in the real world to see if something reminds me of what a dream seems to have expressed in a symbolic way. Dreams symbolize unknown and frequently intimidating and scary situations and aspects of our inner life. Most of the time I don't really want to deal with the dreams' messages. But once I'm willing to dig into their meaning, it often turns out to be quite beneficial and helpful.

"Anyway, here is the dream:

I'm somewhere in the vast wilderness of Russia. It might be Siberia. It is cold, lonely. I don't know how I got there. I feel like a captive, almost like a prisoner. Then I realize that I am not alone. You are there, too. We are looking for a way out of Siberia. We are trying to find a train that will take us out of there, away from the wilderness, away from captivity. To get away we need to get to Moscow first. Our journey can continue only once we have reached Moscow. I feel horrible dread and anxiety, but I don't know why.

Suddenly the scene changes. I start to feel a little better. I realize that we have actually made it to a train station and are now staying at a hotel waiting to take the next train to Moscow. It is supposed to leave the next morning. Again the dream stresses that we have to get to Moscow first before we can head for our real destination. I start to wonder in the dream what our real destination is. I can't figure it out, and it bothers me.

Somehow there was a mix-up of rooms at the hotel where we are staying. Our room is connected with the room of another group of people. These people are quite rowdy. They are having some wild party. They are drinking and seem to be quite out of control. Suddenly I realize that you want to be with them.

This scares me, though I don't know why. I try to keep you away from them. But no matter what I do, their hold on you is stronger and more powerful than mine.

Again I feel trapped. It is hopeless. I am a captive of the circumstances, and I don't know what to do. I am afraid that by now my chance of regaining freedom is gone. Instead I will remain in captivity forever and will

have to go back to where I came from, meaning the hinterland, or Siberia, or whatever that place is. All I know for
sure is that it is a place of captivity.

This realization makes me want to fight for my freedom. I seem to have a clear choice between freedom and
captivity. I don't want to be a captive any longer. There is a
moment in the dream when I seem to be engaged in a real
physical fight with these horrible people. I don't know how
it happened, but I know that as a result of this fight everyone involved in the fight falls into the 'underground,'
including myself. In the dream I know that it is the 'underground,' though I can't understand what that means. But it
turns out to be a real place, right underneath the hotel,
like a cellar. The group, you and I, we all fall through the
floor to this 'underground.'

The horrible experience of falling into the 'underground' finally gives me the strength and energy to
pack up my things in order to get out of there. I have
to get out of there, with or without you. I simply have
to. I am now willing to take the train without you.

Then I realize that you seem to be suffering from a
hangover, caused by partying with those horrible
people. Having been with those people seems to have
impacted you. Then you tell me that you, too, want to
get out of there. I am surprised and not sure if I can
believe you. Earlier on you did not want to leave.
Though it is a struggle, due to your horrible hangover,
we manage to get to the train station. You want to get
on a particular train, one that doesn't seem right to
me. I am sure that this particular train will not get us
to Moscow. I decide to ask somebody about the train you
want to take. Sure enough, I learn that it is heading in the
opposite direction. It would take us back to where we

came from! Full of fear of not making it out of captivity, I ask which train goes to Moscow. I am told that we have to take a train ready to take off momentarily from a track way in the back of the station. So, as fast as we can, we get out of the first train we had boarded and we run to catch the train we really want.

Just as we are getting to the right train and are about to climb in, you realize that you have forgotten something on the first train. I don't know what exactly. It seems to be a suitcase. Though you realize that you might miss the train, you still decide to run back to get your suitcase. Full of terror, I keep telling you that we don't need that suitcase, or whatever it is. All I want for us is to get out of there. For so long I had waited for this moment. For so long I had been held captive. But you insist.

"At this point in the dream I always wake up full of dread."

Angel started crying. She couldn't control herself. She had a horrible sense of finality about something. With tears flooding down her face, she said, "Can you see what this could mean? What if there is no future for you and me? The dream doesn't seem to have an end. I don't know whether you missed the train. What if I had to leave without you? Something dreadful and horrible is about to happen. I feel it. I had hoped that if I could talk you into leaving Silicon Valley, it would mean that you did not miss the train, and we could be happy together in Seattle. Now I have no hope."

Angel sobbed terribly.

Jeff took her in his arms. No, he couldn't see, nor did he understand. Applying the dream situation to their real life made no sense at all. What could the dream possibly have to do with his decision to work at Atlas? Jeff was dumbfounded. But this was not the time to ask Angel why she felt the way she did. She was in despair, and Jeff felt lost and sad. What was he to do?

Chapter 20

News About Loren Grimm

Wednesday morning, October 11, 1995, 11:37 a.m.

The phone rang, and this time Brian picked it up. Michelle had made him feel guilty. The ringing phone also reminded him that he had not yet checked his voicemail messages this morning.

"Brian here."

"This is Lieutenant Woodraw. Hi, how are you today?"

"Just fine, thank you. I had actually thought about calling you."

"Well, here I am. How can I be of assistance?"

"Ahh . . ."

Brian hesitated, unsure about what to do next and how to go about it.

Though the lieutenant sensed Brian's hesitation, she chose to get on with her business and figured this would give Brian time to come around. Without any further ado she said, "I am calling to apologize for a blunder on the part of the department. Due to a miscommunication, you have not yet been informed that your protection actually started this morning. I wanted to let you know that you can rest assured now that your movements outside of Atlas will be monitored at all times. We will also have somebody watching your apartment at night.

"After careful consideration as well as discussions with the head of human resources at Atlas, we decided, for now at least, to limit your protection to outside of Atlas. The human resources manager believes that it would be too disruptive to the work environment if somebody were with you at all times. Since Atlas has security people on site as well as carefully monitored access doors, the risk inside the company is minimal indeed. We've been assured that internal security at Atlas has been increased.

"I hope that you feel comfortable and reassured about the steps we've taken. Again, I apologize that you were not informed earlier about the status of your protection."

"Oh, that's okay. As long as I know now. That's really all that matters." Brian's mind was focused not so much on what the lieutenant had said as on how to ease his way into discussing the subject of Loren and Loren's past. Brian certainly did not want to sound like a foolish busybody.

"So, what was it that you had wanted to call me about?"

Still feeling quite uncomfortable in the role of providing information of such a sensitive nature, and especially in light of the fact that the information was mostly based on hearsay and speculation on the part of various individuals, Brian nonetheless managed to convey the whole story about Safe Systems, Jeff and Loren and possible implications. He concentrated on keeping speculation to a minimum. The main point was to let the police know that Loren Grimm and Jeff Williams had both worked at Safe Systems, possibly during the same time period. Brian related that Loren Grimm had joined Atlas before Jeff, in January 1995. Jeff had joined Atlas several months later, in July. In addition, Brian highlighted the contents of the email message from Ray Beachwood and how significant it might be that Loren and Jeff had worked at Safe Systems during a particular time frame. To learn more and to verify the meaning and implications of Ray's email, the police would have to talk to Ray personally.

Lieutenant Woodraw remained calm. This helped Brian to get over his initial awkwardness. She didn't respond till Brian had concluded his story.

"I agree with you that this is indeed very important information. We have some leads, but so far we've not been able to substantiate any of them, nor have we been able to link what we do have to an overall theme or motive. Where Jeff Williams used to work and for how long and who else was there at the same time are important facts. Do you believe that Loren Grimm might be connected to the murder?"

"Oh, no, I'm sorry! I didn't mean to implicate Loren Grimm!" Brian was mortified.

"I'm not saying that you did." As usual Lieutenant Woodraw remained unruffled.

Brian thought to himself she must have been able to pick up that he didn't like Loren very much. Well, that was okay, because, after all, it was true.

The lieutenant continued, "We'll definitely get in touch with Safe Systems, as well as Ray Beachwood. We've had some contact with members of Jeff Williams' family. They too talked about the young woman referred to in the email you mentioned. We have not been able to locate her yet. She seems to be traveling and is not expected back in the San Francisco Bay Area till October 15.

"So, thanks again for all your cooperation and assistance, and don't hesitate to call me about any further information or concerns."

"Yes, thanks. I will." Brian had broken out into a cold sweat. He hated situations like the one he had just survived and felt terribly uncomfortable. Again he wished he had never gotten involved in this entire mess in the first place. He was drained even though the phone call had been a lot easier than he had anticipated. However, he also had a sense of having accomplished something special, something he had never dared to tackle. In a strange way this actually made him feel good. There were two conflicting feelings inside of him, and Brian couldn't quite bring them into a desired symmetry. He wondered, how he could feel bad *and* good about the same issue.

Well, no more playing detective. Work was calling. But first just one quick thank you note to Ray, informing him that the police might contact him. Brian promised Ray that he would be in touch in case of any new developments. After that it was back to work, and work only!

Brian looked at his watch. He wouldn't be able to go out for lunch after all. Too much time had been wasted already this morning, and by now it was 12:17 p.m. Besides, he wasn't hungry yet. That was good. He would check the break room later on to see if there might be some leftover food from somebody's luncheon. If not, he would get by on a couple of snacks from the snack machine till later in the afternoon. Possibly he could still run out and grab a sandwich at some deli. Well, no, he had forgotten. Somebody would be following him. What a pain! To be "under protection" would certainly influence what he would do and how he would act. Brian felt distraught. Well, that took care of one decision. He would stay inside the building and settle for something from the snack machine.

What next? Oh, yes, the voicemail messages. Brian picked up the phone. There were twelve messages. He sighed. The last one was from Michelle.

"Call me right away! I want to meet with you off campus. Can't talk about it here!"

Now what? So much for good intentions. This probably meant playing detective again.

Brian rang Michelle's number.

"Hi, it's Michelle!"

"It's Brian, you left . . ."

Before Brian could finish his sentence, Michelle jumped in and interrupted him.

"Oh, great! You actually called me! I only left the voicemail because I didn't have time to stop by."

Michelle lowered her voice and whispered, communicating a high degree of conspiracy, "I got the scoop on Safe

Systems. Let's meet somewhere this afternoon, off campus, okay?"

"Oh, gee, Michelle, I don't know. So far today I have not really been able to focus much on my work, and I'm terribly behind . . ." Brian was distraught and felt guilty.

"But Brian! I thought you asked me to find out about Loren and Safe Systems?"

Yes, indeed he had. Brian waffled. Well he hadn't eaten lunch . . .

"Yes, I suppose you're right! Okay, where do you want to go and when?"

"Let's meet in the parking lot in about an hour. I'll be free then. Let's make it 2 p.m. We'll drive to a little coffee shop I know, okay? Not many Atlas people know about that place, and I am sure we won't be seen."

"Okay, let's meet at my car at 2 p.m." This time Brian simply repressed the fact that the murder had taken over his life and that nothing was any more the way it had been. There was a definite limit on how much he could handle!

Wednesday, October 11, 1995, 2:04 p.m.

Where was Michelle? Brian was getting nervous. He hated waiting. And where was the police officer who was supposedly shadowing him? He didn't really want to tell Michelle that they would be followed. That might upset her, especially since she wanted to keep their meeting all hush-hush.

Suddenly Michelle stood right next to him.

"I didn't want to yell to let you know I was coming. I don't want anybody to see me. But everything should be okay. Loren left forty-five minutes ago and aside from him, I don't really care who sees us."

Brian wondered what Michelle meant as he walked over to the driver's side, unlocked the car, and then opened the passenger door from the inside so Michelle could get in.

As Brian started the engine Michelle asked, "Is it okay to start talking to you now, or do you want to wait till we get there? I thought that maybe it would be hard for you to focus while you drive."

Michelle had learned that she had to wait till Brian could focus. Fortunately she wasn't bothered by Brian's peculiarities.

"Well, first you have to tell me where we're going so that I have the directions clear. After that I can listen."

"Good point."

After given Brian directions to the coffee shop, Michelle started her story. The drive would take about ten minutes.

"This morning, just before lunch, I was able to locate the name of the admin at Safe Systems, the one I used to talk with a lot last January and February. Remember I told you about that? I was lucky and reached her right away. Her name is Pat. She was surprised that I didn't know what had been going on back then. Pat was under the impression that the story had leaked out and that Atlas people knew all about it.

"Now get this. Loren was accused of stealing intellectual property from Jeff while they both worked at Safe Systems!

That's why Loren got fired! Can you believe this? Pat didn't know how Jeff had found out that some of his code had been stolen by Loren. But evidently Jeff had been able to convince the president of Safe Systems about the theft. His name is Carl Walter. Walter didn't want a drawn-out legal case. He wanted to protect his company. Jeff had wanted to take Loren to court, and the president evidently persuaded Jeff not to. Loren and Jeff were part of the same team, which had been working on a new software application. Jeff proved to Walter that certain code, which Jeff had developed at home on his own for something totally different, had been used by Loren. Loren, of course, claimed he hadn't done anything of the kind and that it was a simple coincidence. He also maintained that he didn't really write much code anymore but that the people who worked for him did. For whatever reason, the admin didn't know why the president believed Jeff.

"So, after that whole fiasco, Safe Systems got some lawyers involved to cut a deal with Jeff, meaning Jeff sold the code in question to Safe Systems. According to Pat, there was an out-of-court settlement. And, like I said, Loren got fired. Pat thinks Jeff got something in the ballpark of a quarter million dollars, and Loren was terribly ticked about everything. I'm absolutely blown away by all of this! We certainly seem to be getting to the bottom of this whole mess, don't you think?"

Brian had focused very hard to make sense out of Michelle's story. As far as he was concerned she used a strange kind of logic when presenting a point of view. But right now he was mostly shocked by what her story seemed to imply about the murder of Jeff.

"I'm definitely stunned. I hadn't expected anything like this."

Brian always wanted to believe the best about people and went out of his way to give everybody the benefit of the doubt. To get definite validation for Michelle's story, he needed more details, which she wouldn't be able to provide. He also sensed fear in Michelle. Her whole demeanor had changed. Her usual buoyancy and stride seemed to be gone. Now she appeared careful, hesitant, uncertain, and, yes, almost fearful. Brian began to understand why she had wanted to meet off campus. He decided to ask her about her possible fear, knowing only too well how much he himself had been impacted since last week.

"Do you now feel a little apprehensive about working for Loren since learning about these events?" Brian hesitantly inquired.

"Well, yes, actually, I am kind of scared, just a little bit. I mean really. You kind of wonder what the guy is really all about. It's beginning to feel creepy. Ever since last week Loren seems to act so, I don't know, so unlike the way he used to. At first I thought it was because of the police and the trouble he got into with John, our president. Remember, there was that rumor about a possible merger between us and some company in Los Angeles? Supposedly Loren went to meet with them last Friday. But now I'm wondering, why did John want to talk to Loren about that rumor? And I know for sure that's what they talked about. John's admin confirmed it. And remember when I talked to you on Monday about this rumored merger and said that I had a hunch that it might be connected to Jeff's murder? Well, I'm almost convinced now, though, of course, I have absolutely no proof. But it scares me.

"Ever since I spoke to Pat, I wonder about every phone call Loren gets and I even looked through the most recent phone message book for possible clues. I can see that Loren has gotten quite a few calls from a guy called Charlie whose area code is for a Santa Barbara location, not Los Angeles. However, not all specifics of a rumor have to be correct for the rumor to have some truth to it. This mysterious caller never gives a company name when I ask for specifics. He just says, 'Loren knows me. I'm a friend.'

"What if something is going on again, similar to the last time, I mean like at Safe Systems?"

Michelle stopped and waited for Brian to respond. She definitely wanted to hear his opinion. Brian hesitated for a while and then said, "You mean you're wondering whether this could be another case that might have to do with stolen intellectual property?"

"Well, yes. That's what I mean. It could, couldn't it?"

Brian was taken aback by Michelle's suggestion. Such a possibility had not occurred to him yet. However, it didn't seem all that farfetched.

"I suppose you're right, Michelle, it could. But we have nothing to support this speculation." Brian started to feel increasingly uncomfortable.

"I know we don't, but what if Jeff did? He must have known something! I'm convinced of that." It was clear from Michelle's face that the uncertainty about Loren's role in the murder case was beginning to get to her. Her apprehension grew the more she talked about the situation.

By now they had reached their destination, and Brian was looking for a parking spot. Within a couple of minutes they were inside the coffee shop, which also served sandwiches and snacks. Michelle picked a quiet corner for utmost privacy.

"Let's wait till we have ordered, and then we can talk some more."

Brian nodded in agreement.

Michelle chose a peach Odwalla juice and two chocolate chip cookies, explaining she didn't feel like eating a real lunch. Brian opted for a Snapple lemonade, a croissant with ham and cheese, as well as two of the same cookies Michelle had ordered.

Michelle looked around to make sure she didn't recognize anybody in the place. There were only three other customers, all strangers to her.

Brian had been thinking about why Michelle thought it was possible that this, too, might turn out to be a case of stolen intellectual property. They had no proof, no facts, yet what other plausible reason could there be for Jeff's murder? Another case of stolen intellectual property would certainly provide a believable motive for murder, especially in light of what seemed to have happened at Safe Systems.

However, wouldn't that mean that he was willing to assume that just because Loren had done something once, he would do it again? That didn't seem fair.

Their orders came very quickly. Michelle started munching on the cookies and continued, "You know, I'm sure that Loren can't be trusted. That's just how he is. It upsets me. Somehow I feel that I, too, am involved, just because I work for him. It's silly, but that's how I feel all the time now."

"Oh, no, Michelle, you mustn't think that! I know, everything seems so different ever since the murder. I, too, have had very strange feelings." Brian could hardly believe that he was talking this way.

Michelle sounded exasperated as she continued, "I wish the whole thing would be over soon. I want it settled! It's driving me nuts."

Brian had never really seen Michelle like this. She was definitely discouraged as well as angry. He was at a loss what to say or do to make her feel better. At least he could try.

"We'll have to leave it all up to the police to investigate. I talked to Lieutenant Woodraw just before I called you and told her about Loren and Jeff having worked at Safe Systems.

"And there's something I haven't told you yet. I totally forgot and assumed you already knew about it. After you left this morning, I checked my email, and I had a message from an old friend of Jeff's whom I had contacted yesterday. I found his name, Ray, in some of Jeff's files. Jeff had mentioned him some time ago. In the e-mail Ray also talked about Jeff's settlement at Safe Systems. However, Ray didn't seem to know that Loren Grimm was the person involved, and he also couldn't recall the name of Safe Systems itself.

"Remember, I guess it was yesterday afternoon, when you told me about a phone call from an Angel Blank?"

"Oh, yes, yes, what about it? Did you learn more about her? I'm sure she was Jeff's girlfriend!"

"Ray, Jeff's old roommate, mentioned her as well in his e-mail to me. Since January of this year Angel has lived in San Francisco, and she works for a travel agency. The lieutenant also learned about Angel when she talked to Jeff's family. Per the lieutenant's investigation, Angel is not expected back from a trip till October 15. The lieutenant probably talked to the travel agency."

Michelle got excited, and some of her usual energy was back. "Well, that explains a lot of things, don't you see? And how horrible! Can you imagine what this Angel must have been feeling when the human resources manager told her about Jeff? I'm getting goose bumps right now just thinking about it. I bet she's coming back sooner than the fifteenth! Wouldn't you? How could she possibly finish her trip knowing her boyfriend is dead?"

Brian wouldn't know and didn't respond. He had only been meaning to encourage Michelle. Yet now, with the whole story out in the open, it didn't sound encouraging at all. Instead it seemed to confirm and highlight rather shocking possibilities. He started to think about Brigitte and how he would feel if something happened to her, but was interrupted by Michelle.

"Can't we do something, Brian? Anything! I'm going crazy!"

"But what could we possibly do?" Brian was stunned by Michelle's intense desire to want to act on something they couldn't influence at all or do anything about.

"Well, for instance, we could try to contact this Angel, don't you think? Then again, I'd probably start bawling my head off while trying to talk to her because I'm so upset about everything. Trying to call her wouldn't do any good. I guess you're right. There's nothing we can do. But it makes me so angry. I don't like feeling this way!"

They were both quiet for a couple of moments, each preoccupied with their own thoughts and fears. Then Michelle continued, "Well, since we're done eating and talking, we might as well go back to work. No use sitting around and moping about things you can't do anything about!"

Brian was used to Michelle's sudden changes in mood. This time he welcomed it and felt relieved that she wanted to get back to work. Brian felt a lot of anxiety now. He longed for the safety of work, where he could hide and get busy and forget about all these scary speculations!

Michelle in contrast almost looked like a warrior who had to return to battle, not sure about the outcome of the fight, yet prepared to hold her own at all cost.

"Let's go, then. Maybe I'll start to feel better back at work. I guess we have no choice but to wait till this Angel shows up. I am sure that she'll try to get in touch with somebody at Atlas. I'll talk to the operators at Atlas and ask them to send any calls by her to me. Yes, that should work. I want to be there for her! Wouldn't you want to meet the people who saw your friend before he died?"

And then, just like that, without any warning, Michelle started crying, totally overcome by the emotions of the moment. The warrior attitude had just been a mask she put on to ward off her great fears. Brian was terribly relieved that they were already in the car on their way back to work and he could distract himself by focusing on his driving. This was a real mess and he didn't know what to say or do! He could only hope that Michelle would recover soon. And she did . . .

Wednesday October 11, 1995, 8:53 p.m.

As Brian entered his apartment, the phone started ringing. This could be Brigitte. She had promised she would call him tonight if she had more information.

"Hello."

"Brian, I'm so glad you are home early. I've been worried about you."

"Brigitte, you don't have to worry about me, really."

"Well, usually I don't. But you haven't been yourself since last week."

Brian had to admit that she was right.

"Yes, I guess so."

"Did you just get home?"

"Yes, I just walked in. How did you know?"

"Oh, I tried a couple of times over the last thirty minutes. I know that you usually like to work much later than this, but lately nothing has been the same anymore, has it? Anyway, do you now have police protection?"

"Yes, I do."

"Did you see anybody? It must feel so weird."

"Actually, I haven't been able to identify anybody. I think I'm not looking very hard. I suppose I don't really want to know."

"I wouldn't either. But still, I think it's such a relief. I was so worried about that phone call you received Monday night! You want to call me back and settle down first?"

"No, this is okay."

"I got some more information from Alan about Loren Grimm and what it meant for Loren financially to get fired from Safe Systems."

Brian decided to tell Brigitte his own news after she was done.

"Alan couldn't find out why Loren was fired, but Alan learned that because of his dismissal, Loren lost a fortune, well, on paper at least, because most of his options were not yet vested. Remember when we talked about that over dinner? The grapevine says that Loren was livid. As a technical founder Loren had roughly a twenty percent stake in Safe Systems in the form of options, which had to be vested. The company was founded fourteen months before Loren's departure. So, that's a little more than a year and Loren would have had to stay thirty-four more months for all of his options to be vested. Therefore, in the event Safe

Systems goes public, Loren will only get a little more than one-fourth of what he could have gotten if he hadn't left Safe Systems. However, he won't be left totally empty-handed. His remaining options would still be worth in the neighborhood of two to three million dollars, but if he had stayed at Safe Systems, he could have doubled or tripled this amount. Can you imagine that? Incredible! I'm sure Loren was quite upset about his misfortune, but I doubt it would make him murder somebody. I just can't imagine that."

Brigitte paused to give Brian a chance to respond.

"I agree with your conclusions. I have some news as well, and in a strange way what you learned seems to shed light on what Michelle told me this afternoon."

Brian related what he had learned from Michelle. Brigitte got rather excited and intense.

"Well, this means that Loren lost more than a potential fortune. He also got caught in a criminal activity. This puts everything in a different light, and it leads me to believe that Loren might be linked to the murder. Last January Loren was certainly after something that Jeff had invented. What if he still was, and did Jeff know this? And then there's Michelle's hunch about the murder possibly being linked to the rumored merger between Atlas and some other company. Like Michelle, I wonder why Loren is getting phone calls from somebody in Santa Barbara. Is it really from a friend, is it Atlas business, or is it something else? I too wish we could get in touch with Angel. I really want to meet her. I'm sure that she's going to need a lot of support."

Brian couldn't quite understand why Michelle and Brigitte wanted to meet Angel and why they seemed to get emotional when talking about her.

"I guess you're right. We should talk to Angel. But shouldn't we wait till she calls Atlas? Michelle is convinced she will and is giving a heads up to the operators at Atlas in the event of a call. Per Lieutenant Woodraw Angel won't be back till this Saturday, the fifteenth."

"Yes, I'm sure she'll be in touch with us. She will want to know what really happened, and I figure she would want to meet some of the people Jeff worked with. I guess for us that means we're kind of done with our detective work. We actually found out quite a bit, don't you think?"

"What do you mean? Are you saying the case is now closed?" Brian couldn't quite share Brigitte's conclusions.

"Well, I'm convinced that with all of this information the police should find the killer."

Brian wasn't at all convinced. "Well, only if you think it's Loren Grimm and if you believe the murder is linked to what happened last January between Loren and Jeff.

Brigitte sounded very sure. "As far as I'm concerned nothing else makes any sense, unless Angel can provide new information."

Brian's mind still perceived a lot of loose ends, but why share his doubts? Brigitte seemed so sure.

Brigitte continued. "Now all we have to do is wait for Angel to show up. She might have information relating to the murder, and then again she might not. The circumstances surrounding the murder suggest that somebody did something to Jeff's computer at Atlas. But what about Jeff's system at home? According to Ray, Jeff's old friend, Jeff was still fine-tuning his invention. Jeff's murder could be linked to his personal invention or to his work at Atlas, or possibly to both. That will be an important point.

"Also I'm wondering how Angel is feeling about the murder. How will she cope with having lost a good or even intimate friend?" Brigitte's voice sounded quite concerned.

Suddenly there was so much sadness everywhere that even Brian was impacted. He wanted to get off the phone. He no longer wanted to talk or think about the murder. Life in general just was not safe anymore!

They talked for a couple more minutes and made a date for Friday night. Brian almost shared with Brigitte how horrible he would feel if something were to happen to her, but he couldn't make himself say it. It was just as well, he concluded. His life would have to settle down first before he could ever talk about such intimate and scary feelings.

Chapter 21

A New Beginning

Friday, October 13, 1995, 2:12 a.m.

Dazed and feeling terribly frightened and lost, Angel suddenly woke up. She glanced at her alarm clock—2:12 a.m.

"Darn it! I hate jet lag!" Angel was talking out loud, hoping the sound of her own voice might dispel the emptiness and isolation she felt encroaching from all sides.

Now what? Angel was scared. She couldn't sleep. She missed Jeff. Oh, she had been dreaming. Now she remembered. What had the dream been about? Good, it was gone! It was just as well, because by now she hated her dreams. They were too scary, and it was way too tough to make sense out of them.

Then it hit her. She *did* remember. Oh, how she wished she hadn't! The memory was still vague and foggy, but slowly the scenes were coming back to her. She could feel specific images rising up from somewhere deep inside.

She was running, actually eagerly running toward something, something exciting.

Stiff and motionless Angel stared at the ceiling above her bed while listening to the traffic outside. In big cities the hustle and bustle of life never seemed to stop. There was no clear dividing line between day and night. The noise seemed constant. She liked that. Actually, she felt encouraged by it. It meant life went on. That was good. And because life still went on, there was still some hope, somewhere out there. Life wasn't all over yet. But she doubted there was any kind of life left for her. No, definitely not. There was absolutely nothing to look forward to.

How did that go again?

She was running toward something exciting, something she was about to receive. She felt a lot of anticipation. Good anticipation.

Angel pondered this for a moment. Excitement? Anticipation? This was nuts! Impossible! But still more images started bursting forth into consciousness.

Suddenly Angel remembered that in the dream she had not been alone. She had been part of a group of people.

They were all running very hard, driven by a desire to accomplish a specific goal.

What kind of goal? They had all been very intense about it, including herself.

Angel tensed up. She didn't like these thoughts and feelings. What was this mysterious goal? Who were these people? Where were they running to, and, most importantly, why?

The whole situation had felt very competitive. Everyone in the group had wanted to be first. First for what? Oh, yes, Angel remembered now.

> They all wanted to reach a certain store as fast as possible. They were fighting with each other over something. Angel was struggling to recognize and identify the object of everybody's ardent desire. Suddenly she could see! They were all fighting over a sales receipt! Strange. The receipt was supposed to be special. It entitled the holder to a gold ring that would be redeemed by the store they were all running to.

> Angel threw herself full force, withholding nothing, into the competition. She loved competition! Using every one of her talents, she managed to outmaneuver everybody else in the group. As a result she not only captured the receipt but also managed to hold on. Full of exhilaration, she held up the receipt as if it were a trophy. Now there was only one more goal to accomplish—getting the gold ring!

> The last person Angel took the receipt away from reminded her of Jeff, but his face seemed to be blank. She couldn't identify the mysterious male's face features. He definitely reminded her of Jeff.

Still lying in bed reflecting and wondering, Angel started to tense up more and more. What had happened next in the dream? How did it end? Something at the end of the dream had thrown her off and had probably awakened her. Angel felt an unquenchable desire to ward off an unknown yet inevitable truth that was about to reveal itself.

> The group arrived at the store. This was the big moment. Full of excitement and anticipation, Angel

turned in her hard-won trophy. But something seemed to have gone wrong. Oh, no! The store owner said that he did indeed redeem certain receipts for a special gold ring, but Angel had the wrong receipt!

Everybody in the group was so caught up in competing with each other that none of them considered verifying whether this particular receipt fulfilled the store's requirements. Angel's receipt had the correct month and day but the incorrect year. Therefore everybody's efforts were wasted. Angel found herself explaining to the same faceless male figure who reminded her of Jeff that it was okay that everybody in the group had wasted their efforts, because the lesson they had learned was so valuable.

Yes, that had been it. That was all Angel could remember of her dream. What could it mean? Suddenly intense and numbing fear invaded every part of Angel's being. She had to do something. She had to get busy. She definitely felt that so far in her life all of her efforts had been wasted. Then an idea struck her, and she jumped out of bed and ran to her desk. Frantically, as if her life depended on it, she opened drawer after drawer, moving things around and making a big mess. Finally she found what she had been looking for, sighing with great relief and a great sense of inner satisfaction. Tightly clutching the object of her hectic search to her chest, she cradled it in her arms, like a long-lost treasure. It was a notebook, meant to be used as a diary. The cover was made of light tan suede leather, and the edges were lined with gold symbols. Alois had given it to her after she had known him for about a year. His words had been, "Write down what you feel! You will feel better!" Of course, she hadn't paid any attention. It seemed one of her specialties in life was to never listen to any advice from anybody, not even advice from the people who truly loved her!

But this was the moment when Angel would finally follow Alois' advice from years ago. It seemed like an eternity since she had been in Austria! But never mind that now. As of today she would write down her thoughts and feelings. But what where her thoughts and feelings?

Angel was sure Alois had wanted her to write down her feelings because she always got so emotional about everything.

What did she feel?

Angel sat down at her desk. With great hesitation and trepidation, she picked up a pen and started writing:

Early Friday morning, October 13, 1995.
I can't sleep. Jeff is dead. My life seems over.
How do I feel?

Angel paused for a couple of moments, staring outside the window, though not seeing anything at all. And then she started to write again.

I feel like a whimsical bud, blossoming before the end of winter, the time of darkness. Frightened by the harshness of the elements, I freeze, shrivel up, and can never come to full bloom.

What about my life, my beauty? Why does it have to get wasted? Why could I never come to full bloom?

Overcome by an incredible pain rising up from the depth of her being, a horrible rage overtook Angel and shook her forcefully and with great might. It was necessary and unavoidable. The dead leaves on her tree of life had to be shaken off. She wanted to scream. She wanted to yell. She wanted to hurt somebody. Any kind of action would be better than this uncontrollable rage. With utter disgust and dismay, she flung her pen and book halfway across the room. There, that felt better! Alois was wrong. Writing down your feelings didn't make you feel good! It was terribly frightening and made you feel like you were losing yourself into an unknown void!

Angel yelled out loud to nobody in particular, and yet she wanted the whole world to hear, "*I hate this life!*"

After that Angel threw herself into her favorite cozy chair, clutching her knees, hiding her face between her arms, and cried and cried and cried . . .

After thirty minutes, which had seemed like hours, Angel realized that she was getting very cold and looked around for a blanket. Her face looked swollen and was still wet from the flood of tears brought about by the rage. She needed a tissue to blow her nose. And she was freezing! The oversize tee-shirt gave little protection from the dampness of the early morning hours.

Lise had told her on one of their trips that "it always feels the darkest before the dawn." Lise was right about the darkness, but Angel was convinced there was no dawn coming for her, no way. It was just foolish to hope for dawn. Or was it?

An idea had started to take shape inside of Angel. She remembered it now. It had started after she had read Jeff's last letter and all the documents about his invention. He had written the letter not long before he died. He seemed to have been aware of imminent danger. Why hadn't he contacted the police? Why had he been so stupid and naive, thinking he could fix the world and all its woes and injustices?

No, don't think about this now! Angel told herself. It was over. The past had already happened, never to be relived. This was the time to act and not the time to wallow in self-pity. Enough was enough! Nothing could be changed! No "buts" about it! No more running away. It had never worked, and she would never do it again. She had learned that about herself. Yes, she could suddenly see the whole idea coming together inside of her. She would start a company built around Jeff's technological invention. That's what she would do! It had come to her last night before she fell asleep. She could do it. She knew she could. Any doubts would be brushed aside until this thing was launched! Since taking shape inside of her, the idea had slowly molded itself into a tentative plan. A lot of details were still missing, but that didn't matter.

Well, it was time to get going. She might as well get ready by taking a nice long shower. Letting the water roll gently down her body would be like a cleansing of the past and a renewal for the future. That's how she would remember this new beginning and draw strength from the memory. After that she would read Jeff's letter once more—if she could stand it. Would she break down again? *No!* She was committed to a slow healing process. Her wounds were deep, but Angel believed they could heal with the passing of time. Sure, life would be a struggle, yet in the final analysis life was always a struggle. Angel believed many people just kidded themselves wanting a painless life. As for herself, Angel was determined to move forward, prepared to face each step, no matter how painful, using all the energy available to her each passing day. She would let nothing hold her back in the pursuit of her quest. Angel was sure life would get just a little easier once Lise was back from the trip. She longed for somebody to talk to and possibly cry with every now and again. Lise would understand.

Friday, October 13, 1995, 10:25 a.m.

"Brian, I'm glad you finally showed up at work!" Michelle had been sitting around the break room waiting for Brian to enter through the back door of the building. Now she was running toward him. Brian had stopped in his tracks, motionless and frozen. Nothing was registering.

"I've been on needles and pins all morning long. Well, since 8:35 to be exact. Angel called. I talked to her. She wants to meet us for lunch! I already made reservations at Scott's in Palo Alto. It's easy for all of us to get to since it's next to 101. You know, I'm totally in awe of her! She is *really* nice! I mean Angel, of course. And I can't believe how together she was when I talked to her on the phone.

Incredible! She has an idea she wants to run by us. I think it has to do with Jeff's technology. Isn't it exciting? Well, it's sad, too, for sure . . . but still, well, you know what I mean!"

No, Brian didn't know what she meant.

"And before you say anything, like you don't want to meet her or you don't have any time, hear me out first. By the way, you look kind of dazed this morning. Anyway, she's going to the police first, and then she'll meet with us. I gave her Lieutenant Woodraw's name. Can you imagine, she said she has the proof that will convict the murderer! I feel like I'm in a movie and keep pinching myself, making sure I'm truly alive and this is actually happening!"

Brian started to wonder if Michelle would pause to take a breath. She finally did. Brian himself couldn't say anything yet. He felt totally tongue-tied. Finally he managed, "Let me get my espresso first, okay?"

Michelle just nodded, prepared to give Brian his space to recover from such outrageous and exciting news.

As she usually did, Michelle waited patiently until Brian was finished with his morning routine before they both settled down in his cube.

"So, then, are you finally all ears? Are you coming for lunch?"

Brian still acted rather flustered. "Well, I don't know."

"Oh, baloney! It's great, and it's exciting! Don't you have some friend you're really close with? Why don't you give her a call, and she can join us for lunch. Maybe that'll make it easier for you."

"What do you mean?" Brian was stunned that Michelle even knew about Brigitte.

"I told you, I know a lot. I know you have a friend, and I think it's great! You're too much of a loner. It's not good for you."

Brian actually blushed and tried to hide his face by turning around and picking up his espresso. He needed a couple of seconds to regain his composure.

"Well, or maybe you feel it's weird or something to have lunch with two women, and possibly three, if you ask your friend."

Horrors, Brian hadn't even thought about that yet! "Well, really, I wonder. Why would she want to meet us?"

"I told you, she has a plan, and she specifically asked to meet somebody Jeff had worked with. So, are you coming or not? And I don't know if she knows that you found the body. Now stop it. You just looked horrified! It's not your fault, you know."

Brian didn't know why he always acquiesced. Well, actually that wasn't true. He knew why. He didn't know how to say no. And he would definitely call Brigitte. What if she couldn't come?

Friday, October 13, 1995, 11:55 a.m., in the Lobby of Scott's.

"Hi. My name is Michelle, and I made reservations for four."

The hostess checked her book to verify the name. "Is your entire party here?"

"No. We're still waiting for two."

"Just let me know when everybody has arrived, and we'll seat you right away."

Seeing Brigitte hadn't arrived yet, Brian had stepped outside to wait for her. He felt too closed in and exposed in a rather busy lobby buzzing with people arriving for their lunch break. He wondered whether a policeman had been following him to the restaurant, or was that all over now?

Meanwhile Michelle had found a place to sit down while waiting. She didn't mind being by herself. She was excited and eager to get to know Angel and learn about her plan. She wondered what Angel looked like. How would Angel recognize Michelle? When she had asked Angel on the phone, Angel had said, "Don't worry, I'll find you!"

Michelle looked up. That had to be Angel walking in. Before Angel had spotted her, Michelle walked up, saying,

"Are you Angel?"

"Yes, I am. Are you Michelle?"

And with that they fell into each other's arms. It just seemed the right and natural thing to do, and neither of them questioned it. Any onlooker would have been convinced that they had known each other for years.

A few moments later Brian and Brigitte walked in, and Michelle introduced everybody. She was good at helping people get over the first hurdles of feeling strange and awkward. Not many words were exchanged; they were all eager to get seated. Michelle announced to the hostess that their party was now complete, and single file they followed the hostess to one of the tables in the far right corner.

"I'm so excited to meet you all!" Angel said as they sat down. Her face was glowing and looked bright, open, and eager. There was no trace or sign that only a couple of hours ago this face had been washed with tears. "During our phone call Michelle told me a little bit about each of you, but I want to learn and understand a lot more."

Brigitte spoke up first. "I didn't really know Jeff very well. I'm Brian's friend, and it was through him that I got involved." Brigitte had sat down next to Angel. Michelle sat across from Brigitte, and Brian was seated opposite Angel.

"First of all I wanted to tell you all that I'm okay. Of course, I still feel kind of numb. I've had moments, as you can imagine. But it will probably take a couple of weeks for Jeff's death to really sink in." Angel's voice had started to tremble a little, but she caught herself right away.

The others waited for Angel to regain her composure.

"You're probably wondering why I wanted to meet with you. And I'll come straight out and start with my crazy idea before filling you in about what has transpired about the murder. I want to start a company bringing Jeff's invention to market." Angel paused, waiting for a reaction.

"I think that's a wonderful idea!" Again it was Brigitte who responded first, and quite enthusiastically.

Michelle immediately echoed Brigitte's sentiments. Brian could hardly believe what he was hearing. What was he doing here? What was happening? It felt totally unreal.

"I'm glad you guys are with me so far, but I bet you are also dying to learn more about the murder."

"Yes, I can hardly contain my curiosity!" Michelle was always straightforward and blunt.

"Well, here's the story, then."

But at this point the waitress showed up, and they ordered, just water for Brian, iced tea for Brigitte, and a glass of wine each for Michelle and Angel. Angel declared, "I want to make a celebration out of this!"

"Maybe we should look at the menu really fast so that we won't get interrupted while Angel tells her story." Michelle always kept a cool head on her shoulders.

Angel waited for everybody to make their choices. She always knew right away what she wanted to eat. Michelle was quick as well. Brian didn't want to hold things up and asked Brigitte what she had chosen and then picked the same. There was still a lot of tension at the table. Yet Angel took over and continued with her story.

"I guess you'll want to know first about the murder. Do you know anything about what happened in the past between Jeff and Loren Grimm?"

"Yes, we do. We found out quite a bit." Brigitte explained.

"So you know that Loren had stolen Jeff's personal invention while they were both at Safe Systems?"

All three nodded.

"Good. That will make the story easier to tell. Jeff had invented something special. Jeff never figured out exactly how Loren Grimm had learned about his invention or why he wanted it so badly. I figure he learned about it by coincidence and wanted it because of greed. Bottom line, Jeff found out the hard way that Loren knew. This all started back in January 1995. Jeff concluded that Loren had broken into his system at home. They were both working at Safe Systems at the time. Loren stole code from Jeff and used it for one of his own projects. Though there was a financial settlement and Loren was fired from Safe Systems, Jeff was not satisfied. He wanted revenge. I tried to stop him, but it was useless." Again Angel's voice almost broke. But she recovered pretty fast and continued.

"Jeff wanted to catch Loren in the act of stealing code again. He was sure he would." This statement was followed by a gasp from Michelle as Angel went on.

"Jeff had protected his system at home using his invention, which can spot a break-in and trace its source. Only once, in August 1995 was one of Loren's break-in attempts successful. That's because at the time Jeff's invention could not stop the break-ins yet, but could only identify them. After that Loren tried numerous other times, but was always unsuccessful. However, Jeff's invention had compiled a record of every one of Loren's break-ins. Jeff documented the break-ins, and this morning I took that material, together with other important proof to the police.

"Jeff also became suspicious about something he believed was going on at Atlas. By the way, all of this information was recorded by Jeff in a long letter he mailed to me on September 20, two weeks before he was murdered. Jeff never mentioned his suspicions to me when we called each other regularly by phone while I was traveling, yet he believed it was wise to document what had been going on. He must have sensed he was in real danger."

This time there was a short but recognizable sob coming from deep inside of Angel. But again she caught herself and continued.

"Somebody in my building collected the mail for me while I was traveling. Did Michelle tell you that I was working for a travel agency and had been gone for almost three months? Anyway, somebody had a key to my mailbox and took in my mail and left it in my place. This person has a key to my condo. So, when I returned, I found the envelope Jeff had mailed. I don't understand all of the details well, but according to Jeff, Loren was involved in stealing software code of an Atlas product and was passing it on to some small outfit in Santa Barbara."

Michelle could no longer contain herself and exclaimed, "Brian, remember? I told you there was something going on with this guy calling from Santa Barbara all the time!"

"Well, you were right then," Angel said. "Jeff hadn't been acting all kosher either. He had started to snoop around in Loren's system after several break-in attempts into his system at home. From what I can gather, his invention can be used either way. You can use it to break in without leaving a trace, or you can use it as protection from break-ins. That's how he found out about this deal Loren was about to strike. You see, Jeff figured that Loren had never gotten over having lost the potential for a lot of money when he was fired from Safe Systems. Safe Systems went public in August 1995 and Loren lost a chance at millions of dollars because most of his options had not yet been vested. Do you guys understand about the option stuff?"

"Yes, we do and Brian and I had already thought about this being a possible clue to the murder." Brigitte looked at Brian, but Brian looked frozen and stiff and didn't respond. He was still not sure whether all of this was really happening. Michelle just nodded.

"Good, so you understand that part. And that was what was driving Loren to make some kind of crooked deal with the Santa Barbara company. Who knows? Maybe Loren would have ultimately joined them, and that way he was going to make a killing. That's my take, at least."

The waitress showed up, and they all ordered their food as fast as possible. They wanted to get on with the story.

Now it was Brian's turn. He needed to get some specifics clarified. "But who then killed Jeff?"

"I'll get to that next," Angel explained. "I had wanted to talk about the motive first. Bottom line, and I learned this from the police, Loren hired some louse to scare Jeff off, but the guy claims that by mistake he hit Jeff too hard over the head with a pistol he was carrying. Maybe this is true. Who knows? I don't really want to dwell on that part. The lieutenant pieced all of this together after tracing the car that hit some young woman from Atlas."

"Oh, you mean Cathie. Well, that makes sense. Will Loren be arrested now? You know, he is my boss." Michelle looked gleeful.

"Yes, I know. He'll be arrested today."

Brian was still thinking. "How did that person, the murderer, get into the building? And what about Cathie's car accident?"

"The lieutenant thinks that Loren gave that guy his pass or let him in. She did not talk about details relating to the accident."

Now Brian had an explanation for the footsteps he had heard running away, as well as for Loren's behavior that night. But he needed to know more. "Did the lieutenant mention what kind of car this guy was driving?"

"No, that didn't come up."

Brigitte chimed in. "I'm sure it was the car that followed you, Brian!"

Brian still had a number of loose ends in his mind. But there was time to think about the details later on at home. Angel mentioning starting a company had put him on edge. Why had Angel wanted to meet with them? "So what did you mean when you said you're planning to start a company using Jeff's invention?"

"Yes, good point! And actually that's why I wanted to meet you all today. I've already spoken to Ray Beachwood. I called him this morning on the phone. He was Jeff's roommate at MIT, and I've known him ever since then. We need Ray. He has the kind of expertise to understand Jeff's invention and to finish it. So far I have not convinced him. But I think I can get him!" Angel actually started smiling and looked quite confident.

Brigitte intuitively knew what Angel wanted to do and why. "So starting a company is your way of bringing about something good out of something bad, right? Like righting a wrong? No, that's not really what I meant to say. I don't really believe that one can truly right a wrong. What I really wanted to say is, and forgive me, if this sounds like a cliché to you, but I can't think of a better metaphor right now, starting a company based on Jeff's invention would be the equivalent of 'rising phoenix-like from the ashes.' Is that what you want to do?"

For one short moment Angel's eyes got tearful. However, she successfully fought back those relentless tears.

"Yes, that's it! I know that I can't bring Jeff back. And I agree with you, one can't right wrongs, but I can bring his work to fruition and use my own creativity in the process. You see, I have a very personal reason as well. Never before in my life have I been willing to put all of myself on the line to accomplish a specific goal and to stick with it all the way to the end! I don't expect a miracle. Definitely not. I know that it will be a long and arduous road. But it's a new beginning for me, and I'm excited. What do you think?"

"I think its *great!* Really!" Brigitte was truly beaming.

"Good, because I wanted to ask all of you to join me."

They were aghast and stunned. Michelle came around first.

"I want to! I really want to! Can you imagine how much fun this could be? We could have a say in how to work and how to get things done. I've always wanted to have more impact!" She was ecstatic.

Now it was Brigitte's turn. "I agree with Michelle. But what do you want each of us to do?"

"Well, that's the fun part of meeting today and why I wanted to celebrate. We'll figure it out now and make a tentative plan, all right?"

Finally Brian couldn't restrain himself any longer. These women were crazy! Didn't they know that it took a lot of money to start a company? "How are you going to fund your company?"

Totally unfazed, Angel declared, "Oh, money? Money's no problem at all. I have a rather large trust fund. I'm sure that at some point in time we will run out, but by then we should be able to raise more money from outside sources. I'm totally confident."

Brian was speechless. He had never heard anybody talk like that before, nor had he ever met anybody who didn't consider money a necessity. Money was security. As far as he was concerned Angel was gambling away her security, and with it her future. What kind of foolishness was this? But it was not his role to stop her. It was her choice.

Now their food was served and for the next two hours they hatched a plan. Angel would run the company, with Michelle as her office manager. Brigitte would head marketing and sales. Brian would work with Ray, the chief technologist. Brian had said neither yes or no, but Brigitte explained, "Don't worry, I'll get him on board!" Angel would persuade Lise to lead human resources. Angel told everyone to keep their eyes open for people who would fit into the unique culture they wanted to create.

Brian was swept up by a forceful wave of change. Did he really want to join this unbelievable odyssey?